It was impossible to protect herself from the carefully aimed blows. Her pleas for mercy seemed only to incite more violence. There was so much pain from her breasts to her thighs, she couldn't think clearly. There had to be something she could do. An idea came to her, but it was repugnant. Being in New York hadn't changed her that much. She remembered how she felt when she first arrived. That was really something. Seemed longer than five months ago. Maybe if she thought hard enough about the trip, or whatever, she could imagine somebody else was getting beaten up. She'd try to act completely unconscious. That way, the beating might stop before she was more seriously hurt. . . .

GOOD-BYE, DIANE

Faye Kennedy Daly

A BERKLEY MEDALLION BOOK

published by

BERKLEY PUBLISHING CORPORATION

ACKNOWLEDGMENTS

To Pat,
who was always there, encouraging me to hang in.

Also
"The Other Kennedys," Joy, Flo, Lynn and Gay,
for their moral support, and Elaine Markson
and Page Cuddy for their confidence.

BERKLEY PUBLISHING CORPORATION
200 MADISON AVENUE
NEW YORK, N.Y. 10016

SBN 425-03254-X

*BERKLEY MEDALLION BOOKS are published by
Berkley Publishing Corporation
200 Madison Avenue
New York, N.Y. 10016.*

BERKLEY MEDALLION BOOK ® TM 757,375

Printed in the United States of America

Berkley Medallion Edition, NOVEMBER, 1976

Chapter 1

The flight to New York wasn't the enjoyable experience she'd looked forward to. When her Ozark flight first left the airport, she was very excited. She looked out the window until there was nothing left to see of her small Midwestern birthplace, happy as it and similar flat Iowa towns disappeared from view. But changing planes at Chicago and waiting for her flight to La Guardia affected her mood. The chaos and complexity of O'Hare Field. The feeling of being alone and anonymous among so many people traveling in pairs or clustered into groups. The tension of listening to the constant stream of announcements that kept people perched on the alert as she was, or wandering around restlessly until the signal came for them to scurry toward the proper arrival or departure gate. It seemed inconceivable that she'd be able to board the right plane at the right time.

After she was finally settled on the American Airlines jet to New York City, she became concerned about the possibility that her luggage might not arrive when she did, since she'd checked it straight through from Des Moines. Originally, she planned to keep her roomy carry-on with her on the plane. She studied the much smaller, initialed train case she'd carried instead. It would be totally inadequate in the event of a missing-luggage emergency. All it held were some pajamas and underclothes in addition to its well-equipped sewing kit. She was usually more practical. Sitting in an aisle seat with no view to divert her, she realized how much it meant to her as her only going-away present. It was hard to believe she'd been genuinely touched by the unexpected farewell party her co-workers at Miller and Sons had given her. For the rest of the trip, until her arrival at La Guardia, she felt unexpectedly sad and nostalgic.

Returning from lunch on her last day as assistant bookkeeper with the small firm, she could barely conceal her smugness at leaving her boring job and equally dull co-workers behind her. Ten months was more than anyone should have to take of Grace Lukas, Jenny Peters, or Mrs. Corbett. The martyred Mrs. Corbett was the worst, with those drab and shapeless look-alike dresses and navy-bean or peanut-butter sandwiches. Her ceaseless monologues of complaints and sacrifices were her only luxury.

"Annie," she'd begin, "raising five children in a Christian home is a real test for a woman. She deserves a whole lot of credit for not being the selfish kind. If I'd followed my notion about getting me some nurse's training like your aunt, I might've ended up seeing after somebody in a big estate house like they used to show in the movies. No real chores outside of making my patient comfortable and keeping him company. Nobody else to answer to. But everybody said unless I wanted to end up an old maid, I best not waste any money on a fool idea like that.

"A decent woman's got an obligation to find an honest man, satisfy his nature, and raise as many healthy children as the Lord sees fit to give her," she'd go on. "There's been plenty sacrifice, but I'm right proud me and Fred never took no relief, almost own our own home, and kept all five children in good Catholic schools."

The first time she told her story to Diane and showed the curly-edged photo of her oldest son getting his degree from St. Ambrose, and snapshots of the others and their modest frame house, Diane respected her accomplishments. But after a while, she decided there was no self-pity whatsoever, only an unwavering conviction that she was superior to anyone who didn't live by her traditions. She appeared incapable of believing that Diane's secret goal wasn't finding a husband. She subtly offered her solution to Diane's problem.

2

"You wouldn't know it to look at me now, but when I was in my teens, I had more boys wanting to be steadies. I was just as pretty as you, but not as skinny, 'cause I was always more filled out, especially in the sit-down, besides being shorter. Of course, you're lucky to have what little shape you've got, considering your size. But I'd never have no time to spend *my* weekends reading magazines or sewing. At your age, Frank and me was already married. If you could pick up a little weight, you'd be all set in no time."

Actually, Diane had no special concern about being a size nine or ten, although she was five-foot-seven. She was a little sensitive about her breasts, but she knew she'd passed through her really flat-chested stage, and she'd never wanted the kind that might look too conspicuous in clothes, anyway. Although she always went out for lunch alone right up to her last day at work, anyone who assumed she was out stuffing herself with calories was wrong. She wasn't that dissatisfied with her overall figure. Not the type to be openly rude, she was mainly determined to avoid listening to, thinking like, or ever looking like the Mrs. Corbetts of the world.

Jenny Peters was another incentive for escape, with her voluminous bosom, ledgelike behind, tight clothes, and unsolicited intimacies. Jenny was as committed to proselytizing on the physical rewards for the young bride as Mrs. Corbett was the moral ones of parenthood.

"Girl, my Ralph's built like a horse. When we went to Florida for our honeymoon, I was so sore I couldn't hardly sit down or walk for the first week. And, my poor boobs. Forget it! It was all I could do to keep from begging him to let up on me. But I managed not to, and pretty soon I got so I could relax a little, although I was still sore as hell half the time. Well, much as I hate to admit it, before long it got so he couldn't dish out any more than I could take. Now he says he'll be lucky if I don't wear *him* out." She giggled. "We're trying to use rhythm, 'cause he thinks the pill's dangerous, and a diaphragm takes too long, but I don't think it's going to work much longer, 'cause we're both too hot-natured."

After a while, she tried to get confessionals from Diane. "What's with you and Les? Everybody thought you'd probably get married till you started making all these New York plans. He's the only one you've dated at all steady, isn't he?"

"I guess so, more or less. You know my aunt, though. So strict about who could come to the house and everything. With Mr. Haynes being a principal and all, Les was more used to humoring people like her than most of the other boys."

By establishing himself as the best-mannered homework helper around before either he or Diane was being noticed by anyone else, Les became Diane's first steady without being selected for the spot. Although she'd never been partial to curly-haired boys with full-moon faces and pale-blue eyes, her aunt was so pleased with Les, she was almost permissive where he was concerned.

"Yeah, yeah, I know. Most guys don't want to be hassled," Jenny persisted. "But after the first couple of years in high school, you started fixing yourself up and looking so much better, your aunt couldn't have fouled things up too much for you. You ended up being one of the best-looking girls in the senior class. Even Ralph noticed how you'd changed. In fact, now that he thinks that he's such a hot-shot married man, he's always telling me I'd better not leave you two alone together, because he'd completely spoil you for poor Les." She laughed noisily.

Diane could overlook the implication that Jenny's presence would be the only obstacle to her surrender to the oafish Ralph because of her other compliments.

She would've enjoyed talking about her transformation. She hadn't liked being taller, lankier, and less developed than most of her counterparts, especially when the tallest boys usually wound up with the shortest girls. Les was taller than she was, but his stockiness made it less noticeable. On top of that, she didn't have the money to dress decently. Her aunt carefully supervised both her tiny allowance and the sporadic money orders her father sent. The insurance policy her mother left her was inviolable. Unfortunately, her face didn't help either. It was still plain

4

and bare, long after her classmates were doing sneaky things to theirs. Whenever she tried to set her thick hair, it came out fuzzy.

"The main thing that happened," she began proudly, "is that I gained a little weight and started making my own clothes. I got interested in—"

Jenny interrupted her impatiently. "Whatever it was, after you got so much better a few years ago, Les had to get some ideas. You must be a good twenty years old now, and since you've been working and going to college, your aunt can't have that much of a say anymore."

"I'll be twenty this March, just before I leave. I'm hoping that'll make my aunt feel a little better about my going." She disliked giving such naive and unresponsive answers when she knew what was expected of her.

For all her frankness, Jenny would've been surprised if Diane had admitted having sex. Such openness would've been an unexpected windfall, although hasty marriages and premature births were almost a way of life among "nice" girls. But it was definitely considered unsporting not to make any revelations. She could've confined herself to the story of her old semitopless front-seat sessions with Les for starts.

What happened was that she got a bust about the same time he got a graduation car and lost some of his tubbiness. That was when pinching and nibbling were introduced beneath her hitched-up bra. Jenny would've loved hearing about that. But, unlike the bride, any tenderness of her lower parts was negligible. In those days, she only entertained one or two fingers of Les's tireless right hand.

Although they went through a perfunctory rear-seat horizontal stage, when he could only open his fly or scrunch his pants down, and no article of her clothing was completely removed either, it was very brief. Pushing himself back and forth between her clamped thighs, it took forever for him to finish. When they finally got around to the more serious business, he came so quickly she was less satisfied than when she'd relied on his fingers in the old days. To make matters worse, he seemed inappropriately pleased with himself.

After a while, she started making excuses to avoid seeing him as often as before. Although her impending trip was a factor, Les seemed to think it was the only reason. He apparently convinced himself it was a device to get him to propose to her. Fortunately, whatever his other short-comings, he was discreet, largely due to fear of her aunt. Consequently, knowing their affairs were their own, and disliking Jenny's tactlessness, she refused to give her any satisfaction at all, gradually avoiding her instead.

When she returned to the office after her final reclusive lunch, she stopped abruptly in the doorway. She could hardly believe the balloons, paper streamers, and big "Good-bye, Diane" banner were displayed in her honor. Familiar with her routine, but not the motive behind it, Mrs. Corbett, Jenny, and the others had hastily decorated the office with the grudging consent of their generally officious boss. As soon as Diane was inside, they all gathered around her and sang "For She's a Jolly Good Fellow," and followed with toasts of Four Roses and Coke in styrofoam cups. Then Mrs. Corbett presented the box with the small case inside, and self-consciously read a short verse as Diane flushed with shame.

Something borrowed, something blue
Will still be there when the time is due.
This gift will travel by your side.
Don't settle down till you're satisfied.

It was the only parting encouragement Diane was to receive. Her closest girlfriend was upset that she wouldn't be in town for her June wedding. Her father had called from Kansas City the week before to apologize for being "too pinched" for cash to see her off as he'd hoped to.

"Di," he asked hesitantly, "are you sure you want to go? I thought you'd work awhile and decide to go back to the university."

"Don't worry, Dad, I'll be all right. I can always come home if I don't like it in New York. But I'm awfully excited about designing. I know I'll be happier than if I ended up teaching."

"But there must be some schools closer to home you could go to."

"Not like Parsons, Dad. It's really tops."

"Well, I guess you know what you're doing. You've always stuck to your guns once you'd made your mind up, so I guess it's none of my business. But I'm surprised Elizabeth didn't talk you out of it."

To avoid a pointless discussion of her aunt's opinion about her plans, Diane reminded him that he had to watch the time on the call and promised to write to him regularly. He said good-bye with a deep sigh. She could tell that after ten years he still felt guilty for remarrying shortly after her mother's death and taking a job in Missouri a couple of years later. Diane understood his need for more money, since there was scarcely enough of anything during the time she lived with him and his new wife, a widow with two sons. He tried to become a foreman at the Maytag factory, but it didn't work out. Eventually, they might've become comfortable together, but Diane wasn't sure. That was why she accepted her aunt's invitation to stay in Newton with her, instead of tagging along to Kansas City.

She didn't speak to Diane at all the morning before her departure. She remained inside her bedroom and didn't answer when Diane said she was leaving. She'd spoken her last words the night before. Not so much to Diane as to the air around her.

"What more could I expect? I told her mother what would happen if she left this house and her religion behind to marry that Irish trash. I tried to do my duty after the degenerate threw their poor misfit out, but she's just as ungrateful as her mother was after I took care of her. But that's all right, they're the ones who end up suffering. Not me. I've got my life and people who appreciate me."

Her life was that of a highly qualified LPN, as careful about displaying affection and "undue emotion" to her family as to her patients. In age and attitude, she'd been more of a mother than a sister to Diane's mother, a change-of-life child. She'd remained unmarried after their parents died. She was quite content in the role of caretaker of her frail younger sister. But she was almost as authoritarian and undemostrative with her as she was with Diane. She considered them both weaker than they were.

Diane never gave her any "trouble" until she stopped going to Ames University, took a full-time job, and started getting a lot of catalogs from schools all over the country. Her aunt refused to believe she'd follow through until Diane picked up her ticket the week before she was leaving. Her aunt considered her as predictable as her mother seemed until she stubbornly converted to Catholicism and married Diane's father when she was twenty-two.

Diane was sensitive to her aunt's feelings as she summed them up to the four walls and the ceiling their last night together. She wasn't quite sixty, and by no means senile. Her indirect form of address was basically a solution to her lifelong communication problem. She only used it for Diane's benefit when she was very upset. She'd never talk to herself.

"You know I appreciate everything you've done for me," Diane answered. "I never minded going to church with you instead of mass or doing anything you asked me to. But I got so I hated the idea of teaching, especially math, and you always wanted me to have some kind of profession like you. If it wasn't for your influence, I might've had no ambition at all."

"Why would a girl want to go to an unheard-of school in a sewer like New York and live with all kinds of filth?" she continued.

When Diane reminded her aunt it was her own former employer who'd managed to get her an apartment where she lived after Diane had written her for help, her aunt acted like she didn't hear her.

"If it's not a nice place like it's supposed to be, or anything's different from what I expect, I don't have to stay," Diane added appeasingly.

Looking at her for the first time, her aunt said, "And where will you go after your precious New Yorkers are tired of you? At least your mother had the decency to stick closer to her own kind. If you weren't so much like her, you'd stay here and hope to God Lester Haynes married you." She concluded to the ceiling, "I hope she doesn't think this house is going to be waiting for her after she comes back looking like a cheap fool.''

Diane couldn't think of anything to say after that. The next morning she was sorry, but not too surprised that her aunt wouldn't say good-bye. But she knew she could always return, and that if she had any success at all, her aunt would be very pleased. Her biggest P.R. woman back in Waterloo. She'd certainly earned the right to be proud of her, if only to prove she'd made more of her than her father could have. But Diane's evaluation of the reasons why her departure upset her aunt so much inevitably reduced the level of sentiment to a minimum.

Les's last-minute decision to drive her to the airport in Des Moines impressed Diane as a lovely farewell gesture. But it turned out to be a serious mistake. Their relationship had become strained after she realized how wrong he was in his perception of her. No matter what she told him, his delusion that she really wanted marriage was unshakable. After all the years of thinking he was available if she wanted him, it was annoying to see how coy and presumptuous he'd become.

One reason she avoided a complete break during the final weeks was her concern for how others might interpret it. Also, having been intimates, she thought they should at least remain friends. Still, she wasn't too surprised when he'd originally told her to arrange her own transportation because he might not be "free" the morning she was leaving. When he arrived, it turned out he had something important to say. He waited till they were settled in his car. It was clear something was up when he didn't start the motor.

"I've been doing some serious thinking about us," Les began. "I should've realized how badly you felt after Fran got engaged to Ernie, even though he doesn't have a school situation like mine."

"Look, Les, there's no point to this, we've been through it before. I've got a plane to make, you know." She tried to keep the edge out of her voice.

"Just wait a minute, honey, don't interrupt till you hear me out. Now, I'm not making any definite promises yet, but if Dad doesn't mind, he could let us live free in his house on South Third till I graduate. You'd have to go back to Miller's, but maybe only part-time. Now, I haven't discussed any of this with him, and he might not go for my marrying you, even if we didn't need his help. But if you want to cancel your flight and hold on to your ticket for a while, I'll check everything out and let you know for sure within a week or so. So how about that?"

He reached over to pull her toward him, a brilliant, benevolent smile lighting his face. It had never looked so round, moonlike, and idiotic to her before, lightly freckled and topped with his short, reddish-blond curls. As the beaming face moved closer to receive a grateful kiss, she shoved it back violently with the palm of her hand.

"Listen to me, I've tried to tell you every way I know how that I don't want to marry you! I don't know why you and your father think you're such a hot catch all of a sudden. Maybe *you* think you'd be doing me a favor, but you're not. I'm going to New York, and that's that! Now, if you don't mind, I'll say good-bye here. I know you don't want me to miss my flight."

Les had finally confirmed what she'd begun to suspect. That as a semiorphan with an unsuccessful blue-collar father, she had to be more to be equal. Maybe that was a large part of what going to New York was all about.

The NO SMOKING and FASTEN SEAT BELT signs were on. "We are now above New York City. In a few minutes we will be landing at La Guardia Airport. Please remain in your seats with your seat belts fastened until the aircraft has come to a complete stop."

Diane exchanged smiles with the middle-aged man beside her, who had read during most of the two-hour trip.

"Thank God that's over. It's sure good to be home."

"It certainly is," she responded as the plane gently dropped altitude and landed smoothly.

The stewardess sharply reprimanded passengers who rose to reach for belongings in the overhead racks as the plane taxied. Diane picked up her shoulder bag from beneath the seat in front of her and clutched the case she'd held on her lap throughout the trip. When the plane finally stopped, she stood and waited only a minute or so before pushing out into the aisles. She jostled her way into position among the crush of passengers impatiently waiting for the doors to open.

Her seat partner had spoken to her as if she were a returning New Yorker too. She couldn't allow small-town manners to ruin her image. His words, "good to be home," somehow lifted her from the sentimental doldrums. They enabled her to be stimulated by the same sights, sounds, and confusion that had depressed her in Chicago.

Maneuvering aggressively in the crowds, Diane quickly cornered a skycap after exultantly claiming her luggage from the baggage pulley. When he asked, "Taxi?" as they headed toward the street exits, she said she was taking the "limousine." After he deposited her luggage at the side of a large bus, she understood that the term was a misnomer. But she was still glad Mrs. Kraemer had told her about it. She felt like she'd outsmarted her first New Yorker. Finding few other passengers on board, Diane asked if she had time for a phone call before they left. The driver said she did.

Diane found the last letter from her aunt's friend in her bag and dialed her number.

"Yeah?"

She was surprised to hear the voice of a young man. "Is this 695-9592?" she asked.

"Yeah, who do you want to speak to?"

"Mrs. Emily Kraemer?"

Before he replied, a cultured voice answered. Mrs. Kraemer greeted her and told her everything was ready for her. "Remember not to waste your money on a taxi. Ask someone to direct you to the Carey Limousine Service."

"Don't worry, I already have my seat and luggage on the bus. I just wanted to let you and Mr. Hannah know I was on my way."

"Oh, I see. All right, then. We'll be expecting you."

The bus reached the East Side Airline Terminal in

Manhattan by a fast-moving trip along several expressways that took them to the Queens Midtown Tunnel. The route was nondescript until shortly before they reached the tunnel's entrance. Then Diane got her first view of the Manhattan skyline. It was unexpected and awesome on the clear afternoon. By that time, traffic had slowed. The irregular towers rose dramatically behind a low, sprawling cemetery. With a seat to herself, she was able to stare out the window without restraint or embarrassment. She was still heady and flushed when she got off the bus. Fortunately, there was no struggle for baggage attendants or cabs. In minutes she was inside a taxi, moving west in slow traffic toward 341 West Seventy-sixth Street, with no effort on her part.

Her first close-up of Manhattan was a tangle of taxis, Hertz rental trucks, and private cars. The four-lane crosstown street seemed completely inadequate, while sidewalks were barely used. But pedestrians with newspapers, packages, or leashed dogs increased gradually as her cab inched past the mostly small, well-maintained residential buildings. After a couple of long, slow blocks, the sidewalks took on a new vitality. A sign showed they'd reached Lexington Avenue and Thirty-seventh Street. She'd never seen so many interesting-looking people before at one time. No one looked dull. No one overweight. Everybody moved confidently. They defied the traffic, crossing streets, and set their own pace, maneuvering around each other on the sidewalks.

She began looking anxiously for a sign of Madison, Park, or Fifth Avenue. Although she liked to believe she'd come to New York for solid, practical reasons, that afternoon they were clearly secondary. She wished she could run ahead of the slow taxi to find out how close the movies and television portrayals were to the real thing. From her rudimentary knowledge of the city's layout, she knew she was near the legendary streets.

"Could we go by way of Fifth Avenue?" she asked the driver, leaning forward as casually as possible.

"Yeah, if you wanna get us both killed." The diminutive cabbie scrutinized her in his mirror as he continued,

12

"Going the wrong way on a one-way street ain't too healthy, even if the cops wasn't around to stop us."

Diane sat back, embarrassed, wanting to disappear into the worn plastic seat back. Her waist had become damp, and she wondered if a perspiration problem was going to be a side effect of discovering New York. But the driver took pity on her. She was a good-looking kid. Looking at her in his rearview mirror, he wondered what made the slender, auburn-haired girl so attractive.

Her eyes were plain dark brown, but they were large, clear, and a nice distance apart. Her eyelashes were long enough to be false. He was sure they weren't, though, because her eyebrows weren't all plucked, and she didn't have much makeup on. With her high cheekbones and even features, she might've been a model. A girl around twenty-three or so who knew her way around. But a model wouldn't have acted so awkward when she came out of the terminal. And when she talked, he could tell she was a small-town girl who didn't know which end was up.

"New here, huh?"

She admitted he was right, in her humblest manner. He chuckled to himself, thinking how most people wouldn't tab her as easily as he had. She accepted his peace token, a stick of gum, and was given a running commentary for the rest of the trip.

"You notice I don't have a big partition in *my* cab. I like to relate to my fares if I feel like it. I figure if some junkie's gonna rip you off, he'll do it whether there's some plastic between you or not. I just try to stay outta Harlem and Bed Stuy much as I can, but with business so bad lately, I can't do that the way I used to. It's mostly luck, anyway."

After her Fifth Avenue fiasco, Diane contented herself with the route of his choice, although she noticed he could have turned uptown on Park or Madison. The only thing she could tell about them as they passed was that they too were plugged with traffic.

"I'm takin' you up Sixth," he announced, turning up a street identified as Avenue of the Americas. "Sixth Avenue," he repeated argumentatively, although Diane made no comment. "Nobody'll know what you're talkin' about if you use that City Hall crap. Reason we're going this way is so's you can see Radio City and Rockefeller Center."

After pointing them out, he indicated Central Park, straight ahead of them. Blasting a wooden construction barrier that partially hid the entrance, he turned west beside the stone-fenced park. "Usually I'd go through it to Seventy-second Street, but I might as well show you Columbus Circle and Lincoln Center, although I'll never know why every outta-towner gets so excited about any-place with a fountain or statue stuck in the middle of it."

Although Diane enjoyed all the landmarks the driver treated her to, she was apparently too impressed with Central Park South. The canopied hotels, terraced apartments facing the park, and the uniformed doormen and chauffeurs were like her idea of the better-known avenues they'd missed. She could tell she was in trouble again as soon as she joked, "You can let me out right here. Some people really know how to live."

"There might be a lotta dough here, but you couldn't pay me to live anywhere in the city. I sure don't envy the jerks dumb enough to pay what they do to live next to that jungle. I make sure my doors are locked if I drive through late at night without a fare. 'Bout a week ago some little colored bastard stripped a young white girl naked and raped her four times behind some rocks before he finished with her. And it was in the middle of the afternoon, too. Only a little ways from where our fag mayor was shootin' off his mouth to a bunch of other politicians and reporters."

"Really?" Diane was noticing the number of people going in and out as they rounded what appeared to be Columbus Circle, at Fifty-ninth Street.

"Yeah, *really*. Later they got her to say she made it up 'cause she'd played hookey from school, but that was a lot of bull."

Turning onto Broadway, he had to discontinue his narration to honk and fight for his right-of-way. Before he could resume, Diane spotted a complex of low, glass-facaded buildings around a large plaza, and the promised fountain.

"That must be Lincoln Center, huh? It's gorgeous."

"Yeah, it did a lot for the neighborhood, especially considerin' what the rest of Broadway's turnin' into. But they run rock-'n'-roll shows and way-out foreign movies right next to the opera, so you get all kinds comin' here. Not like the *old* Met downtown. That was real class before Lindsay let 'em tear it down. Now they usually run extra buses to take people back to the East Side on big nights, so's they don't hang around too long tryin' to get cabs. Once some people who came with their own chauffeur were even followed home and robbed."

A few blocks later, he said they were almost at her stop. They turned down Seventy-third Street till it met an avenue that ran beside a bench-bordered, tree-sprinkled park. There was a highway behind it that didn't quite hide the glimmer of water slightly below. The driver didn't have to identify this for her. Mrs. Kraemer had made pointed reference to the fact that her house was "right off the Hudson River, Riverside Drive, and a lovely park," in a letter. Naturally, Diane had spent considerable time speculating about her new residence and neighborhood. Rather than be disappointed, she'd tried, characteristically, to keep a rein on her imagination.

It paid off. As they turned off Riverside Drive and stopped before a narrow, reddish-brown building a couple of doors away, Diane was very much taken by the quiet, shady, prosperous-looking block. Most of the buildings were similar to hers, four or five stories high, with low fences in front of them and decorative metal grillwork on the ground-level windows. They too had separate entrances. One seven or eight steps above the street, the other a couple of steps below. Looking up at the windowed door of her own brownstone, she felt a quiet elation.

The cabbie was setting her things on the sidewalk. "Hang in there," he told her after getting an overly generous tip.

April 18, 1973. She'd made it. She eagerly maneuvered

herself and her luggage up to the doorway in stages. As the cab drove off, she wondered briefly about the background of the hopelessly grumpy little man. There would have been a good chance of coming across him again in Newton. For a moment she was reminded of O'Hare. But the feeling passed quickly. She was too happy for loneliness to seem real.

Chapter 2

Diane was admitted by a balding and paunchy middle-aged man who identified himself as Mr. Hannah, the landlord. The tall wiry woman with short, mixed-gray hair and squinting eyes behind bifocal glasses was Emily Kraemer. Although she entered the foyer behind him, Mr. Hannah didn't appear surprised when she took over.

Examining Diane closely, she asked, "Did you have any difficulty after you spoke to me? We expected you sooner."

"Oh, no, everything went very smoothly. There was just so much traffic, that was all."

"Getting in at the height of the rush hour was a mistake. I was surprised you didn't take the earlier flight."

"I hate to get up early if I can help it. It left at the crack of dawn. Besides, I had a cabdriver who gave me a guided tour all the way here, although he had a lot of gripes about living in 'the city.' I don't know where he was from."

"Many people refer to 'the city' when they mean the borough of Manhattan. But taxi drivers are so crude and ignorant, I'm not surprised by anything they say or do. If yours was any different, he would've helped you more with your luggage."

"I can manage these two." Mr. Hannah picked up her largest piece and bent for a smaller one.

"Be careful, it's the old Samsonite, you know. We can make another trip later. I'm sure Diane's anxious to see her apartment."

Diane could see why this woman had become one of her aunt's few friends after she'd attended her late husband.

Although Mrs. Kraemer was better educated, Diane could've closed her eyes and pretended she was listening to her Aunt Elizabeth as they climbed the stairs.

"I'm sure you'll be very comfortable here. I'm in the garden apartment, and I'll expect you to drop in anytime you want to. I'll be able to help you get started on the right foot."

Diane was still analyzing the offer when they reached her third-floor "apartment." It was a narrow, approximately twelve-by-twenty-five-foot studio room. The walls were painted white, including the natural brick on one side. There was also a bricked-up fireplace. Uncoordinated furniture sat on gray-and-white-speckled tile floors. A blue-tweed-covered double bed with a bolster was against the rear wall, a brown Formica cocktail table and spindly wicker end table beside it. A mahogany chest of drawers occupied a side wall, and a maple dinette table was placed near the entrance with one gold and one black director's chair tucked neatly under it.

The kitchen was an indenture in the wall beside the doorway, camouflaged by bamboo blinds you could roll up or down. All the appliances were spotless and modern, but miniatures such as Diane had never seen before. In Iowa, a kitchen was a major family room. The bathroom was similarly modern, but cramped.

"Well?" said Mrs. Kraemer irritatedly as Diane peered through one of the narrow uncurtained front windows for a sideways view of the park.

"It's lovely, very nice and clean. I'm sure I can make it homey in no time." She inadvertently confirmed Mrs. Kraemer's impression that she was dissatisfied with the apartment and trying to figure out what to do about it.

"You won't find many places as nice as this anywhere in the city for what you'll be paying. Not with rent controls off. If you hadn't been recommended so highly by me, Benjamin could've gotten two hundred dollars a month for it."

"A lot of landlords don't rent to single women, either," Mr. Hannah added, looking to Mrs. Kraemer for additional approval.

18

Since they'd only paid $125 a month mortgage on their whole two-story house in Iowa, Diane considered $150 a month a substantial amount. This misconception and her mixed reaction to Mrs. Kraemer were responsible for her disappointment. On his own, the landlord seemed agreeable enough.

Although Mrs. Kraemer had exaggerated about the value of the apartment to make Diane more grateful, she considered it very reasonable from a Manhattanite's view, despite the motley furnishings she'd helped select. She thought it more than adequate for Diane, because she'd assumed she'd be spending a good deal of time down in her own tasteful apartment. The appreciative words Diane mustered as she followed her downstairs to retrieve the remaining luggage didn't sound sincere to Mrs. Kraemer, and she was clearly annoyed. As for Mr. Hannah, he hurried off with his signed lease and Diane's deposit in traveler's checks. A proprietary tenant like Emily Kraemer was always a mixed blessing.

Diane had barely reached her room and closed the door behind her when a gaunt, heavily bearded blond entered the vestibule from the street. Most of the exchange between the disheveled youth and the carefully groomed matron took place after he followed her down to her floor.

"Thought you said the prescription was all made up and waiting for me at the drugstore?"

"Wasn't it?" Mrs. Kraemer asked evenly.

"You know damn well it wasn't. They said you hadn't even called."

"Well, they were mistaken. They're always so busy. I'm sure they just forgot."

"Bullshit! What did you think would've happened if I'd gotten to meet her? I'll meet her sooner or later anyway. So what's the difference if it's now or later? It's never too late to fuck with her if I want to."

"Do exactly as you please. Just remember you have no income whatsoever unless you apply for welfare or think you're ready to look for work. There's no point in my providing you with a place to live and giving you expense

19

money if you persist in trying to disrupt my life. Next month, I'll see to it that you get your check more promptly. So there should be no reason for you to come around unless I want you for something.''

''Okay, I'm leaving, but just for the record, is Diane as pretty as Barbara and Evelyn were?''

''You're disgustingly preoccupied by the sex and physical aspects of anyone with whom I'm in contact. Don't you think it's a little immature to keep punishing yourself and everyone else the way you do? After all these years, I've had enough, if you haven't.''

The young man looked at her in bitter silence. Then turned and left abruptly. Although Mrs. Kraemer and her odd visitor would have a profound impact on her before the year was over, Diane had no way of knowing it. It was so obvious that they hadn't hit it off, Diane rationalized that it would look ''hickish'' to seek her out too often. Everyone knew how much New Yorkers, even converted ones, valued their privacy.

Determined to be self-reliant, she hated to admit she was scared. Confident she could make it, she was shaky about what she'd do if she failed. Her mind was so jumbled, she didn't even know what to do about food the first night. But, hungry, frightened, and filled with contradictory emotions as she was, she never questioned her desire to become a New Yorker. She'd only glimpsed the city, but she knew she was hooked.

There were so many things she couldn't wait to do, that the biggest problem was trying to establish her priorities. Learning to travel about New York and familiarizing herself with her own neighborhood. Seeing what Parsons and the New York fashion scene were like. Personalizing her hodgepodge room until she could afford something unfurnished in the distant fuzure. And picking up where the cabbie left off in seeing the things she'd known New York to be famous for since she was a child.

Within the first few days, Diane had acquired a good enough skeletal knowledge of her immediate area that she was fairly confident of not losing her way home. Her confidence was bolstered by the gleeful discovery of the number-five Riverside Drive-Fifth Avenue bus that stopped practically at her door. She used it first to go to Parsons on lower Fifth. She was determined to avoid the depressing and complicated-looking subway after a brief exploratory ride on a roaring, viewless train.

Diane could hardly believe the narrow sliver of building between a restaurant and a movie theater was the reputable fashion school. But she was reassured by the beautifully designed parent building, the New School for Social Research, around the corner on West Twelfth Street. Parsons' admissions office was located there in a rear wing on the other side of its large courtyard. Although her acceptance was verified by a girl young enough to be a student herself, Diane was impressed by her seriousness, and relieved by the certainty that her portfolio of sketches and the samples of her work hadn't been approved by some terrible error.

Since there were uniformed guards in the lobby of the various buildings where the classes would be held, she didn't think she could roam through the floors very long. But her glimpses into the uncrowded rooms with abstract graphics on the walls and long work tables revealed that the students were mostly girls around her age, with a smaller number of young men. She left feeling a little like an outsider, but resolved to use the months before fall classes began to acquire more professionalism than she had arrived with.

Posing as a very discriminating buyer, she devoured the construction, lines, and finishing touches on the best garments from Bendel's to Altman's on Fifth Avenue. She made a few tentative forays into some prestigious old Madison Avenue shops before their snobbishness convinced her her pose wasn't as convincing as she hoped. After that she moved on to Bloomingdale's, Alexander's and Ohrbach's and the younger designer's showrooms.

Although they didn't make her think she'd committed a social breach by crossing their thresholds, even at the acclaimed Halston's she felt guilty when she left empty-handed, because the casual shirtdresses and fluid styles were so appropriate for her figure. She was able to return a couple of times after she realized the sales staff let the clothes sell themselves. Their main concern was putting together the proper look and safeguarding the designer's image. Diane had much to learn.

"That bra completely kills the effect. Your bust doesn't look as if you have to wear one. Do you?"

Or, "You'd be surprised at how many of our biggest names don't wear anything at all under their clothes. They let you know they're naked every chance they get. If you must wear something, you'll have to get yourself some body stockings. That panty girdle is impossible."

Her simple sling-backed pumps were also scored. "These pants have to have very high platforms or clogs; otherwise they just drag and look frumpy."

She began to wonder if she'd chosen the right career for herself. Despite her innate interest, it was hard to overlook the arbitrariness and superficiality of the industry. Some of the things designed to be taken seriously were like practical jokes to her. Styles she'd considered outrageously faddy before were almost commonplace in New York. Especially in the East Fifties and Sixties near Bloomingdale's. The more she saw of the trendy young disciples of the 1930's jazz-age look, the less like a potential leader she felt.

It was easy enough to buy more natural-looking underclothes and higher heels, to stop teasing her slightly bouffant hair to conform to New York standards, and to wear a bit more makeup. But the more dramatic cosmetics remained unused after she bought them, and she still kept her hair shoulder-length with a slight wave rather than mimick the longer, dead-straight styles.

In short, while unusually adept at spotting the subtlest of differences, she simply wasn't prepared to shed her old image overnight. Hesitant about fitting into any old mold. This was one of the earliest indications that after years of identification with New York, she wasn't ready to embrace everything as wholeheartedly as she'd anticipated. This ambivalence about her new role would underscore some of her later problems.

During her first busy week, Diane saw nothing of Mrs. Kraemer, but she did meet her other downstairs neighbors, Mr. and Mrs. Stern. They and their infant daughter occupied the duplex apartment on the first and second floors. She was a small, trim brunette whose erect posture and carriage made her seem taller than she actually was. Her face was narrow and tapered, with little teeth and thin lips. Her voice was huskier than you'd expect, and somewhat theatrical, but she came across as genuine and down-to-earth to Diane. Mr. Stern had an average build, with light crimpy hair, and a receding hairline. A mustache made him less bland-looking than he might've been otherwise. They appeared to be in their mid-thirties.

It was very cordial when they first met. However, they didn't act as friendly as she expected after their initial welcome. She didn't know whether it was due to their different backgrounds, their preoccupation with their own lives, or possibly her own awkwardness as a result of an incident that occurred a short time after their first meeting.

While both a radio and a sewing machine were high on her list of necessities, Diane was well into her second week without finding a good buy in either. With no one to talk to, she was going through the quietest period of her life. It was a relief to hear sounds of her neighbors when they were home. Even the baby's occasional crying didn't last long enough to disturb her, under the circumstances. But since they were usually in the downstairs half of the duplex, where their living and dining area evidently was, it was as if Diane was alone in the house.

One night she was up later than usual, making striped denim curtains and matching pillows by hand. She was startled by a sudden moaning. Concerned that someone was ill, she stopped her work to listen more closely. When it was repeated again, louder and more intense, it was obvious what was happening below. She started sewing again, but a few uninhibited words were also audible enough to reach her. Graphic demands by Mrs. Stern. Then there was the sound of Mr. Stern's voice, very low, after which there was complete silence. A few minutes later, Diane heard the toilet being flushed.

Diane was ashamed of the unfairness of her position. She hadn't been in New York long enough to know that the walls and floors of the partially renovated brownstone were less flimsy than many in the newer luxury apartments. Sharing your neighbors' private lives wasn't that unusual. Especially for a single person with a typical pair of neighbors. Despite her efforts to stop thinking about what she'd heard, she couldn't help wondering whether "Eddie" had satisfied Mrs. Stern. Had she reached an orgasm before they finished, or had Mr. Stern reminded her they had a new neighbor upstairs and spoiled everything?

She often speculated about what a real climax would be like, and whether she'd ever had one. Certainly not during the one-minute intercourse with Les. It was over before she was even aroused. She used to get very excited when he was only using his fingers, but she couldn't pinpoint any one moment as a definite peak. She'd stop him after she'd enjoyed herself sufficiently. Whatever peaks she'd known were probably those she'd experienced by herself. Most likely there was something else more dramatic that she'd recognize for sure when it happened.

She realized she was becoming aroused. The sounds from her neighbors, her own thoughts . . . She laid the material aside and stretched out on the daybed, untying the belt of her wraparound. With her right hand beneath the elastic top of her pajamas, she began running her forefinger beneath the shaft of her clitoris. As it stiffened, she used the fingers of her left hand to hold back the flesh around the extended button in order to have greater access to it. Moving her hips up and down, slowly at first, she worked on herself deftly until she began to get a charged, tingling sensation that was almost agonizing. It made her moan softly and move more and more spastically, until she could take no more. She relaxed with a shivery sense of release.

She felt very weak-willed and loathsome whenever she masturbated. Until she went to college, she didn't believe it was possible to satisfy yourself with your own hands, as many of the other girls claimed. She only knew you could

24

make yourself feel good by wedging a doubled-up pillow tight up between your legs and moving on top of it. Or bunching up something furry to rub on.

But those things didn't seem so bad. She'd done them off and on since she'd become too old, around six or seven, to "play nasty" with Regina Hicks. They used to take turns lying, in their clothes, face down on the floor of Regina's barn. The one who "did it" to the other one held the other girl around her hips and rodes up and down on her moving behind. Diane usually liked it best on the top.

During her year commuting to college, the word was out about quite a few girls who hadn't outgrown such childish experimentation. She was careful to avoid all but the most casual of contacts with these suspects. She wasn't too at ease with coeds who boasted about their sexual activities and relished discussions about which contraceptives they preferred, either. She didn't see how they could be as casual about sex as they tried to appear. It occurred to her that the most cosmopolitan girls probably did what they wanted with their boyfriends and didn't bother to advertise it. At the time, her rut with Les was getting a little tiresome, but he acted fairly complacent about it.

There were any number of fellows at Ames she would've preferred to him. The trouble was that the type that appealed to her was usually too popular to be as attentive and reliable as she was accustomed to. Not only that, they were much more experienced and aggressive, coming from all over the country. It was annoying to see how many expected sex after one or two dates. Although she tried to screen them out, it was practically impossible.

Within the first semester, she lost her virginity to a virtual stranger. On their second date, she was reluctantly necking with him after a basketball game. He'd drunk spiked sodas throughout the evening, and afterward, she couldn't budge him from the parking lot. He slid his front seat back so far, it was almost as roomy as Les's famous rear seat. Perfectly willing to go along with him up to a point, Diane misjudged his single-minded, intoxicated persistence. They were so far along when he clamped back her thighs and penetrated her, she knew her protests sounded ridiculous. What made the experience so humiliating was that while it hurt, she didn't bleed or suffer great pain. As a result, the self-centered premed student refused to believe she'd been a virgin. He stopped because she resisted so much he decided she was too cold and phony to be worth the effort.

Perhaps the sourest note of all was that she ended up on the defensive whenever their paths crossed in the future. But that experience gave her the impetus to have sex with Les. Les never knew why the old rules were suddenly dropped or that he wasn't the "first." But whatever sexual rewards Diane expected from him weren't forthcoming.

She was glad that both men were behind her.

Rising from the bed to wash her hands, she sighed resignedly about her situation. Was it sick to have to masturbate as she did? Her sex drive wasn't that compelling, but surely it wasn't unreasonable to want a stable relationship with someone who'd respect you as a person and also make some effort to satisfy you. With all the eligible-looking men around New York, she was certain she'd meet one a lot better than Les, sooner or later.

The next day she bought a small combination AM-FM radio and cassette recorder, resisting the salesman's efforts to sell her a television set too, because a sewing machine was her next must. The kind she wanted was around two hundred dollars, so she settled on a portable advertised as a "special" at eighty-eight dollars from the Singer Center on Seventy-second Street. Everything was more expensive than she'd anticipated. Her plan to come for the summer and be all settled by the time school started was draining much more of her savings than she'd expected.

She'd started out with her mother's five thousand dollars and almost sixteen hundred dollars savings after buying her one-way plane ticket. In less than a month she could see that the careful budget she'd planned to cover her living expenses and roughly twenty-three hundred dollars yearly tuition for three years, without working until the following summer, was completely unrealistic. Food prices along Broadway, as elsewhere, had everyone outraged. Paying a dollar-nineteen a pound for ground chuck at Gristedes to make sure it wasn't fresh-looking on the outside but brown and stale on the inside made her consider going vegetarian. Some of the best manicured and bejeweled hands dug through the meat packages more furiously than she did. Shedding their habitual reserve, some shoppers lamented the fact they weren't on welfare. "At least I'd be entitled to food stamps then." However, since the neat cellophane-wrapped packages of two or three vegetables were priced like rare heirlooms, a single Bermuda onion as high as forty cents, and fresh fruit also going like gems, Diane soon had a choice to make. Eventually starve, find a full-time summer job, or work nights after school.

She hated to give up her leisurely afternoons shopping, enjoying the park, and getting into the feel and tempo of her cosmopolitan neighborhood. She window-shopped and browsed uninhibitedly in shops selling everything from bohemian exotica to antique bric-a-brac. She was continually amazed at the equally fantastic variety of places to eat and drink. There was something for every taste. Kosher delicatessens and restaurants. Chinese and Japanese. French and Italian. Latin and soul.

The area she'd come to was an unusually mixed one in every way. It ranged from luxurious apartments and private brownstones to seedy hotels and furnished rooms. The majority of the residents were middle- and upper-income. But they coexisted with alcoholic old transients and young men who hung around corners or slumped and nodded on benches around the busy Seventy-second and Broadway square. When the young ones idled along Broadway in their mismatched costumes with funny hair or funny hats and inevitable dark glasses, Diane found them more colorful than sinister. Although she walked more briskly if any of them came too close or made a remark of any kind, it rarely happened.

It occurred to her that the relaxed atmosphere during the

early-summer days and nights might disappear when fall came and went. The crowds would thin out, and the square wouldn't welcome the transients when the days grew short and colder. She could imagine how chilly the streets near the river would be. The Riverside Drive vicinity could be particularly desolate and changed. Especially after dark.

These almost subconscious ideas decided Diane on finding an immediate summer job to alleviate her finances, rather than waiting to find a night job after school. She saw it as the lesser of two evils. At least she wouldn't have to come home regularly after dark. It was to be an important decision. She might have worked at home a little longer if she'd realized she'd have money problems so soon. But that was doubtful. She'd been too anxious to come for too long, and her overall mood was still one of great optimism at that stage of the summer.

It was the first week of June when she set out to find employment. Her spirits remained so high, she actually looked forward to working. She wanted a job in the garment center, to learn more about the trade and get paid at the same time. As it turned out, the idea was snuffed out at the first employment agency she visited. Since she hadn't admitted she'd be going to fashion school in the fall and only sought a temporary summer job, she couldn't oppose logically the interviewer's arguments against her preference.

"Most of the better firms are on the East Side or in the Wall Street area. Unless you were looking for showroom work as a model, there's no reason for an attractive girl like you to do clerical work in that kind of atmosphere. It's a cruddy mob scene all around there. Even where the top Seventh Avenue houses are located. You'd spend all your free time dodging hand trucks and looking for a decent place to lunch. They're slow summers, anyway."

Flipping through cards, she first offered her an advertising-agency job that didn't pay much because it was considered "glamorous." Diane declined the next two Wall Street offers because of the traveling, although one paid a very good salary. When the young woman returned impatiently to her cards, Diane accepted the next referral. A top insurance firm on East Forty-first Street with an opening for an assistant bookkeeper.

"You're just the type we like," the violet-haired, sturdily corsetted interviewer told her after efficiently scanning her application and eyeing her appreciatively. "We don't pay the agency's fee for everyone we hire, you know."

Diane thought she was hired as the woman continued that it was a "permanent" job.

"We try to avoid turnover as much as possible. Are you sure you'll be satisfied here in our bookkeeping department instead of doing something more exciting?"

"I know bookkeeping sounds kind of dull, but I've always loved working with figures, and if you'd seen the last little place I worked at, you'd realize that working in a beautiful building like this would be terrific to me, although some people might take it for granted."

"And you're sure you're not interested in trying to get into modeling or the theater, or something like that?"

It upset Diane that she'd devoted so much attention to her appearance and grooming that she might be penalized for it. Thinking quickly, she alluded to her aunt's "stabilizing influence" on her. "I can't help feeling sorry for girls who come to New York looking for the limelight."

After adding that she hoped they wouldn't object to her going to business school to try to advance herself if hired, she was warmly asked to start work the following Monday. She wouldn't have accepted the referral if she'd known permanence was such a big factor, and she certainly wouldn't have tricked her way into it if she'd anticipated all the consequences.

The next few days were a time of indolence for Diane. No pressures of any kind. Only the residual discomfort of an unpleasant encounter with Mrs. Kraemer the afternoon she found the job. In an expansive mood, she hurried to catch up with her as she walked toward the house.

She invited her up to see her new curtains and pillows. "I have almost as much fun decorating as I do making clothes. I used to refinish everything at home. I could antique the cocktail table and chest in a light blue if it's okay with you. Since the curtains have olive and white stripes on the blue, I don't think it would be too much of the same color. And now that I've got a job, I can get fresh covers for the director's chairs, too,'' she chirped. ''Olive and white I think.''

''I already saw the curtains from the street. Most tenants in furnished apartments get the landlord's permission before they start making changes. With outside shutters, I personally prefer simple shades like there were before. If we'd known you'd be so particular, Mr. Hannah would've gladly rented to you unfurnished. I told him you couldn't afford furniture because you'd be a *student*. I didn't understand you were coming here to work.''

That rebuff and Mrs. Kraemer's subsequent iciness were largely responsible for Diane's early concern about a social life. It also increased her dependence on the park. From her earliest days in New York, she always enjoyed going there whenever she got a chance. After it was apparent that her room would never be a home to her, she took to spending hours there, whenever the weather permitted.

By the end of the weekend before she started to work, she'd become familiar with most of the regulars. Many were the elderly retired. Some were young mothers. She exchanged nods and greetings with those who seemed safe and friendly. But there were others whose presence she tried to ignore. The unkempt types who sometimes straggled over from Broadway or other regular haunts. Young men molded into tight pants accompanied by pedigreed dogs. Young women who were conspicuously provocative, in her opinion, and men who ogled all females indiscriminately. And, finally, the interracial couples.

Generally they were casually dressed young black men with young white girls in Levi's. If the girls were pretty and the fellows ordinary, it was especially difficult to force her eyes away from them, because she was so curious about the girls. But whatever the couple was like, she always tried to look at them unobtrusively if she could. They usually acted surprisingly natural.

The funny thing about it was that in New York she was more conscious of blacks, whether they were in mixed couples, or not. The numbers had a lot to do with it, but it was also the way they carried themselves. Since she hadn't come in contact with many blacks until she went to college, she'd never thought much about them before. Although people like her aunt were prejudiced, her mother had taught her not to "look down" on people who were "different." Sometimes certain blacks tended to minimize their differences in order to blend in. Even so, interracial dating was quite unusual back home, and she didn't think she'd ever be very comfortable with the idea, even in New York. Personally, she was much too thin-skinned.

She'd been very shy during her plain, lanky years, although she took pains to hide it. She'd walked erectly and tried to act indifferent to people. After she found she could look attractive, she became more assured, but she still wasn't a self-confident person. For instance, in the park she always wanted to look occupied. She had to have a *Vogue* or *Harper's Bazaar* or book before her as a prop. She instinctively sought the most private spot on a beach or the grass to sit on. Once seated in the sun, she wouldn't have cared if she were invisible.

Chapter 3

Despite her early-summer tan and striking appearance, Diane found that being from Iowa had a disarming effect on people when she showed up for her first day of work. She also made a conscious effort to act as warm and outgoing as her personality permitted.

"I'd have to spend every single weekend on the beach to get a tan like that, and you probably got yours walking around a farm without even thinking about it," a pale but pretty girl declared when they were introduced.

Although Diane told her she spent a lot of time sunning in her neighborhood park in New York, the girl bubbled on. "It must've been fantastic, living out west where you don't have the fresh air and sunshine fouled up with soot and exhaust fumes."

Diane didn't point out that Iowa was a Midwestern state. She agreed that her hometown was clean, but joked about the numerous Iowa meat-packing houses. "If you ever spent any time around one of them, you'd be glad to get back to exhaust fumes or anything else." She laughed.

One or two co-workers mentioned that she didn't have "much accent," and nearly everyone marveled at her outfit, a beige linen dress and matching cardigan jacket with tan piping. They were amazed when she said she'd made it herself.

"Sewing's a hobby that saves me a lot of money," she told them, in deference to her dedicated bookkeeper's role.

There was one reaction of surprise, that she didn't knit

and crochet too. When Diane acknowledged she could quilt, she could see the girl's faith restored. It was obvious that to her and many of the others, Diane had much in common with the frontierswomen.

Diane easily detected the condescension in some of the comments. But she was objective enough to attribute it to their preconceived ideas about heartland Americans, rather than anything personal. In a way, their attitude toward her was flattering, because she was obviously such a remarkable specimen to them. But she was very relieved when the introductions were over. The few men she met were remarkably forgettable despite their enthusuastic greetings. Women outnumbered them about four to one.

At lunch she was invited to join a young woman with blond-tipped brown hair that looked like a home job, and jeweled, harlequin-shaped glasses. About five-four or so, her figure wasn't bad except that her knees and thighs were somewhat large for a miniskirt holdout.

The first thing Mona Chernock did was confirm Diane's impression of the males in their section, advising that all the important ones were in the management and promotional departments.

"But almost all of them are married. Most of the single guys are such creeps, you wonder where they find them. Some of the girls are silly enough to sneak around with the big shots, but it always gets out. I don't know if you remember Dorene, the skinny blond with bangs you met, but everybody found out she had to get an abortion after thinking one of the bosses was going to leave his wife for her. And they say she's seeing him again already."

"I can't remember her, but she must really be desperate. That's a shame."

"Yeah, it's a drag, all right, but if you haven't got anything going for you by the time you're in your late thirties, like she is, there's not much to choose from. It's bad enough at our age." She looked at Diane's hands. "You're not married, are you?"

"Heavens no." In spite of her juvenile-looking dress, Mona appeared to be around twenty-five or so.

"I didn't think so. Where do you live?"

"In a small brownstone off Riverside Drive. It's just a little furnished studio, but the neighborhood's nice."

"Yeah? How far up are you?"

"In the Seventies, Seventy-sixth Street."

"Well, at least you're not too far up, but I'd be careful if I were you, in a building like that, with no doorman or anything. Make sure you haven't got your full name on your mailbox or bell, so no one will know you're a single girl."

"I don't have to worry about anything like that. One of my neighbors is a lady from home, and the only others are a nice couple. The block's very quiet. Of course, if I made a better salary, I'd be in the Schwab House or one of those other beautiful buildings on West End or Riverside."

"I've always been a Brooklynite myself. We have a two-family house in Bay Ridge. I was going to share an apartment in Park Slope with this friend of mine, but she got a thing about Manhattan and ended up with another girl in the East Eighties. The rent was so much more than we would've been paying, she had to leave here for a much worse job, just because the pay was better. She claims it's worth it, but I feel sorry for her. At least in Brooklyn you get something for your money."

Mona didn't come right out and say it, but by the end of their hour, Diane was pretty sure she'd been selected as her friend's lunchtime replacement. She was relieved to have her old solitary meals behind her. And while she thought Mona could've been better turned-out, she was looking forward to having her as a partner for the after-work activities that interested her. A week or so passed before she found she wasn't available.

"There's a terrace-restaurant near me on Amsterdam Avenue that the *Times* says is good and not expensive. Victor's. It's Cuban, but all kinds of people go there, and it looks like a nice crowd. Want to go some evening after work?"

"I don't know," Mona hedged. "I don't like going
34

home alone and using the subways too late at night, unless we got through pretty early.''

"Boy, for someone who was about to leave home and be out on their own, you're kind of scary," Diane teased. "I'm supposed to be the one from the sticks."

"I hate to be the one to break the news to you, but you're the only one who thinks it's so safe alone with all those junkies and welfare people where you are. You're worse than Rita about Manhattan, but at least she knows the difference between Needle Park and Bryant Park.''

"Well, I know Bryant Park's where the main Forty-second Street library is." She figured it was best to play the straight man for a while.

"Uh-huh, and Needle Park's what they call that square at Seventy-second and Broadway. You probably never heard of the movie *Panic in Needle Park* about the addicts around there?''

"Afraid not, but it's funny how people with a lot more than we'll ever have stay and pay so much more than they would in the other boroughs, if things are so terrible.'' She was coming to suspect an element of sour grapes with people like Mona and the cabdriver she'd talked to, who spent more time worrying about Manhattan than the residents themselves.

"Honey, a lot of the older Jewish residents don't pay what you or I would have to. They've been in those fabulous old rent-controlled apartments so long, they're not about to give them up. You should come out to Bay Ridge and see how much more at home you'd feel. But if you're determined to go out in Manhattan, I'd rather try the East Side singles scene than the kind of places you're talking about. And that really turns me off.''

"So, thank heavens for the Knights of Columbus socials, right?''

Although Diane had noticed the arrival of the long-legged, angular-faced young woman with straight dark hair reaching well down her back, and a prominent Roman nose, she didn't realize she'd intentionally paused near them until she spoke.

35

Mona looked around and flushed. "What're you up to? I never would've expected such a busy lady as you to have time to be checking on me."

"I've got your Speedwriting book for you. Rita asked me to give it to you last week, but this is the first chance I've had, sorry."

"That's okay, thanks. This is my girlfriend, Diane. You're welcome to join us if you want to."

"I'm on my way to Bloomie's. If I get too starved, I'll probably grab something from P.J.'s. You're the new gal from Idaho, huh?"

Without being pretty, she had the mannerisms of someone accustomed to being noticed. Although the space between Diane and Mona was negligible in the small booth, she required both a head toss and a backhand sweep of her hair to transfer her attention fully to Diane.

Diane was determined to act. unintimidated. "That's me, Newton, Idaho. It's right near Des Moines."

Jacky looked confused. Then she laughed genuinely. "I'm sorry. Even I know where Des Moines is. You're all right. I really wish I didn't have to run, but maybe we can get together another time." She extended her hand. "By the way, I'm Jacky Peretti." She and Diane shook warmly.

Before she could leave, Mona managed to get in that Diane was practically convinced she should move to Park Slope, and that it looked like everything was "shaping up" and they'd soon "have it made."

"It all sounds very exciting, I'm happy for you. I'll be sure and tell Rita. Afraid I've got to make it now. . . . Ciao," she called back airily from several booths away.

"You were fabulous. That's the roommate of my girlfriend I was telling you about. She's got a pretty good job up in advertising and acts like no one's got anything going for them but her."

It was obvious that Mona would've welcomed her friendship. But considering how limited and provincial she was, she could imagine what someone like Jacky would think of her. After the business about Brooklyn, she probably lumped them in the same bag. It wouldn't have been so annoying if Mona had been more available, even with her shortcomings. Her resigned expression evidently made Mona feel guilty. She offered to introduce Diane to a recently divorced Staten Island cousin.

"He drives a new Impala and doesn't pay any alimony because his wife left him for an unemployment interviewer. He isn't much over thirty, although being kind of bald makes him look a little older. But what a sense of humor! Everybody cracks up over his imitations. I'll bet he'd jump at the chance to pick us up for a drink after work some evening. He might even take us to that Puerto Rican place you mentioned, but I don't know. He goes more for big midtown places like Jack Dempsey's and Mamma Leone's."

Although she acted as appreciative as possible of Mona's offer, Diane considered herself fortunate when the threatened introduction never materialized. She was also relieved after reaching a standoff with some of the gutsier office rejects. As bad as predicted, their offers of such inexpensive thrills as Coney Island, Chinatown, the Statue of Liberty, and the top of the Empire State Building were as unimaginative and ludicrous as they were.

One evening, as she was lugging groceries home from Broadway, she was consoling herself that her life would be more interesting once she started school. Although she'd originally had notions about eating out in the neighborhood from time to time, she'd come to accept the fact that she'd be uncomfortable eating alone. After all the boutiques had been browsed and the novelty of discovery was behind her, she'd become increasingly conscious of being an unattached female alone.

Sometimes she ate a big lunch and almost nothing at night. More often she picked up a pizza on her way home, or chicken from Merit Farms, when she found herself pronouncing her r's as l's from all her visits to Ming Ming for Chinese takeouts. She realized she could've spent less by cooking, but TV dinners and very short orders were the only things she dared risk in her unbelievable kitchen. She had visions of getting trapped inside between an open stove and refrigerator door and never being heard of again.

37

If the bamboo blinds accidentally rolled down on her, she could imagine suffocating.

She'd almost reached her building with her heavy load of staples when she almost tripped over a large wolfhound that ran past her, dragging his leash. More annoyed than frightened, she turned to berate the owner. He turned out to be a tall, well-built young black man. Late twenties to early thirties. She found him unusually fine-featured and handsome, in spite of his large afro and muttonchop sideburns, which she didn't usually care for.

"You don't believe in 'curbing your dog' apparently," she said, less forcefully than if he'd been white, because she didn't want him to think she was prejudiced, and since he was also smiling apologetically as she spoke.

"I'm sorry if Lobo frightened you, but I usually let him loose when we get near the park. He's traffic-trained, for one thing, and if I don't, he almost yanks my arm off when he knows we're almost there. Besides, practically everyone around here likes him and knows he's harmless. I'm surprised you haven't noticed how popular he is, since you're in the park so much yourself."

"How would you know that?" she snapped, embarrassed.

"You're not too easy to miss." He responded easily, oozing self-confidence and lowering his eyes to give her a frank, upward-moving appraisal. He acted like she was an object up for bids.

Very resentful of his presumptuousness, she hoped the flush of anger that warmed her cheeks didn't look like a blush. "Don't let it worry you." She couldn't think of anything to really put him into his place without being very nasty. She angrily turned to climb the stairs of her residence.

"I'm Chuck Johnson," he called out. "I'm right up on West End. Hope you won't still be so down on Lobo and me the next time you see us since we're neighbors."

She looked back to acknowledge his apology. He was stooping to pick up the dog's leash and didn't bother to look around again as he headed toward the park.

It wasn't necessary to push it. Chuck was well aware of

his assets. He knew he was sharp, and how he looked from behind in his snug chinos and denim work shirt with the sleeves rolled back. He didn't want it to be too obvious that he'd created the dog incident to meet her. She had the tall, groovy looks he liked, but he was accustomed to meeting good-looking white girls. Some of the sharpest turned out to be the easiest to make. He had no special shortage, but his sporting instincts were particularly aroused after the brief exchange with Diane. Apart from her looks, she had a certain reserve that made him curious and anxious to break through.

Diane kept thinking about him that evening and the next day at work, although she tried not to. She realized that if he'd been white she would've given him her name and probably ended up friendlier, although she didn't like the idea of pickups. It would've been great to have someone to do things with. Just to sit looking out from a sidewalk café, rather than marching past the other people pitifully, was a constant dream. But as anxious as she was to become a part of the local scene, the prospect of being one of the white girls who held hands with black men made her nervous just thinking about it.

She brought up the subject of interracial dating at work, although she was pretty sure what Mona's reaction would be.

"It's definitely on the rise in certain parts of Manhattan, and it's practically all you see in the Village. But the girls who do it have no self-respect and couldn't possibly care about anything but sex. They don't seem to mind that all those fellows want to do is show them off and take advantage of them. It's a sick scene as far as I'm concerned. Rita could laugh at me all she wanted to, but I personally don't believe in any kind of mixed dating if you can help it, let alone interracial."

Diane hadn't expected to find any people like Mona when she came east. She'd assumed everyone would be much more broad-minded than they were at home. But in some ways, she didn't find the expected differences. For instance, her firm was pretty well integrated, and everyone was friendly, but there was much of the same clannishness that there'd been at Ames. On top of that, Mona claimed that most of their top insurance bosses were not only white, but Christian, and teased Diane because she couldn't tell who was what by their looks.

What it boiled down to was that after nearly three months in New York, Diane was more conscious of other groups than when she'd first arrived. Perhaps that was typical in cases like hers, and not necessarily bad. But she wasn't sure, and she hadn't come east to become like the disgruntled people like Mona and her counterparts at home who were invariably the most bigoted. She hoped she could sort it all out soon and forget about it. She had enough other things to worry about. Something was radically wrong to be in New York so long without a single date.

After the humiliation of being jammed into the park on the Fourth of July with no real alternative from anyone, she was beginning to wonder if she'd been too snobbish about the available office clods and Mona's cousin, the comic. She'd become especially discouraged after reaching the elevator-speaking stage with a handsome young VIP, and thinking her drought was over when he'd invited her up to his prestigious department. But it turned out he was one of the smoother married playboys, and she had to call it off.

One afternoon later in July, during a break, a young man in accounting who'd made no previous overtures toward her offered Diane a quarter for a Fanta orange soda. He saw her digging unsuccessfully in her purse.

"Thanks, I'll pay you back as soon as I finish my pop and get some change."

"Don't worry about it." He paused. "Did you say 'pop'?"

"Yeah, why, what do you say, 'soda pop'?"

"No, just soda. You've got to be from the Midwest. I was stationed in Fort Riley a few years ago, and everybody out there used to say 'pop.' How do you pronounce 'water'?"

"Water. Is there more than one way?"

"See, you can't even hear the difference. In New York, there's more of an 'r' sound instead of the 'wahter' way you say it."

No escape, she was thinking, when he continued. "I thought it was great out there. I wanted to go back after my tour in 'Nam and start a gym or a health club, but things didn't work out that way. Maybe I'll get back there yet. People were very friendly and down-to-earth. Not like they are here."

Diane liked hearing such sentiments for a change. She always felt she should defend her area, although she'd left voluntarily.

"Fort Riley's in Kansas, isn't it? My dad lives in Kansas City, Missouri. I've visited him a couple of times, but I'm from Iowa."

"Really? Once I was in Des Moines and had a helluva time in a little club there. It reminded me of Reno Sweeney's."

"I never heard of him."

"That's the name of a place here in the city," he corrected her gently. "It's supposed to have come from some character in a novel or something. Would you like to go some night for dinner?"

He'd never been attractive to her. He looked somewhat underweight, and only slightly taller than she was in heels. He kept his hair short and usually wore white shirts, very narrow ties, and bluish-gray, narrow lapel suits, whenever she'd noticed him. Sometimes he wore white socks. But when he spoke, his gray eyes crinkled and lit up his face. He dimpled on his right cheek and appeared an entirely different person.

She said she'd love to go.

"Great! I think I'll make us reservations so we'll be all set. How about this Friday evening? Saturdays are probably pretty packed."

"That sounds swell to me."

"Would you feel more comfortable going home and having me pick you up later around seven or so? Or would you just as soon have a couple of drinks up this way right from work, and make it down there for the early show? It's probably around eight. Either way is okay with me. I live in Washington Heights. Where do you live?''

For some reason, going after work seemed more casual and less like a formal date to Diane. She told him where she lived, and they agreed to meet at Longchamps at five-thirty and have a reservation at Reno Sweeney for seven.

Diane couldn't decide whether or not to tell Mona about her upcoming date. She decided not to. If it was the first and last, no harm would've been done. If she heard about it, she could always say it was too trivial to mention. If she found she enjoyed his company, she'd tell her then and build up his assets. They were quite underwhelming on the surface.

Richard Fenster was as amiable and comfortable on their first date as he was two days earlier in the office. There were no conversational lags at either Longchamps or Reno Sweeney's. The tiny, dimly lit club with exposed brick walls had a casual, bohemian atmosphere. She enjoyed the low-keyed, intimate music and Richard's inexhaustible supply of anecdotes about his adolescence and army days. She was surprised he used to like to fight and had become a middleweight boxing champion in his division.

''I was ten and fifteen pounds heavier than I am now. Most guys put it on as they get older, but not me. My posture was always lousy too, and it makes me look more out of shape now than I am. Here, feel this,'' he told her, indicating his upper right arm.

''Very impressive. What do you do to stay so muscular—you don't still fight, do you?''

''No, I'm taking some karate, but I don't know how long I'll stick with it. Haven't got the stamina I had before. Maybe it's all in the mind.'' His manner was wistful. ''Girls go for you if you look like you can handle yourself. I always liked to dance. I could've had a different date every night if I wanted to when I was fighting. But the kind of dancing they do in these crazy discotheques, you couldn't pay me to do. All you do is get your eardrums burst."

Diane said she didn't like loud, fast music either, and agreed when he said he wished you could dance there. When they left he asked her if she'd ever been in the Village before. They walked a few blocks down to Eighth Street and moved along the narrow crowded streets. Many of those they passed were in such odd getups, it reminded her of a carnival. There was a toughness about some of them that contrasted sharply with the innocent vulnerability of others. She was relieved when he flagged a cab and took her home. That was a place she definitely wouldn't want to live in. It was odd that her school was just a few blocks away, and yet the atmosphere there was so different. In some ways it was an exaggerated version of her neighborhood. An ugly caricature.

When Richard dismissed the cab, he explained it was because he would take the bus home. Diane said she'd be lost without it and wondered what people did who had to use the subway all the time. He answered, "Suffer," and they had a nice silly laugh.

"I hope you enjoyed yourself as much as I did tonight. Can I take you out again?"

"Definitely. You're the first person I've gone out with since I came to New York."

"Honest? Now I really feel special. That's one thing I liked about the girls I met back in Kansas. They were honest. Most chicks always pretend they're so popular. I wouldn't come within twenty feet of a girl who looks like you if she were a New Yorker. They're so superficial you can't even hold a decent conversation. Everything bores them."

"It'll be awhile before I'm bored in anyone's company. I'm practically talking to myself nights."

He made another date for the following Wednesday to have dinner in Chinatown. "We'll go right from work so we'll get in early, since it's a weekday and we'll both have to get up early the next morning. We'll save the clubs for weekends, okay?"

He didn't try to kiss her, but squeezed her hand so tightly as he said, "I can hardly wait for Wednesday evening to come, I've been lonely too," that she wondered if she should've accepted another date so soon or admitted she hadn't gone out with anyone else.

She found him very pleasant company, but she couldn't see herself getting serious about him. It occurred to her that if they went Dutch treat that Wednesday, they'd be more like buddies.

Richard's behavior was so circumspect whenever he saw her during the next two work days, she was reasonably certain he hadn't mentioned their date to anyone. But on Wednesday, since they were meeting in front of the building, she casually mentioned to Mona that she was having dinner with him in Chinatown.

"You're kidding! Why him, of all the creeps? He's a joke, the way he dresses. I think he gets some kind of disability too." Mona shook her head in amazement.

Diane tried to describe the spontaneity of their friendship, based on his fondness of the Midwest and his ingratiating personality. It didn't go over at all. When she said, "Well, one dinner date can't hurt anyone," Diane realized she didn't understand she'd already gone out with him. She didn't dare admit it after that.

Diane had trouble matching Richard's gay mood as he steered her through the narrow, colorful streets crowded with orientals, tourists, and personnel from nearby courts. They passed a variety of souvenir, trinket, and food shops until they reached the stairs leading down to the restaurant he'd chosen. It was simply decorated and unpretentious. Tables with pastel cloths and comfortable chairs were spaced for privacy, and a jukebox played relaxing, unobtrusive musuc.

"You have nice taste." She could see him as she had before, but she realized their friendship had been clouded by Mona's comments about him. She was disgusted with herself for being affected.

"If you say that now, wait till you have some of their specialties. They have some kitchen here, not like some of these tourist traps. Their shrimps in black-bean sauce are out of sight." He named several other dishes, some of which were among the more expensive.

Diane hesitated to choose, then decided to approach the matter of splitting the cost.

"Hell, no! What kind of a guy do you think I am? I'm glad I'm the first guy you got hooked up with here. The wrong type of fellow could really take advantage of you. Now don't worry about the price. Read the menu from the left side, as they say. After all, this is a very special night. Money's the last thing I'm thinking about."

When the check came and he got back only a couple of dollars' change from a twenty-dollar bill after the tip, Diane stifled another offer to pay half.

"That was absolutely delicious." If he got some kind of an army pension, maybe she shouldn't worry.

"Yeah, let's hope we won't be hungry again half an hour after we reach your house," he answered, hailing a cab.

Although she might have asked him if he'd like to come in, to be polite, Diane was surprised he took an invitation for granted.

"This is great," he told her, once they were inside. He looked around approvingly, then settled back comfortably on the sofa bed.

"I hope coffee's all right. I don't keep any liquor around, but I've got some beer if you'd prefer that."

"Don't worry, coffee's perfect. Do you have milk or cream?"

"Milk."

"That'll do. We'll have Irish coffee."

"But you need whiskey or something for that, don't you?"

"That's right, I came prepared." Bending over, he opened his briefcase and proudly extracted a pint-size bottle of John Jameson's. "This should be enough. I figured we wouldn't want to get smashed and not be able to go to work tomorrow! You don't have many tapes yet, huh?" He turned on the radio after looking over her limited supply disapprovingly.

Diane could see they were on different wavelengths.

There he sat, making himself at home, planning to be there from the start, while she'd nearly called off their date before it began. But he'd been so generous, she didn't want to look like a bad sport.

She served the coffee in big earthen mugs she'd found in the neighborhood, at Zabar's. He poured in the whiskey as she joined him on the bed. Some of the wariness left her as he continued to chat casually and made no sudden lunges in her direction. Then he suggested that they dance.

"No, I think we'd better not. My downstairs neighbors have a baby. I'd hate to do anything to disturb them."

He reminded her it wasn't yet nine o'clock. "We'll be quiet enough." He turned down the radio. The FM station he'd selected played uninterrupted romantic standards and blues.

"I thought you liked jazz."

"Not at a time like this." He pulled her up gently by the hand.

When the first song ended, he didn't release her. Diane felt his hold tighten uncomfortably around her waist as she was reluctantly moving to the second number. "Watch the old muscles." She managed to laugh. "Between the liquor and a couple of bruised ribs, I won't be able to go to work all week, let alone tomorrow."

"Excuse me, sugar, I didn't mean to get carried away."

He relaxed his grip, but he still pressed her closely enough that she couldn't overlook an erection building in his pants. He put his lips to her neck.

"It's getting late. I'm afraid I've had it for the night. Maybe we can go dancing sometime. It might be fun."

A quizzical look came over Richard's face. Diane's words didn't hit him right. What she said next confirmed his doubts.

"I've really had a nice time, though."

"What's all this *had* a nice-time jazz?" he exploded. "We agreed the last time I took you out that we'd get together early this evening so we could spend the night together and still not be too messed up to make it to work in the morning."

"I don't know how you could've gotten an idea like
46

that," she replied, backing away from him. "I never agreed to anything of the kind! You said we'd have dinner early so we wouldn't be tired, since we had to work the next day. But no one ever said anything about us spending the night together."

"Are you crazy? You told me you hadn't met anyone since you've been in New York, you even admitted you were lonely. But I still put it to you straight about tonight from the jump, so there wouldn't be any misunderstanding. You think I'd be taking you out like that in the middle of the week if it wasn't for something special like we planned?"

"I know you spent a lot. I offered to pay my own way. I can still give you my part."

"Its not just the money. What the hell do you think I've been lugging around in this briefcase all day? You think I carry my toothbrush and razor and a fresh shirt every time I go out on a date, for Chrissake? Oh, man, I know how the local broads operate, but you fooled me with that poor new-in-town bit."

"Okay. I see your point. Apparently I gave you the wrong impression. I *have* been lonely, but not the way you mean. The only thing I can do now is accept the blame for accidentally misleading you and make sure it doesn't happen with anyone else. I don't think I'd ever have to deliberately trick anyone to take me out. What I'll do is give you ten dollars back now, and if you think we should've split the other evening, I'll do that too. After that, I'm willing to still be friends if you are."

"Okay, honey. Maybe it was a misunderstanding. But I'm here now. Don't send me away. After all, we're both human. I know I could satisfy you if you let me. No one would ever know the difference. While we're wasting all this time b.s.-ing, we could be getting undressed and taking a hot shower together. Come on, baby," he whispered. He reached for her hand.

"I'm sorry, Richard, I'm sure you're great, but there's no point in discussing it. If I *was* in the market for a lover, I'd have to know him better than I do you. I shouldn't have invited you up in the first place."

"What would you do if I took off all my things, anyway, and got into your bed and just lay there?"

"I wouldn't do anything, because I know you have too much self-respect to do anything like that. Besides, the walls are like tissue paper. My neighbors can hear me if I cough."

"Self-respect, my ass. If I really wanted it, I could give a well-placed chop that would have you begging me to screw you, if you were able to talk at all. But I'm not going to risk my job on a broad like you."

Diane got her purse as he spoke and took out a ten-dollar bill. As he picked up his case and hurried toward the door, she tried to stick it in his pocket. He knocked her hand from him with a painful blow to her wrist.

"Don't worry about me, I'll survive. Guys like me who get fucked over when they try to treat a girl decently aren't the dumb bastards you think they are. You'll need a lot more pity than I will in the long run. You can count on that."

Slamming the downstairs door as he left, he charged down the outside stairs and nearly collided with Mrs. Kraemer's former visitor on the sidewalk.

"Hey, fella, don't run over me. What's the matter, house on fire?"

Richard glowered at him and brushed past angrily without answering.

Diane had trouble getting to sleep. Whatever happened, she'd never go out with anyone from her office again. It might be better not to have anyone in her room anymore, either, unless she was ready to sleep with the man. She was nervous at the thought of having to see Richard so soon after what happened.

But the next day, to her surprise, he acted perfectly normal, except more friendly and familiar than before.

He greeted her as "Di" or "honey" whenever he saw her, and once, when several people were within their hearing distance asked, "Are you feeling all right this morning?"

"Sure, fine. Why? Do I look like something's wrong with me?" she shot back.

"Oh, no, I was just concerned, that's all. I feel pretty good my own self."

There was nothing subtle about his strategy, but she didn't know how to fight it. Having told a half-truth to Mona before, it was practically impossible to give the details of what happened at her house. She wouldn't understand why she'd let him come up in the first place. Diane certainly couldn't deny he'd been there, since he could describe it in detail. She'd never expected him to be so spiteful. It made her less upset when she decided he could have been just as indiscreet if she'd slept with him.

When she met Jacky Peretti entering their office building the following Monday, she didn't know whether any of the Richard Fenster affair had reached her or not. She was concerned that people might see her a little differently than they had before, but there was nothing tangible to go on.

"My ass is dragging," she groaned, when Diane asked her how she was doing.

"What's wrong, don't you feel well?" She looked as smart as before, but beneath her eyes was a little dark.

"How well can you feel on only three hours' sleep? I was at Southampton for the weekend and wouldn't have come in at all except that I'm out so much, I hate to call in sick on Mondays. What's with you? How do you manage to stay so tan?"

"All I've been doing is warming the park benches on Riverside Drive, but at least it beats being bothered with some of these characters who come out of the woodwork if they think you're new and stupid. I've just about had it, and Mona's not in much better shape than I am."

They'd reached Diane's floor by then. "I'm on extension two-fourteen. That coffee shop you always go to turns me off, but if you're ever at loose ends and want to try someplace different, call me anytime."

Diane was very pleased. If there had been any fallout from the Richard incident, at least she'd been able to use it in a positive way with Jacky.

Diane called her a few mornings later on payday. Since

she and Mona used different banks, their lunch plans were always left loose. That meant there was no routine to upset when it became plain that Jacky didn't require her presence any more than Diane did. She wasn't even mentioned.

They met at the pub-type restaurant Jacky suggested. She arrived a few minutes late with the flourishes Diane took to be her trademark. She introduced Diane to the headwaiter and their waitress, specifically, but no one was actually excluded if their tables were in their vicinity. Diane found that she talked so quickly, it took her a while to get accustomed to it. She'd noticed it before, but thought it was because she was in a rush. However, she was very complimentary about Diane's short-sleeve safari-type jacket in white with green and blue epaulets and navy slacks, while Diane was equally enthusiastic about her well-tailored mattress-ticking pants suit.

Although Diane was somewhat uncomfortable at first, she felt better when she realized that the majority of the customers were very presentable males who seemed to regard them with flattering interest. As she and Jacky talked, however, it tapered off until there were only occasional discreet glances that she was barely conscious of.

At twenty-four, Jacky was married and separated, the apartment she shared with Rita being the one she'd furnished with her husband. She'd expected the extra bedroom to be his painting studio, but it didn't work out that way.

"The poor soul had given up his big loft on the Bowery, and even though he was making a fortune with the galleries, he couldn't get used to living decently. I wasn't that fussy, but there's a limit to how many good things you can junk when different-colored fingerprints and globs keep turning up all over the place. When he got another floor-through down in SoHo, it was supposed to be just for working, but he was so glad to be able to run all around in his sweat shirt and army boots and do his thing without offending the doormen and everyone else, he ended up staying there permanently. He'll give me anything I ask him for as long as I don't bug him. Every now and then we'll have a little light scene down there with a couple of my friends, and that's about it. So what's with you? You don't do too much partying, huh?''

It was as much a statement as a question, made dutifully in the manner of someone yielding to another because of parliamentary procedure.

"I'm afraid not." With no one to mention besides Richard, Mona, or a neighborhood black man whose dog had run past her, Diane felt so limited; she quickly returned the floor to Jacky. Although Jacky seemed at home on center stage, Diane was worried that she might appear too dull to her.

They were about ready to leave when Jacky produced some printed cards with her address and telephone number.

"For the last couple of weeks I've been making it with this engineer I met at Southampton, but it's just about run its course. So you can try me if you're over my way, and hang out with Rita and me if you're ever in the mood to. In fact, we'll probably be making the rounds on Friday night. If you're not seeing anyone, you can meet us at Gregory's if you want to."

Diane was trying to get up the nerve to suggest going from her apartment, but Jacky thought her hesitancy came from not knowing where the bar was. Diane was too grateful to correct her.

"It's on First Avenue, the corner of Sixty-third, I think. I'm never quite sure of any of those streets, but you can't miss it. If you get to Maxwell's Plum, you've gone a block above it, and don't worry, it's very small, so there's no way we can miss each other."

Chapter 4

Diane made her first appearance on the East Side singles scene on Friday, July 20. She came by cab. Both sides of First Avenue were crowded and spilling over with young people. Many of the young women didn't look much different from her. Most of the men were in their twenties or early thirties. There were occasional blacks, but nothing like on the West Side. She and the taxi driver both spotted Gregory's at about the same time on the southwest corner of the street. It was indeed small. Friday's, diagonally across from it, looked much larger.

Anyone who saw Diane get out of the cab and cross the busy sidewalk toward the bar's entrance would've seen a slim, fashionable young woman who was unhurried and somewhat aloof in her manner. She was good-looking enough that her confidence appeared justified, although homely people were clearly outnumbered by attractive ones. However, the reason she was so unrushed was that she hoped Jacky might see her arriving and come out to meet her.

When Jacky wasn't among those seated at the tiny tables behind the picture-windowed front walls, Diane walked in and found her on the outskirts of a small, crowded bar. She kissed her on the cheek and welcomed her as effusively as if she were the hostess at her own party.

"This is Rita, and this is Paul Slattery." Rita was a petite and bubbly brunette with an overbite and none of her roommate's affectations. She said she'd heard all about Diane from Mona. Husky and sandy-haired, Paul looked about six-four and spoke from invisible lips hidden by a thick walrus mustache. Rita and Jacky were both so relaxed that Diane almost forgot she was in a singles bar. She suspected it might not be typical even before they told her it used to be a hamburger stand. She'd noticed that some of the customers looked a little more mature than the crowds in the street, and it also had a live trio on an incredibly small round platform. Paul appeared more interested in the jazz music than most of those standing around them.

Although he didn't have much to say, he insisted on treating her to her first drink. She protested, because Jacky and Rita appeared to be taking care of their own.

"Don't worry about it. I'm supposed to be your first offering of the evening."

Diane shook her head and groaned. "Aren't things like that against the rules? My invitation was just for me and no date. I thought it was going to be just the three of us against the world when I talked to Jacky. Now I feel guilty."

"Don't, I'm the one who should feel like an ass. I had no idea you'd be so attractive."

Paul was nothing like the predatory types she'd expected. But she couldn't figure out why he acted so awkward. He seemed especially sensitive for one his size. Most of the men around them acted very much at ease. If alone, they were looking around coolly, sizing up the unattached girls like a bettor might do before picking a racehorse. If they'd just connected, she could hear bits and pieces of clichéd things people said to impress each other. If they'd gotten beyond that, some had reached the mouth-to-ear whispering stage, occasionally accompanied by inconspicuous touching or testing.

After some floating around, Jacky and Rita were ready to leave. It wasn't clear whether they expected Diane and Paul to come along or not. But neither one of them wanted to be left behind. They'd only been making polite conversation, and Diane was curious to see as many of the singles spots as possible. When, once outside, the two girls decided to cross over to Friday's, she didn't know if it was their usual routine, or altered for her benefit.

Jacky saw a fellow she knew before they'd walked through the jammed outdoor terrace. She ruffled his hair without stopping. It was just as well she didn't, considering the affronted look of the young woman seated with him. Inside, you could hardly move. To Diane it had more of a frantic quality than there'd been at their first stop. However, flanked by friends, she found it exciting. She felt sorry for girls all alone.

She imagined you could spend the whole night in a place like that and never get a drink if you didn't want one. Waiters could hardly squeeze through to the tables with red-and-white cloths that matched their shirts as well as the outside awning. When Paul told her the shirts were the kind worn by rugby players, she thought that was most appropriate.

Paul quietly managed to get their drinks while they were still a good distance from the chrome-railed bar. It was her third daiquiri compared to his fifth or sixth vodka. This time he ordered for Jacky and Rita before they started mingling. Diane nursed her drink because her arms and legs were already a little heavy and her neck and temples warm. The alcohol and sexually charged atmosphere all around them finally loosened Paul's tongue. "Are you sorry you're not more a part of the action?" His gray eyes had gotten so heavy-lidded, a few more vodkas would probably make them as mysterious as his mouth.

"Not at all, I'm fine, but don't let me keep you from circulating," she answered stoutly. .

"For such a beautiful girl, you're quite a sport. Putting up with me the way you do."

"Why do you say that?"

He changed the subject, and between half-listening to him and watching the progressive explorations of a couple up in front of them, Diane didn't realize when Jacky and Rita left.

"Well, I guess that's that. They've formally ditched us."

Diane found that it was almost one-thirty. "Are you sure they're gone? Maybe they're in the ladies' room?"

"They're gone. They left with some clown about half an hour ago."

Diane suggested they might be coming back but that she was about ready to go home.

"Okay by me. We can go anytime, my tab's straight."

She told him she could get home all right and wouldn't blame him in the least if he wanted to stay.

"Forget it, and don't worry, I'm not trying to make out."

Diane wondered how Jacky had come up with a person like him. He was very easy to like, especially considering how much he'd drunk. That was one thing that usually turned her off. But the way Paul drank was more like a person with something bothering him than someone who did it habitually. In the cab she still couldn't find out what the trouble was, as he hardly talked at all. He had the cab wait as he accompanied her up the steps, somewhat unsteadily by then. She was afraid to ask him if he was all right for fear of embarrassing him. "Well, thanks for everything."

"Sorry I wasn't better company," he mumbled. "Guess I'll be seeing you." He looked very vulnerable holding on to the stone railing to get down safely. Diane hated watching him leave like that.

She was feeling less appreciated than ever when she saw Chuck Johnson in the park again that Saturday. His dog was bounding around him and a slim blond woman in a tennis outfit. Diane didn't think he'd noticed her until his companion left. When she walked briskly uptown, he immediately came toward her.

"Am I still regarded as the enemy?" he asked, smiling, when he reached her.

Seeing him leave the other attractive woman to join her was especially flattering after the night before. It would've been hard to pretend she wasn't glad to see him. "Not at all." She extended her hand. "I'm Diane Keely." She glanced around involuntarily to see who was looking as he shook her hand and sat down beside her.

"Whew." He wiped his forehead exaggeratedly. "I

55

needed that. Before I saw you, I'd promised to throw some balls for the gal who just left, so she could practice her backhand. She might not be speaking to me after the way I backed out. I don't think I could've coped with having to face two hostile females back to back.''

"I don't think you could call me hostile, as a rule. But hauling groceries home from Broadway on some of these muggy days doesn't exactly bring out the best in me.''

"Why don't you get a shopping cart, if you must cook and eat in? If you're single, I'm surprised you haven't discovered it's not that much more bread to eat out, and a lot more fun.''

"I guess it depends on the person." If she'd learned anything from the Richard experience, it was not to volunteer anything about how few friends she had. Not only that, she didn't want to encourage him to invite her to dinner, accidentally.

"Yeah, as they say, 'different strokes for different folks.' Some people enjoy doing their thing alone. I'd say I'm pretty gregarious, though. It's hard to be anything else with so many sharp chicks all around. Where do you hang out, by the way?''

Diane shifted uncomfortably. "Nowhere special. Sometimes I go to East Side places, or Greenwich Village,'' she said weakly.

"Greenwich Village? You mean the Village? How long have you lived in New York?''

"Just a few months." A real detective.

"How about that! I should've known. I wondered why you were always alone whenever I saw you. Where're you from?''

She hated him. "Iowa. But you shouldn't assume that being by yourself has to mean you're lonely. Some people like to be selective.'' She was ready for combat, waiting for his answer.

"I think most girls *try* to be." He smiled tolerantly. "Take the girl I was with just now, Janet. She's pretty together. She was married to a broker and took up tennis after they split, as a good way to meet guys. She usually goes over to Central Park, where most of the action is, and saves Ninety-sixth on the Drive for trying to concentrate on her game, like today. I was supposed to throw some balls to her. The trouble is, most of the fellows who take the game seriously don't mix that much.''

"What do you mean?"

"They hardly ever play with girls unless they're something special. Every now and then a fox will show up in something that turns everyone on, and they'll all be on top of her to give lessons or whatever. But most of the time, the girls end up together.''

"Maybe they're better off. If a girl has to look like a go-go dancer to have a male tennis partner, who needs it? It sounds like the fellows are the ones making a big to-do about sex.''

"You miss the point. The girls spoil your game because most of them can't hit and don't come regularly enough to get any better. Some can volley a little, but aren't strong enough to give you a real workout. Most of them can't hit the ball back unless you hit it straight to them, so you end up spending half the time chasing balls. It's a real drag. You can blow your whole hour giving free lessons. "But"—he grinned—"I don't think you'd have anything to worry about if you ever showed up.''

"Gee, thanks, that's big of you.'' She was sorry she'd allowed him to sit down. Apparently he couldn't help being obnoxious, like he was doing her a favor. She wondered if he was really as much of a wise guy as he seemed, or just had a chip on his shoulder when he talked to white people.

Chuck usually knew when he was being offensive. But he figured there weren't many blacks where she came from, and even fewer who were "together" like he was. There was no question she'd ever dated one before. He was anxious to show her he wasn't intimidated by being a first. But as important as that was, he could tell that if he didn't tone it down a little, he'd turn her off completely. "What kind of things did you do back in Iowa?" he asked pleasantly.

"Mostly hoe the fields, seed the corn, and feed the sows," Diane replied straight-faced.

"Oh, come on." He laughed. I know you weren't that much of a farm girl—were you?" He was pretty sure she was kidding, but he hadn't expected such a facetious reply from her.

"Not really."

"So, seriously, what do people go in for, say, in the way of sports?"

"Well, we do have tennis courts. I only play a little, but there're tournament players from out our way. Obviously, we don't have any beaches, but there're a few lakes and enough pools for anyone who wants to swim. Golf's fairly popular, and a lot of men enjoy hunting, but there's mostly pheasant and small game."

"Too bad, that's the worst kind. Around here most people disapprove of hunting. But when the animal can fight back, at least it's more equal."

"I thought deer hunting was popular in New York."

"I suppose it is with the upstaters and the suburban beer-drinking brigade, but not with most of the educated city guys, and definitely not with our local environmentalists. The cats who go for that are usually the ones with the flags on their windows or stickers all over their bumpers. You've seen them, like, 'Your Country—Love It or Leave It,' or 'Support Your Local Police.' But they wouldn't have any trouble out of me, they have a million guns. Anything to show how much man they are, especially if they're over the hump. Pardon the expression."

"Do I have any choice? I thought I'd just be getting a little sun. I didn't know I'd be getting a free lecture on people's politics and sex problems. It's a shame I didn't come prepared with a notebook. I'd feel terrible if I woke up tomorrow morning and found I couldn't keep all your theories straight." She didn't see why he had to knock people because they were patriotic, and she hated the idea that she couldn't mention anything without having it picked apart.

She wasn't too surprised when he smiled at her indulgently. "You don't bite your tongue, do you? Okay, I don't want to overstate my case and bug you, but if you stay in New York, you'll have a hard time trying to ignore what's happening in this country and staying in a bubble. They predict that by the year 2000, all but the wealthiest whites will have moved to the suburbs, and Manhattan will be predominantly black and Puerto Rican. Unless you're going to join the exodus, you'd better start trying to get your head together. Otherwise, you're going to be out of it in certain circles. Most people aren't all that liberal underneath, but it's still in to pretend you are, around here."

"Maybe so." It was the least controversial answer she could think of. She wished he hadn't turned the conversation to that type of thing. If her aunt's friend had lived somewhere else, her life would've been simpler. It was unpleasant enough being on the defensive with a person like Mona at work, without being challenged as a nonliberal by someone like him. Once in New York, she'd expected everything to fall into place. It was disheartening to find herself in the familiar position of being neither fish nor fowl.

"Guess I'd better split before I'm evicted from the bench." Chuck looked at his fashionably large sports watch. "It's time for me to get going anyway. I always forget the time when I start b.s.-ing. Later on, I'm going to be in Tweed's around seven. After the tennis business, I won't be with a date, if you feel like dropping in. You must've seen it on Seventy-second Street, so you know it's no big deal. But some people dig it anyway, if you find you can make it, beautiful. But if you can't because of some other gig or something, don't worry about it. I'll be there with some friends anyway."

"Okay, thanks. I'm not sure if I can make it tonight, but if not, I . . . uh, hope I'll be seeing you around." She could tell her forced smile was tight and unnatural.

"Groovy. If you don't show, at least I'll know who I'm nodding at if we should run into each other again. Nice meeting you, Diane Keely from Iowa. Have fun."

59

"So long." She shook hands again, resolutely. Anything to terminate their conversation. In a way, "confrontation" was a better word.

Chuck called Lobo, sniffing at other dogs nearby, and left the park. He would've made book that Diane would arrive at Tweed's, flustered and defensive, no later than seven-thirty. He was wrong . . . by ten minutes.

As Chuck rose to wave and saunter toward her, Diane didn't exactly consider him her date, since she hadn't come with him. But when he put his arm around her shoulder casually, she realized she'd been splitting hairs and felt extremely uncomfortable and embarrassed. He led her to a table where he'd been sitting with a deeply tanned dark-haired white fellow who appeared a few years older. When he stood to meet her, he was broad-shouldered and more muscularly built and stocky than she liked. But she imagined some women would find him appealing. With a custom-look summer suit and French cuffs, he looked expensively dressed but a bit overdone for the casual spot.

"Diane, say hello to my favorite guinea, Tony Ferrara. Tony, Diane Keely."

Tony was glad high heels were in for men when he stood. He didn't like girls he had to look up to. Even sharp ones. "Glad you could make it. For once Chuck didn't exaggerate about his discovery. But why you'd let a spook like him get his hooks in you beats the hell out of me. Sometimes I think I'm in the wrong racket. Trying to make it with my scrap-metal business, instead of being a playboy on unemployment checks. Like, I'm really out of it, I don't even have a dog going for me."

For the first time in the past few hours, Diane found something to laugh about. She'd changed her mind a thousand times about what to do. Tweed's was one of the small cafés she liked the most from the outside. Still, if Chuck hadn't mentioned other friends, she wouldn't have considered going. It was possible they might be worth meeting. But on the other hand, she was afraid they might be like him. It helped that he hadn't offered to pick her up.

In the end, she decided she couldn't afford to pass up her first chance to get acquainted with at least one of the local spots, although she hated to give Chuck so much satisfaction. Unfortunately, she hadn't bowled anyone over on the East Side.

After meeting Tony, and seeing how he teased Chuck and made fun of the famous Lobo, she recognized him as a natural ally. "You two have quite a friendship," she chortled. "What do you do when you're feeling especially chummy, play Russian roulette?"

Chuck didn't consider Diane's comment amusing enough to justify the conspiratorial laugh she and Tony enjoyed. As they talked about Diane's impression of New York, and a wide range of other subjects, Chuck remained subdued. He became interested when Watergate came up, but Tony said it was being blown out of proportion by "sore McGovern losers." "I'm too busy making a living to be hung up with that crap," he sneered.

The only thing that kept Diane from becoming sorry for Chuck was that he knew more people than Tony. Especially girls. Because of this, he'd regained much of his self-confidence by the time they were ready to leave. Diane liked the dim, congenial pub and the fact that people weren't necessarily coupled off. She was pretty sure that if she joined them there, maybe one more time, she might be comfortable enough to come in alone. A major breakthrough, at last.

They all left after Tony paid the bill. Chuck didn't press his offer to split the check, and made no mention of paying for the two of them. Diane was glad, because it confirmed that, technically, she wasn't his date. If Tony hadn't been there, she'd planned to ask for a separate check, if necessary. The thought of any obligation to Chuck at the end of the evening was intolerable.

Her worries turned out to be so unnecessary she felt foolish for having entertained them. Tony had a white Lincoln Continental parked practically in the doorway. "Man, I don't know how you can take some of those dogs in there. Thank God I'm meeting Gloria at Rust Brown's.

61

Afterward, we'll be going to Hippopotamus. Why don't you two hang out with us for a while? Show Diane a little class."

Chuck said he was tired before Diane could get out something similar.

"Do you want to walk the few blocks in the moonlight or take a short air-conditioned ride?"

"A ride's okay with me," Chuck answered.

"Me too," Diane echoed.

She dutifully complimented Tony on his flashy car as he proudly worked switches for seat adjustments and loud taped music. Since she was seated in the middle, it was obligatory for Chuck to get out with her at her door. But he showed no intention of lingering.

"Tonight was a lot of fun," she volunteered. "Thanks for inviting me."

"Not at all, it was a groove," he answered unenthusiastically. "Take care."

The night would've ended on that flat note if Tony hadn't called out. "Hey, I almost forgot, Liz is giving a cocktail party tomorrow. There'll be a lot of heavy people, if you want to make it."

Chuck acted hesitant, but Diane saw it as another chance to get out of her social rut. "I wouldn't mind going. I hadn't planned anything of consequence for tomorrow." She thought she detected a raised eyebrow from Chuck, but he didn't say anything snide. She hoped they'd all go together. However, it was agreed that Chuck would pick her up around seven. Tony said it would be early in deference to "working slobs."

The next day, July 29, Diane spent half the evening trying to put on false eyelashes for the first time, tweezing her eyebrows, and trying to decide what to wear. The day was overcast. When it started to rain, she was afraid the clinging beige jersey dress she'd decided to wear might get wet and look messy, if not vulgar. She also worried that her hair might become wilted from the dampness. When it was practically seven, she was in a state of near-panic, undressed, and expecting her bell to ring momentarily.

She settled on a totally different look out of desperation.

She put on a forest-green heavy-crepe pants suit with a fitted tailored jacket and a pale-green halter that matched the lining. She brushed her hair back severely into a clasp at her neck, allowing only gypsy curls to dangle down her cheeks to soften the effect. When she finished, she saw it was nearly seven-thirty. The street below was empty when she looked out, hoping to see Chuck in sight. The rain would give him a perfect excuse for not coming. The dread of being stood up became more intense than the fear of looking wrong.

A few minutes before eight, she was almost in tears, ready to remove her makeup and prepare for bed, when her doorbell rang twice. She grabbed her bag and rushed down the stairs like she was after the last train out of the station. Chuck was standing in the entrance beneath a large umbrella when she opened the street door. From her breathlessness and the short time it took her to reach him, it was obvious she'd been ready and waiting anxiously. She didn't try to hide her relief that he'd finally arrived.

He was very pleased. "Sorry I was late. I got hung up. I'd of called if I'd had your number."

"I don't have a phone yet," she apologized.

"Well, I won't make this a habit. Especially after seeing how much trouble you went to for me. You look wild! No one would ever take you for a small-town chick tonight. You look more like a high-priced fashion model or a gal who only parties with the beautiful people."

"I was going to wear something altogether different until it rained. You're sure I don't look too severe with my hair like this and all?"

"I don't see how you can call it severe, but whatever it is, I dig it. It really knocks me out."

Getting in the cab Chuck came in, Diane was amused at the idea that men were supposed to go for a soft, feminine look so much and be outraged when miniskirts were no longer in style. But there she was practically unisex along side Chuck, and he loved it. She hadn't dressed to attract *him*, but she was glad he approved.

He told the driver they were going to the Colosseum House on West Fifty-eighth Street. When they reached the entrance on the circular driveway, a friendly black doorman greeted and announced them. Upstairs they were admitted by a male guest apparently nearest the door when they rang. The foyer had a bar and tortoiseshell wet-look walls. Inside, the living and dining rooms were a pale gold with a large white area rug and white canvas sofa and chairs, piped with gold. The brown-and-white-tile flooring in the foyer was repeated in the dining area.

Despite some forty or fifty guests, the apartment didn't seem overcrowded. Some sat on the sofa around a glass-topped cocktail table, some of the younger ones were down on the long-haired rug, and the dining area absorbed some more of the crowd. They'd passed a few guests stationed at the illuminated, cabinet-styled bar.

"What a fabulous apartment. I never thought I'd see anything like this outside of *House Beautiful*. Where's the hostess? What's she like?"

"She's okay. I don't see her, but she must be around someplace. Let's get something to drink. What do you want, same as the other night?"

"Who cares, I'm drunk already. Don't you think this place is terrific?"

"She has a nice layout, but I've seen better. I could take you to friends of mine where you'd really flip. People with their own townhouses and valuable antique and art collections. Now, that's what you call fabulous. This isn't raising that much hell. But who wants to spend all night talking about interior decorating? If anything's going to get you all shook up, I'd rather it was me."

She'd forgotten how competitive he and Tony were. Naturally it annoyed him for her to keep raving about an apartment Tony had invited them to.

"The daiquiris were nice last night. Do you think they have the makings for them here?"

"Yeah, most likely. Let's see what's what."

Chuck was looking for the rum when Tony spotted them for the first time. He rushed over and kissed Diane on the cheek. "Hey, you look great. I was in the kitchen. When I saw you just now, for a minute I thought Chuck had brought someone else. Come on, let me introduce you around.''

Chuck blocked his efforts to separate them. ''Cool it, man. Can't you see we're trying to get something to dry us out? These jive artists aren't going anyplace.''

''Okay, man, be a drag. Diane, I'll make sure you at least meet the hostess later.''

''That's fine. Don't forget.'' Diane had no objection to remaining with Chuck for the time being. There was plenty of time to meet people informally without enduring an awkward series of introductions. Looking around, she noticed that guests ranged from white-haired, pink-faced banker types to young colored girls with elaborate rows of braids all over their heads, and a tall shaved-head black man with an earring in one ear, who had an entourage about him. She was glad to see an encouraging assortment of eligible-looking men, although there were some very beautiful females too.

''There're some gorgeous girls here,'' she told Chuck as they remained in a spot near the bar with their drinks.

''No competition, don't worry.'' He slipped his arm around her waist as he spoke.

''Seriously,'' she continued, temporarily doing nothing about his arm, ''which ones appeal to you the most?''

Reluctantly, he chose a willowy blond and a slender brunette with a very deep cleavage for her size.

''What about that gorgeous black girl with the slit to her thigh? She seems to be making quite a hit. I wonder who she is.''

''She's all right, but not my type.''

''What do you mean, do you know her?''

''No, not personally, just the type. I know she'd be a real ball-buster.''

''Why do you say that? You know plenty of attractive girls, why would she be any different? I thought they were your specialty.''

''A girl's got to have looks before I'm interested in her, but she's got to know how to behave like a woman too. Not like some goddamned Queen of Sheba!''

Diane hadn't expected him to get so worked up. She

65

moved out of his hold and turned toward him quizzically. "You sound like you think a good-looking black girl is more difficult than a good-looking white one. This girl at work says Jewish girls can be the most demanding of all sometimes, and you get along with them, don't you?"

"I don't limit myself to any one group, but I do all right. This chick with all the theories, what is she?"

"Catholic, if that's what you mean. But I don't pay that much attention to what she says. I'm just curious about what you think."

"Uh-huh, well, I think this whole conversation's a little silly, but if it'll make you any happier, the point I was making is that a white broad who might give an ofay trick a hard time would know better than to try it with me. Someone like your pal might turn out to be a pushover if anyone felt like being so bothered with her."

She assumed "ofay" was white. Sometimes she thought he went out of his way to sound hip. "You mean white girls make fewer demands on you?"

"Maybe, but why are you so hung up with how I get along with other women? Isn't how we relate to each other what counts?"

"I don't want to bug you, but I get the impression you avoid dating black girls with a lot to offer because white ones let you get away with more and maybe even spoil you because you're . . . uh, different, and they don't expect you to be as responsible as they would otherwise." For some reason, she didn't mind getting a rise out of him when she realized she might be carrying her comments too far.

His expression became tense and angry. "First of all, I don't relate to people who say 'different' when they mean 'black.' I don't know how you refer to black people in Newton. But what is this, anyway? Birds-of-a-feather-should-flock-together time? I don't have to be defensive because white girls happen to dig me more than most gray cats. What's the matter, afraid you'll feel the same way if you stop fighting it? I know you're getting the same vibes I am, you're just ashamed to admit it. I know where you're coming from, you're not the first girl I've known who

66

never made it with a black cat before." He didn't look angry anymore. His eyes met hers challengingly.

Although Diane conceded to herself that there might be an attraction there, she was sure it was far less than he assumed. "I give up," she said simply. "Let's change the subject. Is the hostess around yet?"

"Now she wants to change the subject. Why, what are you so afraid of? I really dig you, I wouldn't try to con you. You're even afraid to look at me all of a sudden."

She stopped looking around to satisfy him. When she faced him, he put a hand beneath her chin and brought his mouth to hers so unexpectedly, she couldn't turn her head away in time to avoid a moist contact with his lips. He acted like he expected her indignant response. As if it was a joke on her.

"What makes you think you can pull something like that? You must be crazy. I never saw anything so nervy in my life," Diane railed.

"You're right. Public displays of emotion. Very poor taste, et cetera, et cetera. But wasn't it delish?" He ran his tongue lightly over his lips and grinned.

Tony returned then, guiding a full-figured, elegantly gowned black woman with a mixed-gray afro. Chuck was only mildly disturbed at their appearance, because he figured he'd managed already to get to Diane, in spite of herself. Diane was still very annoyed, especially since she couldn't tell how much anyone had seen and didn't want to draw unneccessary attention to them.

"Liz, you know Chuck," Tony said, "and this is the girl I told you about, Diane Kelly. Diane, this is Liz Cooper. Wasn't I right, would anyone believe she was from Newton, Iowa?"

"I don't know," she answered, winking at Diane as they shook hands, "I've never met anyone from there before."

Diane pumped her hand enthusiastically. She liked her on the spot, although she wasn't what she expected.

"He doesn't even know her name right, it's Keely," Chuck interrupted, shaking his head disgustedly. When Diane said it was a common mistake and started telling

Mrs. Cooper how much she liked her apartment, Chuck looked more disgusted. Then he excused himself "to rap with some brothers across the room." Diane thought he was pretty phony, joining the group of black men with hard slaps and clenched fists, when he insisted he couldn't get along with colored girls.

"I get the impression I'm being manipulated," Liz said as Tony hurried to freshen Diane's drink. "This is about the first time I've seen them interested in the same person. Usually there's no conflict, because they stick to strict boundaries, Tony uptown and Chuck downtown. Apparently Newton hasn't been decided yet. Or if it has, Tony doesn't think so."

He quickly produced Diane's drink and tried unsuccessfully to take her limp free hand in his. "Chuck's crazy if he thinks I invited you here so he could monopolize you all night. It's bad enough he brought you as late as he did."

"I think I'd better be checking on the rest of the mob. I'm glad they invited you tonight, Diane, but you'll have more fun if you start circulating a bit. I'm sure you won't come across anyone any nicer than these two, but it won't do you any harm to exercise all your options."

"Well, I'll be damned," Tony exclaimed as Liz glided off. "She acted like I wasn't even here. She never would've talked like that in the old days before Lindsay gave her a fancy title. I could've been the door prize then. Now, I'm just another slob. No wonder a lot of people hate to see people like that get ahead. It doesn't take them long to forget who they are."

"She was just being nice to me. If she was like you said, I'd be the last person she'd show any interest in. Who am I? Besides, she has all kinds of people here. Some actually look a little weird. If she was all that snobbish, she wouldn't have them."

"Are you kidding? See that dirty-looking blond guy over there? He's one of the most popular composers in the city. He does classical and chamber music for things like the Shakespeare Festival, and gives jazz concerts too. The fellow in the sandals speaking French is a famous documentary producer. That heavy black woman on the floor is a Broadway actress. Not all the important people she's got look far out, though some of them don't want to be noticed one way or the other. That's one thing I have to give her credit for, whether I'm pissed at her or not—she does know plenty of big shots.'' He surveyed the scene with pride before focusing again on the composer, frowning. "I couldn't make it like that myself, though. I like to be clean. The kind of women I go for won't have anything to do with you if you're in that raggedy bag."

She almost let his words pass without comment. Then she remembered what Mrs. Cooper had said earlier. She hoped she sounded casual as she asked, "Do you go out much with black women?"

"Yeah, why not? I'm not looking to settle down yet, and black chicks turn me on. Now that the white ones are all into women's lib, I really go out of my way to avoid them, present company not included. You're nothing like the kooks I'm talking about. Of course, black girls have gotten more uptight than they used to be. They're a little hard on you if you're not a brother. I'd be lying if I said they weren't. But as long as they treat me right, I'll treat them right. I can do them a lot more good than most of the black cats they go for."

"It sounds a little commercial to me."

"Not to me, it comes out a lot cheaper than getting sucked in by some Italian virgin. They're worse than the libbers. One kiss and you're engaged, and next time you look up, you've got a heavyweight and a bunch of little leeches to feed. Who needs it?"

"So Liz really has you and Chuck pegged. 'Jack Sprat could eat no fat, his wife could eat no lean,' huh?" She was fascinated by what she'd unearthed.

He had no trouble figuring out what she meant. "Chuck's more hung up than I am. I go out with white girls sometimes if they don't get on my back. But the kind of girls I'd take out, who'd be bugging me about marriage, wouldn't give Chuck the time of day. He doesn't have enough to offer. Looks and a front don't always make it. He attracts only a certain type. They might look good on paper, but they've all got problems. I could see last night you weren't falling for him and his bullshit. That's why I made sure I'd see you again.''

"People talk about women. I thought you two were supposed to be such buddies.''

"I'm not trying to put him down. He's a real dynamite guy in some ways. But I know him. He only looks out for Chuck. A girl's got to be a little masochistic to make it with him. He wouldn't know what to do with a girl like you except mess over her. He couldn't relate to any one chick if he tried. He judges broads by things like how much head they can give. I'm not knocking it, but he won't even take care of business without that. There's a lot I could tell you about him if I wanted to, but I think you're too smart to waste your time with him as it is.''

Diane thought Tony was beautiful when he gave Chuck a hard time to his face, but hearing such personal things behind his back offended her. She wouldn't trust him as a friend, no matter how many parties he knew about. "Don't worry about me, we're barely friends. I'm sure it won't go much farther than that.'' She began to fidget. "Where's the rest room? I haven't done anything to myself since I came in out of the rain.''

He insisted that nothing was wrong with her, but indicated the direction anyway. "We'll get together again later, okay?''

Under most circumstances, an increase from zero to two suitors would've been flattering. But she was sure Tony was interested in her only to deflate Chuck. And Chuck had no idea of his own limitations. She didn't know what to do about him. When she reached the bathroom, the sophisticated reflection in the mirror was so inconsistent with her self-image, she was surprised by it. No repair work was needed, but she brushed her hair anyway and dabbed some Miss Dior on her throat and wrists. She went out determined to measure up to her deceptive appearance.

She'd left her drink on the other side of the room. She looked for a cigarette to hold nonchalantly instead. A pack lasted her forever, but she found she didn't have one with her. She started across the room, but before advancing very far, a dark-haired, mustached man asked her if she'd like to dance. There was only a handful of other couples who'd started while she and Tony talked. After a few strained minutes in an uncoordinated imitation of the solo style that seemed to be called for, her partner suggested they give it up and talk.

Diane liked his simple apology for not waiting for a formal introduction. She also liked the way he looked in his blue blazer, plaid pants, and tinted aviator glasses. When he asked her how long she'd known Liz, he passed over her answer with a comment about how few native New Yorkers he met. "I'm one, but don't hold it against me," he told her. "I get away from here every chance I get. You're looking at a frustrated beach bum. I'd rather sail and snorkel and scuba-dive than make money, but unfortunately I can't do one without the other. You look like you must spend a good deal of time on the beach too. Where do you go?"

"Nowhere very interesting, I'm afraid."

"That's too bad. I was lucky, we got a pretty good deal on a little less than an acre right on the ocean at Quogue. I love privacy, but most of what's left of good beachfront property is being broken up into small, crowded lots. Do you know the Grenadines?"

"No."

"I'm not surprised. They're a chain of tiny eastern Caribbean islands, one of the Windwards. Absolutely beautiful, but still relatively undiscovered. They've spoiled me as far as beaches go. Petit St. Vincent would be my Shangri-la if I could manage it. Unfortunately, I have to make do with a couple of months there every winter."

"My heart goes out to you, having to struggle along with what you have here in the meantime. Do you have a house built yet?"

"Oh, yes, I'd enjoy having you out some weekend when you're free. Is there a long waiting list?"

Although Diane didn't plan to accept a weekend invitation from him so soon, she was enthusiastic about getting to know him better. She was about to suggest he call her at work when she remembered he'd said something about "*our* good deal" before. She glanced at his hands. He wore no rings. If he were free to invite her for a weekend of her choice, it didn't seem likely he was married.

"Did you buy your house with a co-partner for expenses? Even a good buy must've cost a small fortune."

"I was able to swing it."

"So you have a big place like that all alone?"

"I'm not always alone, but I am this summer."

"What arrangement do you usually have?"

"The usual, I suppose. My family stays there all summer, and I go up weekends. This summer they're in Greece."

"Your 'family'?"

"That's right."

"You mean a wife?"

"Yes, my wife and children. Two boys, seven and nine. I hope your questionnaire isn't much longer. After all, I'm only suggesting a weekend away from the city if you'd enjoy it. Or we could see each other for dinner or cocktails in town if you'd prefer. I'm not proposing anything complicated. If you're concerned about any problems, don't be. I'm in advertising and I've been married long enough for my wife to be relaxed about the women I come in contact with, even though most of them are beautiful like you. I move about freely, and so does she, but I'm not a fly-by-night. So don't get the idea I'm interested in you only as a one-night stand. I can see that's not your style. Who knows, if we hit it off, we might get a nice arrangement going. Is anything wrong with that?"

It all sounded so plausible and natural Diane thought something might be wrong with her thought processes. She looked around again, hoping for a graceful way to excuse herself. Chuck was nowhere in sight. Tony was concentrating on an uninterested-looking black girl.

"I'm afraid it might be awkward. I can only be reached in my office, and there's no privacy there at all. It would be a problem just keeping in touch."

"Look, luv, here's my business card. If you decide you'd like to see me, don't worry about calling. Just give my secretary your name, and there'll be no hassle in reaching me any morning or afternoon."

She took the card and put it in her purse.

"Okay, thanks. I guess I'll be checking on my friends now. If we don't get a chance to talk later, you'll most likely be hearing from me."

As she left the bathroom earlier, she'd passed a dimly lit, partially opened room with conversation and soft music coming from inside. She decided this might be an alternative to another bathroom retreat. She'd never suspected her first New York cocktail party would be so hard. Opening the door tentatively, uncertain about what she'd find, she was struck by the spicy, pungent aroma that dominated the room. It wasn't the first time she'd smelled marijuana, but it was the first time she'd voluntarily joined a group where it was being smoked. Hesitating in the doorway, she got welcoming gestures from some of the dozen or so guests lounging about on the bed and carpeted floor.

"Hi." Her cheeriness was manufactured, as she entered smiling.

Before she saw him, she heard Chuck call out. "Hey there, what've you been up to? Come on over here."

Sitting on the floor in a corner near the windows, he cleared a spot for her next to him. He was in a group with another fellow and a couple of girls.

"I was about to come looking for you. Beginning to think you might've split with Tony or some other dude. See the effect you have on me. Insecure already."

She found she didn't mind him saying things like that to her in front of those people. It could've been worse. "I talked to a couple of people and danced awhile. I thought I'd take a break."

"Well, it's more real in here. None of that 'and what line are you in?' jazz."

She could sympathize with him, thinking about the affected advertising man she'd just met.

The scrub-faced girl in granny glasses next to her was nudging her to pass along the joint their immediate group was sharing. "This is quality stuff," she volunteered, as Diane accepted it, turning to Chuck.

"Here, I'm not curious," she whispered to him. Until

73

she'd reached college, she'd never smoked plain ciga-
rettes. She didn't inhale after she started. She wasn't
surprised when Chuck took a couple of deep drags. If they
hadn't been in a group, she would've asked him not to use
it around her, although she realized she was more squeamish about the possibility of arrest than many people. But
still, considering Mona's theories about interracial
couples and "pot parties," they'd be prime suspects even
if they weren't using it, she thought.

"So what do you think of the party?" Chuck asked.

"I'm not sorry I came," she was responding, when she
saw something she considered the most shocking she'd
ever witnessed. A few people across the room were using
folded bills to sniff a white powder into their nostrils. They
did it so openly, she knew that it too was accepted by the
group. The man wasn't much different from the one she'd
been speaking with before, except for graying temples and
sideburns, which made him more distinguished-looking.
The girls could've been pretty young secretaries or school-
teachers.

There was no point in expressing her outrage to Chuck.
Apparently this was his scene. Grass, cocaine, and God
alone knew what else. Trying to appear composed, she got
up, saying she'd be right back, and left the room.

In the rest of the apartment a few more people were
dancing. The atmosphere appeared more relaxed because
people were less separated into groups. Working her way
to the front door as quickly as possible, she pushed aside
momentary guilt feelings about not saying good-bye to the
hostess. If she permitted things like that to go on in her
home, Diane wasn't concerned about her own manners.

Chapter 5

Waiting anxiously for an elevator to come before Chuck or Tony realized she was leaving, Diane was jarred when she heard the door being opened again. When she saw it was a slender, bespectacled young man, she was greatly relieved. Just before the elevator arrived, he spoke for the first time.

"I wasn't enjoying myself either." His tone didn't suggest he expected an answer.

Diane offered none, focusing her attention on the numbers of the floors until they reached the lobby. The doorman assumed they were together and made no offer to get her a taxi. As Diane was unaccustomed to such services, she walked quickly through the entrance and down the curved walk. She hesitated only after she reached the sidewalk.

It was drizzling. The West Fifty-eighth Street block was almost empty. Ninth Avenue was closer but appeared equally dark and deserted. Columbus Circle and Eighth Avenue or Broadway would be a longer walk, but there was plenty of light and activity there. A cab should be no problem, but there were plenty buses as a last resort. It wasn't yet eleven o'clock, although it seemed her ordeal had been interminable.

"I don't suppose you'd be willing to accept a ride from a partial stranger?" the young man from the elevator asked over her shoulder.

"Thanks, but I'm sure I won't have any trouble getting a cab," she responded firmly. She was resolved never to be picked up again.

"I could get one for you on Ninth Avenue, and you could go back under the canopy and wait so you don't get all wet, if you'd like."

"I appreciate your offer, but there's no need for you to trouble yourself. I'm sure I can get one at Columbus Circle with no problem."

"It's no trouble. I'd be happy to get one if you don't mind waiting a few minutes."

There was no point in overdoing the independent theme. She agreed to wait while he walked toward Ninth. Seeing no sign of him or a taxi after a few minutes, she decided to start off for Columbus Circle before Chuck came looking for her. She'd walked only a short distance from the building when she heard a car honk lightly, as it pulled over beside her. Instead of a brightly colored taxi, she saw a dark-brown, expensive-looking European car. Frightened, she was about to retreat to the building when the car stopped a little ahead of her. But then the young man got out.

Bowing slightly, he said, "Please forgive me for being late, madam, I was delayed in traffic, but I assure you it won't happen again."

Diane smiled at him, shaking her head with amusement at his tenacity. "So this is your version of a cab?"

"Excuse me, madam?" he asked innocently, opening the rear door of the sedan and standing aside erectly for her to enter.

His performance was so realistic, she could almost believe he was someone's chauffeur. He had on an expensive-looking dark suit, but that wasn't necessarily inappropriate for a certain type of driver. But then he closed the back door, opened the front, and said, "I'm Bob Smith. Don't worry, I'm harmless."

"You're taking as much of a chance as I am," she said, getting in. "I could live in Hackensack."

"You don't suggest Hackensack to me, but I'm prepared to take you wherever you want to go. I noticed you before you left the party. When I saw you rushing out, I was very disappointed, until it occurred to me that you might allow me to accompany you if I could catch you and

76

you weren't driving. So the farther away you live the better. The more proof you'll have that I'm completely at your disposal.''

"You're lucky. You won't have to be tested. I'm on West Seventy-sixth Street. Maybe I seemed phony by not accepting your offer sooner, but you know how it is, certain things are 'no-nos.' This certainly beats a taxi any day, though. It's very nice.''

"Thanks, I'm glad you like it, even though it's a few years old. It's a hand-me-down.''

The tan-leather upholstery and the interior in general looked as new and rich as the outside.

"Well, you keep it beautifully, and no one expects people to go out and buy a new Rolls-Royce or Mercedes-Benz every year like they would a Ford or something.'' She wasn't sure what kind of car it was, but since he didn't seem to realize it, she decided to gamble.

"I suppose not, especially a Rolls, but they're too rich for me, old or new. If I'm not being too personal, though, why'd you leave the party in such a hurry?''

"God, I didn't know it was that conspicuous, but I don't mind telling you at all. I was in the bedroom with the friend I came with, and everyone was smoking marijuana. Then I saw some of them using cocaine. Cocaine! I've never seen anything so incredible in my life. The idea of being at a party where that kind of thing was going on was disgusting. I'll bet you would've gotten out sooner yourself if you'd known what was happening.''

"That was it? That's the last thing I would've thought of. I imagined you'd probably become bored.''

"You did? Why?''

"I suppose because you looked so . . . uh blasé. Not like a young woman who'd be disturbed about what you just described. Maybe you would've reacted differently if there weren't so many unfamiliar people around.''

"What difference would that make? It's still sick. Especially since Mrs. Carpenter and her guests are supposed to be so distinguished.''

"I think that's part of what I mean. I don't know how most people think, but at a large party like that, it's almost impossible to know everyone. Of course I'm not, but someone like me could be an undercover man. You wouldn't expect to find intelligent people using cocaine so indiscriminately under such circumstances. When they did, I can understand your leaving. Why take such unnecessary risks for something other people are doing?''

''That's right. Can you imagine how crazy people must be who'd become drug addicts, with so much to lose?''

''They say you can't get addicted to cocaine, and it's so expensive that most people couldn't make it a habit if they wanted to. I think that's why it's getting to be something of a status symbol among some successful people. They probably figure it's all right as long as they can afford it and are careful to use it discreetly. A lot of people need something to give them a boost, but anyone can tell that you wouldn't need any crutches.''

''Why do you say that?''

''Just looking at you, the way you were dressed and carried yourself. You had to know how you stood out from the women who looked so busy in those bright, printed tents and long skimpy dresses. The girls in blue jeans gave the impression they were trying too hard in a different way. You looked like you were accustomed to 'doing your own thing,' as they say. Hearing your strong opinions reinforces what I thought. You'd be the last one to be intimidated into going along with the crowd in a situation where you had nothing to gain. Most girls would've sat there waiting for their boyfriends to take the lead. It's a good thing your friend was smart enough not to try to stop you,'' he concluded admiringly.

Having endured her Sunny Brook Farm image so long, she could resist the urge to set his thinking straight. He had her so typecast, she was surprised he didn't try to name her astrological sign. They'd reached Broadway and Seventy-fifty by then.

''Do you realize we're practically at your door and I don't know your name, although I know so much about you?''

''Diane Keely. It was fun talking to you. Do you have far to go after you drop me?''

78

"Not at all, only to the East Eighties."

"That's good. Have you always lived in that area?"

"Since I've been in New York, but I like it over here too. The Drive's one of the most beautiful parts of the city."

"Yeah, I love it. I only wish I was right on it so I'd have a view."

"I wouldn't think you'd stay here if you weren't satisfied. Do you share the brownstone with friends or . . . anything?"

"No, but the woman in the garden apartment used to be kind of a friend when I first moved in. It's not that bad for something temporary."

"Well, I hope you can move soon." He'd stopped at her building and turned off the motor. "Could I see you again? I'd be very grateful."

"Sure, I don't see why not." She was deliberately nonchalant so she wouldn't look too available, considering the way they'd met and his illusions about her personality.

He insisted on walking around to open her door, in spite of the rain. He reached in and put his hand under her elbow, in such a solicitous way it avoided any suggestion of intimacy. After opening her door at the top of the street stairs, he asked, "Is it possible to see you next weekend? Will you have any free time?"

"Sure, if you let me know early enough what day you'd like to see me."

"Next Saturday?"

"Fine."

"Shall I plan on taking you to dinner or do you prefer doing something else?"

"Dinner's fine."

"What time would you like me to come?"

They agreed on eight o'clock. He'd remained out on the stoop as they talked. "You'd better get back to your car before I have your pneumonia on my conscience."

"Yes, Diane," he said, bowing slightly, reminiscent of his earlier behavior, "I'll be careful."

For a quiet, rainy Sunday, there was an unaccustomed

amount of activity in front of the house. Mrs. Kraemer looked out to see what it was this time. Seeing Diane return with a different man in such a short period of time was very upsetting to her.

That Monday, Diane was so heady with all she had to report, she could hardly wait until lunchtime. She was trying to think of some way to get Mona and Jacky together when Jacky rang to say she was on a different schedule but could meet her the next day. She apologized for not seeing her again before she left Friday's, but didn't elaborate. Although meeting Bob had lessened Diane's sensitivity about her flop with Paul Slattery, she was relieved when Jacky didn't mention him, and she didn't either.

To keep Mona from feeling too left out, Diane minimized her East Side singles evening and moved quickly to Bob Smith. She said she'd met him at a party her "neighbors" had invited her to. Mona thought he sounded so perfect, Diane was unprepared for Jacky's reservations about him the next day.

Until she heard his name, Jacky's only criticism was that he sounded a little "too straight" for her taste.

"Bob *Smith*? Well, I guess it could have been 'John Doe,'" she said disappointedly. "Do you think he's married? In a way, he doesn't sound smooth enough for a player."

"If he were married, I don't think he could've been free anytime on the weekend I was, do you?"

"Nowadays, almost anyone can pull that off if they don't overdo it. Then, of course they could have an arrangement, or she could be on vacation."

Naturally Diane thought of the ad man, but considered them complete opposites. "Well if he *is* married, he's some actor."

"Personally, I don't think it's that big a deal, as long as you don't get too hung up until you find out what his story is."

"Mona thought he sounded so eligible there'd be all

kinds of girls after him, although I told her he really wasn't all that handsome.''

Jacky had become too quiet and contemplative for her. When Diane asked if something else was bothering her, she answered apologetically. ''You don't suppose he could be gay, do you?''

Diane didn't know what to think by that time. If he wasn't married or gay, Bob might be so busy he'd only been kidding around when they'd met, and she'd never see him again. But since Jacky wasn't naturally inquisitive, more given to nonstop talking about herself, Diane could hardly resent her questions about him. It wasn't much consolation when she showed no promise of becoming a hypocritical office threesome with Mona, either. When Diane mentioned several movies and she said she'd seen them, Diane thought they'd reached a premature dead end until Jacky told her she could still call her if she was in the neighborhood.

Although Jacky didn't make any specific plans with her, Mona became more flexible as a result of their previous activities. She agreed to see a movie of Diane's choice without insisting on a bowling date out her way first. While that was progress, Diane was still upset about Bob. Her uncertainty made her concerned that her abrupt departure from the party might have finished her brief friendship with Chuck. She didn't want things to be so strained they couldn't be casual friends anymore when it was so hard to avoid him.

She decided to see if he was in the phone book. He was. She waited until her afternoon break and still felt funny about calling a man who'd never given her his number, and whom she'd been ashamed to admit having gone out with. However, with Jacky in the picture, it didn't seem so out of place.

Chuck answered, ''Hi,'' on the third ring in a contrived, sexy voice. It was so apparent he expected the caller to be some female or other, Diane almost hung up.

''Hi, this is Diane Keely,'' she said instead. She realized too late how humble it sounded to give her full name. "I called to explain about Sunday night."

"Hey, baby, I'm glad to hear from you. I was worried about you. I figured you must've gotten uptight about that scene when you didn't come back after a while, but it never occurred to me you'd split altogether. I would've come out right away if I had. But I didn't want it to be too obvious what was going down, so I cooled it a while before I left. Why didn't you wait for me?"

"Maybe I would have if I'd known more people, but I doubt it. All I know is, I never expected to be anyplace where people were using that kind of stuff. I still haven't gotten over it. You don't use that other business, do you? You know what I mean."

"I've snorted it a couple of times, but it's not my bag. I was glad you were cool about the grass, though. It's almost impossible to avoid that. At most of the parties I make, there're more smokers than drinkers. Liz is so square she doesn't like anything but alcohol around. That's why anyone who wanted to get high had to do it in the bedroom. She would've flipped if she'd known about the coke. But don't worry, you'll never be put through any changes like that again when you're with me."

"Okay, that's settled. I just didn't want you to think I'd gone off without saying good-bye or anything for no good reason. I've got to get back to work now, though."

"Hold it a minute, sugar. When are we going to get together again? You've got the advantage on me now. You have my number, but I don't have one for you."

"Maybe I'll get a phone sometime soon."

"So how're we supposed to keep in touch? I'm not into ESP, and keeping up your social contacts through the park can get a little creepy after a while. We could get run in for loitering. Besides, I'm not always in town on weekends."

She realized he had to try to be smart the minute he thought she wasn't properly responsive to him. Who needed that?

"Don't worry about my social life, I don't need the park for anything of consequence," she snapped. "Take care." She hung up before he could answer, disgusted

82

with herself for calling in the first place. Even if she never saw Bob Smith again, she'd call the family man before she'd bother with Chuck anymore, and she was sure she'd never be desperate enough for that. She didn't know what his background was, although she liked his particular dark, continental looks. She wondered if there might be various cultural differences that sometimes made men like him and Chuck cockier toward women when they were good-looking or successful. But then, remembering the conceit behind Les's last-minute proposal, she couldn't make up her mind if they were any worse or not.

Seeing *Last Tango in Paris* with Mona had more of an impact on Diane's thinking about relations between the sexes than she recognized at the time. She'd previously seen a couple of movies alone after Mona rejected them as being too "arty," too serious, or having no plot. She saw *Cries and Whispers* when it reached the Embassy, a few blocks from her house, although Mona knocked the ads of a bare-breasted woman holding another one to her. Diane found the movie depressing but still liked having access to it. It was very unlikely she would've seen an Ingmar Bergman film of that nature in Newton, although everything from Fritz the Cat to *Blacula* was rated for decency by the *Witness,* the local Catholic monthly.

Going to a crowded first-run East Side movie was something she'd tried only once. She'd hated standing on the line with no one to talk to. She knew she'd have to wait forever for *Tango* to reach the local theaters near her, but she didn't have the courage to go to such a publicized erotic movie by herself. She was delighted when Mona agreed to accompany her. She rushed to get their reserved-seat tickets. The demand was so great, they wound up practically on the front row to get the hour and day they wanted.

Arriving apprehensively at the Trans-Lux East Theater, they were relieved to see females well-represented among those waiting around the theater. Few of the men fit Diane's naive stereotype of Forty-second Street porno fans with shifty eyes and newspapers or hats over their laps. It was a fairly typical East Side movie audience, and there was a festive mood as they filled their seats and waited for the movie to begin.

Within the first ten minutes, the trench-coated Marlon was having intercourse with a strange young woman against the wall of the vacant apartment where they'd just met, her legs wrapped around his waist before they finished frantically on the dirty floor. Since this was what Diane had expected, she settled back to enjoy it vicariously, as so many other sexually inactive people like her. But as the movie progressed, she was disappointed by the unexpected shift to obscene language and the sadistic rectal penetrations that Brando's character was obsessed with either giving or receiving.

She found the collateral movie-within-a-movie about the girl's life silly, and the story of his life unbelievable. But what ultimately disturbed her most was the consequence of Brando's determination to end their nonverbal, animal relationship and persuade her to marry him. When the movie ended with him dying from the girl's bullet as she rationalized that he was "just a stranger," Diane resented it as an undeserved indictment of women.

She and Mona agreed that it was generally the female, not the male, who wanted an emotional commitment rather than a casual affair, and that the film was farfetched and overrated. However, Diane was happy she'd been able to see it.

"A five-dollar ripoff if there ever was one," Mona declared. "All these foreign movies are alike. I'm glad I saw it, though, because it was so awful it'll keep me from wasting my money on any of the others they make such a fuss over."

They were both hungry, but Mona was rushing home to eat. When Diane told her she thought she'd call Jacky to see if she was free to meet her, Mona did her best to discourage her. "Why eat out and spend all that money?"

"I don't mind, I don't do it that often."

"But it'll be late by the time you finish."

"Not that late, and besides, there're plenty people around."

"Sure, maybe you'll be okay here, but what about when you have to go home?"

"Don't worry, I'll be all right," Diane answered firmly.

"You know Herb's been after me to have a serious talk with you about your attitude," she began. Diane braced herself. He was the policeman she'd met bowling recently. "He says you should at least carry something for your protection if you're determined to stay where you are. Some hair spray and a whistle is better than nothing, but a gas gun would be safest."

"What's that?" she asked resignedly.

"It looks like a real gun but shoots pellets instead of bullets. It could still kill someone if they were close enough. They're illegal, but he says he'd rather see a girl up before some grand jury than in the hospital or morgue. He's thinking of getting me one."

"Good luck, Bonnie."

"Okay, be funny. I don't like to scare you, but I don't think you realize how many unsolved cases there are around you. Not just robberies and muggings, but cases where women have been killed in their own apartments in buildings right near yours, and they never found who did it. Those street people might look like they're out of it, but they spot girls like you, and once they size up your situation, anything can happen. Herb says a phone's an absolute must, and to get one right away, even if it means telling the precinct and the telephone company you've been followed or something if it looks like a long wait. We're really concerned about you."

"Yeah, I guess so. Tell Herb I said thanks," Diane replied flatly when she finished. After all that, no one answered at Jacky's. She decided to go to the Zum Zum nearby, but found she wasn't hungry anymore. She partially attributed it to the stern-faced service of the unattractive counter women. Homeliness and brusqueness could have been job requirements, although they were less stern with men. But when she left before getting waited on, she knew that the service was the least of it.

Walking across Fifty-seventh Street to catch the number-five bus uptown on Sixth Avenue, she envied, for the first time, the homogeneity of the people she passed. When she got off the bus at her corner, the Drive was typically quiet and semideserted. Only an occasional car, and no pedestrians in sight. It couldn't have been much later than other times she'd come home from late shopping nights, but nothing was the same. Everything was sinister and threatening.

The shady trees scattered about the park could hide vicious assailants. The sunken playground between Seventy-sixth and Seventy-seventh could conceal the most horrible crimes from passing traffic, and the empty rows of benches above looked so cold and grim she could hardly imagine them with people. She quickly turned the corner to her house, clutching the keys she'd removed from her purse before leaving the bus. She peered around continuously as she opened the outer door, closing it nervously behind her as she unlocked the inner one. Shaking and breathing hard, she reached her own door and locked it behind her.

Mona had finally accomplished her goal. On Thursday, July 26, less than four months since Diane's arrival, she'd finally lost her prized defenses against the virulent fear that immobilized so many. She made coffee with trembly hands and tried to figure what to do. On her school budget, she couldn't think of anyplace else in Manhattan she could afford to live and would consider herself safer. She dreaded a distant family-oriented suburb. The most accessible parts of other boroughs might be all right, but were probably no great bargain. Farther away, she'd be dependent on the subway to get back and forth to an inconvenient location she didn't want to be at in the first place.

Considering her limited options made her calmer. She'd get a telephone as quickly as possible. Maybe a whistle. After that, what? Hair spray, lemon juice, hat pins? Illegal weapons? Where would she draw the line? There was no telling how effective they'd be, and only one thing was sure. They'd constantly remind her of possible danger. Whatever she did, she knew she could never regard her neighborhood as before, in spite of having no friends to share it with. It was impossible not to be angry at Mona for what she'd done. She couldn't help being bitter toward her. She'd forced a major change in her attitude, but with what effect on the odds for her safety?

When Diane arrived home from work the next day, she found an unstamped envelope for her stuck above the mailbox. Her first thought was of an apologetic note from Bob, canceling their date. She unsealed it gloomily, and was surprised to find a studio-type card from Chuck inside. A picture of a crying clown was on the front, and the handwritten message on the inside said, "In mourning for a dying friendship . . . at Teacher's, seven to eight this evening," above Chuck's tiny signature. She could tell he'd made it like that deliberately.

Coming from Chuck, it was pretty humble. She recognized Teacher's as a restauraunt on Broadway and Eightieth. It wasn't particularly interesting-looking from the outside, but she'd heard the food was good. She hated the timing of the note, arriving the day before she'd find out if she was still comparatively friendless or not. If it had been more presumptuous, she would've ignored it regardless.

As it was, her earlier concern about burning her bridges behind her prematurely made her decide to go. She decided that if she left before dark she shouldn't have too much to worry about. When she set out around seven-thirty, she was uncomfortable until she got to Broadway, but once there she was all right.

At first she saw no sign of Chuck among the people inside. He wasn't at the small bar, and she didn't have to enter very far to see he wasn't at any of the tables of the modest-sized restaurant. Almost relieved, she was turning to leave when she saw him coming from the unused rear part of the restaurant.

"Man, lucky I got a busy signal on the phone just now," he said, grinning when he reached her near the doorway. "I thought you weren't going to come and was trying to reach someone else to lift my morale. It was groovy of you to show after the way I acted on the phone the other day." After they were seated at his small table, he radiated warmth as he looked across at her. "I've missed you."

"Thanks, I'm sorry you thought I wasn't coming." She was getting to know him. He'd probably become nervous when she didn't arrive earlier and devised the telephone-booth business so he could disappear in there from time to time so she wouldn't catch him watching the door for her and looking anxious. Once she decided how transparent his behavior was, it surprised her that Tony hadn't figured him out too. That evening, without his needling or her own resentment, she got to know Chuck better than she expected to.

His parents lived in Baltimore. His father was a postal clerk and his mother a saleswoman. They encouraged him to go to college, but it was a football scholarship that made it possible. He was in his sophomore year, studying to be an architect, when he made his girlfriend pregnant.

"It wasn't much of a love match. I was something of a big man on campus, and she was the only daughter of a successful West Indian doctor. Neither of us was really strung out on the other one when it happened."

"If her father was a doctor, she must've known about birth control. She probably liked you more than you thought and wanted to have your child."

"Definitely not. That was about ten years ago. The pill was pretty new, and she wouldn't have anything to do with a diaphragm or anything that would show we were consciously planning to make it. She used to talk all the time about how 'loose' the lower classes were in the islands, and all the illegitimacy. I didn't think we'd ever go as far as we did."

"So how did you start having sex?" she asked hesitantly. She was afraid she'd gone too far when he raised his eyebrows slightly at the question and said something about "kissing and telling" not being "too cool." But he seemed more than willing to go on after that.

They'd been going together fairly steady for over a year, although both were popular and had other dates from time to time, when she got the idea he was getting interested in another girl who was very good-looking and "fast" by her standards. Although she considered Chuck basically unsuitable in much the same way that Lester's family regarded Diane, she didn't want to lose him to the other girl.

The first time they made love was in her finished basement after a party. She later claimed she was too high to know what was happening. He used a rubber, but after that, if she found he had one, she got insulted because it looked too premeditated. He'd been withdrawing, coming on her stomach, when she got pregnant.

They planned to get rid of it before either of their families found out, but neither horseback riding, nor quinine, nor steam baths, nor pills from friends worked. But then a doctor's injections brought on her period lightly, and she thought she was all right. But when nothing happened the following month, she got reexamined and found she was still pregnant.

"I couldn't find a doctor or nurse to do an abortion, only this woman who'd do it if we provided the place. When she showed up with liquor on her breath and started laying newspapers on the floor of the motel, I told her to get the hell out. Denise wound up telling her father everything when she wanted to go to Puerto Rico with a girlfriend in the middle of the summer and he got suspicious. Normally, the whole family went to Canada or England summers, and the Caribbbean in the winter.

"By then it was almost four months, and he ordered us to get married immediately because he didn't want to risk a late abortion. We agreed to tell people we'd been secretly married before but were afraid to tell her family."

"That's really something. You're the last person I'd ever have expected to have had a wife and child. What happened, didn't it work at all?"

"Of course not, neither one of us wanted a marriage like that. I had to stop school in the middle of my junior year. I was trying to study and play ball and work too. We were ashamed to live the way we could've afforded to, so her father was helping us a little at first, but that came to a dead halt when our son turned out anemic. Her old man blamed me and the abortion attempts and refused to have anything to do with his treatment or medical bills. Even working full time, I couldn't have come up with all the money I was supposed to if she hadn't remarried shortly after our annulment.''

"How long were you together?"

"About eight months after the baby was born."

"I guess she kept the child, huh?"

"Are you kidding? She married a white Trinidadian. They moved to England, and I heard her old man helped set him up in a business. Our kid was the last thing she would've wanted around."

"Was she very . . . uh, fair?" Diane asked.

"No, quite dark. She was gorgeous but very defensive about her color. She used to embarrass me talking about her Carib Indian blood. I tried to tell her how old-fashioned that shit was. She was so proud of her delicate features and straight hair, she couldn't get over it when our son looked like any other little black baby. The funny thing is, I felt closer to her after he was born."

When Diane asked where the boy was, Chuck looked down at the neglected beef stew before him before giving his barely audible answer. "He died a couple of years ago. He was staying with my parents, but I hadn't seen much of him. At first I thought it was a weight off my back, but later . . . I don't know. I almost went into analysis . . . . But what the hell, how'd we get into all that anyway? It looks like every time we're together you end up trying to psych me. That's usually my game. I figure I've paid my dues, I don't have to do any soul-searching about where I'm at now. But you'd better cool it unless you're trying to bring out the serious side of me."

It was Diane's turn to work on the food. Before she could think of anything to say, he continued.

"When I told you I'd missed you, earlier, all you said was 'thanks.' Does that mean I was all by myself?"

She hated to lie or say something phony and evasive when he'd been so open with her. She carefully kept her eyes away from his face. "Not really, I've thought about you too, sometimes."

She tried to appear nonchalant as he reached across the

table and pressed her hand gently between both of his, running his fingers sensuously through hers.

"Wouldn't you like to leave here and come to my place with me?"

From his point of view, she imagined it was a natural sequence of events. He hadn't proposed anything directly, and if he had, it probably would've seemed reasonable to most of the girls he met. But even if he were white, she couldn't have pictured herself becoming intimate with him after such a brief relationship. Under the circumstances, it was out of the question. But since he'd only asked her to his apartment, it was hard to find a suitable answer.

"It's a little late to see it tonight. I'd just have to rush in and rush out. Maybe I'll run by some other time, on my way from work or something."

"Tomorrow's Saturday, you wouldn't have to rush in and out unless you wanted to. I've got a big pad, very together. I was lucky, got it before decontrol. We can listen to some sounds and relax."

"It sounds very nice."

"So?"

"I'd hate to go, and risk some misunderstanding that might spoil our friendship just when I'm getting to know you."

"I don't think that would happen. There's no reason for a misunderstanding if we only enjoy each other and do whatever comes naturally. We wouldn't have any blueprint, as far as I'm concerned. I'd just like to be alone with you. I'm too big for hand holding and stealing kisses in public, if I can avoid it."

"I'm not sure I'm ready for that much at this stage, although I'll admit I feel closer to you tonight than I did before. Sometimes I don't know what to think of you."

"In other words, I'm still on trial. Sort of a probationary period."

"I wouldn't say that. Give me a chance. After all, I haven't known too many big-city playboys like you." She tried to sound light.

"Oh, sure, that would naturally make you uptight about getting closer to me."

They both knew what he meant as, in silence, they finished the cheesecake he'd recommended. When they left, he walked her home without touching her except to mechanically touch her elbow whenever they came to a curb.

"Here you are, safe and undefiled. Have a fun weekend."

"Thanks for dinner, I'm glad you thought of the note. I applied for a phone today. Would you like my number at work in the meantime?"

"Why? You know how to reach me if you feel like it." He took it anyway when she found some paper and wrote down the number. He'd hoped she might break down and invite him in at the last minute. But he could tell from the narrowness of the building what her studio was probably like and figured she didn't do much entertaining if any.

She was turning out to be more difficult than he expected, but she had a way of responding to him just enough to keep him interested in her. More than anyone he'd met in a long time. Although his interest wasn't only physical, he'd become very turned on when he thought they were going to be alone together. He decided to see who he could turn up on such short notice.

Within the hour, he was lying back sideways across his king-sized bed with Sheila Gresh kneeling on the floor in front of him, alternately sucking his penis, licking his balls, and sticking her strong tongue in and out of his anus while he pressed down on her head. Heaving, moaning, and fantasizing about what it would be like making love to Diane.

Chapter 6

Diane was having trouble concentrating on her scheduled date with Bob Smith the next evening. She was sorry Chuck had told her so much about himself. It was easier to minimize him as long as he remained one-dimensional. She managed to sleep later than usual that morning so the day wouldn't seem so long. Since it was slightly overcast, she decided to stay in and write to her father, her aunt, and Fran. She wanted to make Fran's a nice long one, but after she asked everything she could about her wedding, she realized they didn't have much in common anymore. She didn't want to exaggerate about her life in New York, but she knew she couldn't tell her the truth either.

Later she dressed without enthusiasm, pulling her hair back as before, but avoiding any special efforts because of the uncertainty of the date. She prepared herself as best she could for a disappointment. Glancing out the window idly about quarter to eight, she saw a parked car that looked like Bob's, but she couldn't see the driver clearly. She waited awhile to see if he'd get out to ring her bell. When this didn't happen, she decided to go down anyway to see if it were he, since she was ready. Bob saw her through the side-view mirror and got out of the car as soon as she appeared on the stoop.

"Hi, I got here earlier than I intended to. I didn't think you'd be ready yet, so I decided not to ring your bell ahead of schedule and look like I was trying to rush you."

Diane couldn't laugh the way she wanted to over the irony of his statement, for fear he'd want to know why.

She confined herself to an enigmatic smile. "Sometimes I'm pretty disorganized. Don't let tonight fool you. But don't ever worry about being too punctual. It's nice to see you're so reliable."

"You didn't think I'd be reliable before? You're not serious, are you?"

"I figured you probably were, since you were so accommodating the other night. But since I've been in New York, I've stopped taking too much for granted."

"You didn't tell me you were from out of town. How long have you been here?" he asked, starting the car.

She tried to improve on her stock answer. "Not long enough. I'm still recovering."

"How about that. It couldn't have been as bad as the part of New England I was born in. There were only a few dozen families. But we left when I was a kid. I'm surprised you had the patience to stay as long as you did," he continued after she got where she was from out of the way without his asking.

"If I'd known before, I wouldn't have been so worried about tonight."

"Why were *you* worried?"

"I assumed you'd probably been everywhere of consequence, and was worried about making a reservation someplace you might not care for. Then too, until I saw you, I wasn't sure if you'd remember our date, or have other plans. Now I have no reservation, mind you, but I thought of the Sign of the Dove, unless you'd rather go somewhere else."

"That sounds good. I hadn't forgotten tonight. I had you in my appointment book, with a reminder, 'Kept me from getting wet,' so I wouldn't get confused." She could tell she hadn't overdone it when he laughed delightedly. She found herself surprisingly comfortable in their unexpectedly reversed roles.

They went through Central Park on Sixty-fifth Street. When they reached Sixty-fourth and Third, he turned uptown and slowed down to look briefly for a nonexistent parking place in the street. She spotted the restaurant's name on the bright-yellow corner building decorated with masses of greenery and hanging vines. She'd been attracted by its singular appearance whenever she passed that way. It was so hard to overlook that the name had sounded familiar to her. As the passed the glass-enclosed, intimate cocktail terrace and reached the wide stairway to the main dining room, she found it unintimidating despite its elegance. The mirrored walls and elaborate chandeliers were softened by the profusion of trees and plants that looked like they were there before everything else. There was a fashionable but unpretentious-looking crowd.

When Bob spoke with assurance to the maître d' and they were seated at a table of his choice, alongside the windows, Diane enjoyed the feeling of being "in." She didn't think it was fair to compare the restaurant with the other places she'd gone to, but she was also more confident being there with him.

The gigantic menus printed in French and English had no visible prices. Although she started out gamely reading the French side, she found that her school courses couldn't help her with the names of dishes that often included a regional description. She had no trouble recognizing the *escalope de veau* as veal scallops, and wavered over having that with only her drink before. But Bob suggested an artichoke appetizer and recommended the filet mignon with mushroom caps. She had great admiration for him when he chose the escargots for himself and ordered venison to follow the frogs' legs. Although she had the impression he wasn't a hard drinker, Diane found Bob took considerable care with the wine list before ordering.

"This is great, you couldn't have made a better choice," she told him, unobtrusively taking everything in over their drinks.

"I'm glad. I tried to think of someplace I liked that was large enough to get in without calling ahead of time. Otherwise I would've taken you to the Lutèce garden. As far as I'm concerned, it's in a class by itself, although with the Côte Basque, La Caravelle, and La Grenouille getting so much more publicity, I know a lot of people prefer them. Especially women. Somehow they're very attracted

95

to places with a reputation for snobbishness. Are you like that?''

''Not me. I've heard of some of the things they do. Like not admitting women in pants or men without ties, even if they're famous. I read where one won't allow women to wear their sunglasses pushed up on top of their heads. I started to wear a long skirt tonight just in case, but I decided this jumpsuit was wide-legged enough that hardly anyone could object to it.''

''I didn't want to say so before, but I'd never voluntarily patronize a restaurant where people paid to serve you have the audacity to tell you what to wear. If I went, it would only be to satisfy someone else. I don't see why someone like me has to be judged by people with no real credentials outside of the limited field they're trained in.''

''You dress so conservatively yourself, it's a wonder you feel so strongly about it. They'd love you anywhere if there wasn't any question about your date.''

''I've gotten accustomed to wearing my regular business clothes whenever I go out. If I look too conservative, though, I could try to be more casual if *you* wanted me to.''

He sounded so apologetic she regretted the comment before he went on, ''But as far as you're concerned, I wouldn't ever wear flared slacks or a dress either, considering the way you look in more fitted, tailored ones.''

''Really, I didn't know you noticed the *fit* of my outfit last week. I thought it was only the fact that it was different from the other ones there.'' She couldn't account for her desire to tease him. Perhaps because he seemed so serious, with his longish face, sober, close-set eyes, and careful speech.

His reply, however, was completely unexpected. ''When you moved, it was difficult to restrain myself from following you around all night.''

Diane would've been embarrassed herself it it weren't for the color that came to his face and the way he dropped his eyes self-consciously after his admission. Her impulse was to pat his hand or his cheek, but she was afraid it

96

would be inappropriate. "I'm flattered. You weren't afraid of offending me, were you?"

"I didn't know. Until you've known a person awhile, it's hard to predict their reactions."

"The other night, I thought you had me all figured out. What happened?"

"Nothing. Perhaps you seemed a little different, a little—"he hesitated—"older."

She didn't think that was exactly what he meant, but she responded to it anyway. "Maybe it was all the makeup. How old do you think I am now?"

"Twenty-two or -three."

She was used to people thinking she was more mature than she was, but she was young enough not to mind. "You sound prejudiced. You can't be more than thirty-one or -two yourself."

"Thirty-three, but I certainly didn't mean you're too young. All I worry about is taking anything for granted with young girls who're unpredictable and keep you confused all the time."

"Have you found that? I get the impression the men are the ones playing all the games, the married ones and the single ones both." She hoped for a clue.

"I suppose quite a few do, but they're usually more open about it, I think. With women, you don't know what to expect."

"You know, that sounds so much like the *Last Tango* theme. Did you see it yet?"

"No, but I know the subject matter fairly well from what I've read about it. Have you gone?" He sounded very interested.

"Yeah, I saw it recently with a couple of girls I work with. We thought it was ridiculous, but I'll bet most men liked it. It gives them a good argument for acting superficial and not making commitments to anyone if they can help it. But I think the kind of girl who'd want a relationship like she did would usually want money. I can't see anyone having a well-to-do family and a fiancé she was about to marry doing what she did with a stranger. It doesn't make sense. If there are girls like her running around looking for people to use them like that, I wish they'd make sure people know where to find them, so the rest of us can take advantage of the good guys.''

''Is that what you like to do?''

''What?''

''You know, what you said, take advantage of . . . uh easygoing men?''

''I can see where I'm going to have to watch my words with you, but you know what I meant. I should've said I *appreciate* fellows who're attentive and considerate, but not to exploit them or anything. Is that better? I don't want to sound like a villain.''

''Don't think I was trying to judge you before. I wasn't at all. I was just wondering. I don't hold anything against girls like that. The only thing that makes it hard is that most girls don't really know what they want, and if they do, they don't say. At least you're more open and easy to talk to, although I'll admit I may have distorted you a little when I first saw you.''

Diane couldn't pursue it; Bob's attention had turned to the waiter. He considered it time for their first course. Although Diane found the service excellent, he had an air of watchfulness for any flaws. When their wine came, he examined it, sniffed it, and tasted it so carefully, she was relieved when he finally approved it. She concluded he was at home giving orders, despite his attitude with her.

''What kind of business are you in?'' She accepted it as the kind of question you had to ask when you met the way they had.

''We have a family business. I run the New York branch. My mother and stepfather handle our main office in Zurich.''

''Do you have any brothers or sisters or anyone to help you here?''

''No, I wish I did, now. I'm an only child. Do you have a large family in Iowa?''

''No, but they're much more common there than here. The only reason my parents didn't have more children is because my mother had a diabetic condition and was always down with something. I think I liked having them all to myself, though. But then Mom died when I was eight.''

"That's too bad. She sounds like the opposite of my mother. No one can believe she's in her fifties. She has more energy than most people half her age. She's managed to stay about the same size you are, but I think she's a little taller. How tall are you?''

"Maybe a touch over five-seven.''

"I knew I was close. She's five-eight. You should see her on skis, or handling a horse. She's competitive at tennis, too, but that's not really her game.''

"She sounds like quite a person. Are you athletic too?''

"I'm not too bad in those things, but I never went in for any team sports in school. The thing about Mother, though, is that she has much more discipline than most nonprofessionals in anything she does. For instance, she rarely did the cooking, but when she did, it had to be authentic cordon bleu or mandarin or whatever. She always looked so young, people were surprised she was such a perfectionist. They used to think I was her kid brother when I was little. When I grew up, she could've gotten around much easier without me, but she still took me everyplace, no matter what people thought who didn't know us.''

"You're lucky. I was raised by my mother's sister. If she'd had her way, neither one of us would've breathed until she was sure it looked all right to everyone. She was really strict.''

"Actually, Mother wasn't as permissive as she sounds. She didn't have much patience with you if you didn't have the same approach she did. She could be a very rough Yankee lady if things around her weren't done the way she thought they should be.''

"Yeah? So maybe you didn't have it much easier than I did.''

"Don't get me wrong, we usually got along so well, I almost forgot she was my mother. You just had to understand her, that's all. She was only thirty-one when she and my father broke up. She had all kinds of offers, but she didn't remarry until a few years ago. Not many attractive women would've done that.''

"I know it. My father was only a widower a little while before he married again.''

They ate a few minutes in silence. She tried to think of something less personal to talk about in case he was tired of talking about their families. She looked at the wine label. Chateau Latour, 1964. "I love the wine.''

"I hoped you would, it's a fairly respectable year. My stepfather used to get a kick out of going to good French or Italian restaurants and ordering beer.''

"Really?''

"That's right. He'd done light feature stories for the *Tribune* before it folded. After that, he had an advertising job he hated because he thought it was too phony. He still liked to be around his old crowd, but Mother wasn't that enthusiastic about them. Whenever she didn't want to do something with him, he'd take me. We mostly went to the Garden, but he even took me to a few stag parties she didn't know about. He liked the idea of rounding out my education, I think, but I didn't mind.''

"It sounds like you must've really hit it off if you were going to see sports events without your mother, as interested as she was.''

"Not in the boxing and wrestling matches he liked. She didn't like body-contact sports at all. Wrestling might be for laughs, but boxing can be awfully rough, and ice hockey can shake a person up. Once when I saw Phil Esposito get slammed across the face so hard he got a mouth full of blood, I—''

"You'd better save the gory details for later. I know you wouldn't want me to lose a great dinner like this.''

"I'm sorry, I wasn't thinking.''

"I was only teasing. I'm not at all squeamish. My aunt who raised me was a nurse, and her cases were one of the few things she liked to talk about. I'd probably outlast you if it came right down to it.''

"It sounds like you've got me pegged. I think I'd better stop bothering to compare you to other girls altogether. I'd ask you to let me get us tickets to something, but I'm afraid

I might seem dull enough as it is compared to some of those ladies' men you were talking to at the party.''

Diane was about to ask him who he'd seen her with, when she remembered the scene with Chuck. "I can do without fellows like that. They take themselves too seriously. But as far as the way anyone looks, you could look like as much of a ladies' man as anyone around if you wanted to. Not that you don't look fine as you are,'' she added vigorously.

"And how would I go about that?'' he asked amiably.

"Nothing's wrong with you now,'' she repeated cautiously. "You're a nice size. When you're tall and slender you always look well in your clothes, and yours look very expensive. But if you wore turtlenecks or sports shirts and jackets instead of dark suits, you wouldn't look so serious. Or even lighter-colored, sportier suits. Then you could still wear a tie without looking so businesslike.'' She paused for his reaction, afraid of irritating him.

He smiled encouragingly. "Is that all, anything else?''

"Well, you could let your hair grow a little bit longer, unless you like to keep it short for the summer. It's funny how so many men who're practically bald on the top grow the biggest sideburns and leave their hair almost too long in the back. You're lucky, you have all yours. All you'd have to do is let it grow an inch or two in the back and fill out a little on the sides, and you wouldn't have to wear the front much longer than it is now. With those gray highlights you have, your sideburns would probably be beautiful if they were a little longer. Then if you tried the tinted, wire-rimmed glasses instead of those hornrims, you'd look so fabulous, you'd have to fight women off.''

His whole face had transformed as she spoke. His eyes wouldn't have appeared capable of radiating such delight. Words tumbled on top of each other when he responded.

"I can stop going to my barber entirely until you think my hair's long enough. You can tell me when. And we can shop together too, if you'd like. There's a place called Sills that I've never shopped at before, but I think it specializes in the kind of things you have in mind, although they also make up traditional clothes like I usu-

101

ally wear too. We can pick up a few things for you while we're at it.''

"Hold on, this is going to be your shopping trip exclusively. I don't mind going along, though, to help you find some good buys. I'm usually pretty good on women's clothes. I don't know if I told you, but I came here to study fashion design. Of course, I don't know as much about mens' wear, so I hope you don't mind being a guinea pig.''

"I don't mind anything as long as you're not kidding about being interested.''

"I'm not kidding. I'm glad to see you're so open-minded. Most people have such strong feelings about the way they're used to looking, they get offended if you have any suggestions for changes, even though they're minor.''

"Do you often have the desire to make people over?'' He made an unsuccessful effort to still sound cheerful.

"No, you'll be my first project.''

On that upbeat note, they completed their coffee, Bob settled the bill, and they left the cool room for the muggy Third Avenue pavement. Then he became stiff and awkward.

"What are you accustomed to doing after dinner? Do you like to go someplace else for a drink?''

"Whatever you'd like, it's up to you. You've shown me a swell time already.''

"If that means you're ready to be taken home, you can say so. I don't want to bore you.''

"I'm not at all bored. I told you, it's up to you.''

"If you want to make a night of it now, it's all right with me,'' he replied morosely.

When she said "Okay," he looked disappointed, but she didn't know how she could say anything else when it was possible he had something else to do. She thought it was most likely that he'd simply run out of things to talk about. Whatever it was, they'd lost the closeness they'd had inside, and Diane saw no point in prolonging the evening if it was going to be strained.

They rode across town in silence. "Do you want to see me again?'' he asked when they were near her house.

It reminded her of the first night they'd met, except for sounding more pessimistic. "Of course, how else can I supervise your hair and do all the other things we talked about? It sounds like you're trying to chicken out on our agreement already."

"No I'm not. I only want to be sure I'm not imposing on you and that you really have time for me."

"I wish you'd stop that. I have plenty of free time. If I didn't, I'd say so. Now, when do you want to get together again? Remember, you're fine if we never shop. We can just have a plain, ordinary date and leave that for later or skip it altogether." It was getting hard to conceal her impatience.

"It's up to you," he insisted. "Would you like to think it over, and I'll call you to see what you want to do?"

He was acting so indecisive, she decided to make a definite plan then, rather than spend another week worrying about what he was going to do. "Let's make it for next Friday evening. Then, if you want to, we still have Saturday afternoon if you decide to buy anything, and you don't have to make up your mind so far ahead of time."

Bob agreed unhesitantly and appeared to be very pleased with the way things had been worked out. He was helping her out of the car cheerfully when the Sterns arrived on foot with their baby. Diane said hello and introduced him to them, although she rarely saw them and didn't regard them as potential friends anymore. But Bob was very outgoing, volunteering to help raise the carriage up the stairs and complimenting them on the baby. She was glad he'd brought her straight home so they could see she was doing all right socially. She was also pleased he didn't expect to come in, not because she was worried about a pass, but because she didn't want the Sterns to think she automatically invited her dates upstairs.

Diane extended her hand for a good-night handshake when it was clear he had nothing more daring in mind. When he took it, bent slightly, and pressed first the back of her fingers then her open palm to his parted lips, she was astounded. It was as provocative as a French kiss would've been from someone else.

"Good night, Diana," he said tenderly.

"Uh, good night, see you Friday," she stammered.

She was excited by the possibility that behind his timidity and restraint Bob might be a sexual person. One she could handle and move along at her own pace, like Lester, but who wouldn't let her down once she was ready for him. Bob reminded her of Lester, although she realized that by being older and more desirable, he was more unusual. In fact, after her early experiences, she'd never expected to find such an unaggressive man in New York.

The idea of becoming intimate with someone who wasn't coercing her or giving her ultimatums had considerable appeal. She liked the idea that he was experienced, but diffident. In the beginning, she didn't think it would be hard for her to take the initiative if they reached the point where she felt closer to him. She tried to imagine how he'd react if she invited him up after a while, excused herself, and returned from the bathroom with hardly anything on. Although she knew she'd never do exactly that, she studied herself in the mirror as she undressed, considering how she'd look to him. When she was nude, she pushed her small breasts together and inspected her supple, well-proportioned body from different angles.

Diane showered in the same narcissistic, sensual mood, lathering herself caressingly and placing herself so the stinging spray played against her nipples till they became taut. She permitted her hands to linger over her body's crevices well beyond the requirements of hygiene. She finally became so stimulated, she could hardly hold back from masturbating herself outright to relieve the tension she'd built up. But the prospect of having a capable lover made her finish her shower without satisfying herself. It was getting to be too much of a habit, and she wanted to be as receptive to Bob as possible.

The next morning she awoke feeling more like her regular self. Cautious, resolved to avoid anything premature with Bob, and distracted by Chuck.

Chapter 7

Jacky was out that Monday, but Diane couldn't have avoided lunch with Mona anyway. She was anxious to know what had happened with Bob. She wanted to hear about where they'd gone, but would've been more excited hearing a firsthand report on somewhere "famous like the Top of the Sixes or the Rainbow Room." When Diane mentioned their shopping plans and her plans for redoing Bob, she was unprepared for Mona's response.

"I know how hard it is to meet fellows, but you should try not to get involved with them so soon."

"What do you mean 'involved?' I don't know who I've gotten involved with, but as excited as you are about a policeman like Herb, I'd love to see how you'd act if you met someone in Bob's category."

"If he's single, fine, but you still don't know if Jacky's right. But it's not just him, it's your attitude with men in general. You make it too easy for them."

" 'Easy?' " I have no idea what you're talking about, but if you've got something to say, I wish you'd say it. Otherwise, I think you've got a helluva nerve."

"Now, don't jump down my throat. I was just trying to be a friend. If you want to be angry with someone, Richard's the one. You shouldn't have had so much to do with him, especially when you were so new and everyone had noticed you."

Although Diane had suspected that a distorted version of that unfortunate episode might've been circulated around the office, she hoped it wouldn't be believed. Or that by her ignoring it, it would be forgotten.

"I don't know what lies that poor thing has spread

around, but the truth is that we went out twice, and when I let him come up for coffee on the second date, he had his briefcase filled with things to spend the night because he somehow got the idea it was all set. I tried to pay my part of the expenses so he'd stop insisting I owed him something and begging to stay. The only way I finally got him to leave was by telling him my neighbors would hear me if he tried to make a scene."

"Well, at least I can tell people what actually happened, *now*, but I wish you'd taken me more into your confidence in the first place. After all, I thought I was supposed to be your best friend."

Diane couldn't think of anyone she disliked more, but hoped she could put up with her until she didn't have to see her anymore.

Although, as previously, there were no outward signs that she was a topic of speculation or interest, Diane was disturbed about the incorrect impression people might have of her and knew she would be until she resigned. Her only satisfaction was the furious expression that darkened Richard's face whenever he met her and no one was around. In the presence of others, he continued to act as if there was a delicious secret between them.

On that Thursday evening, after dragging herself to the office every morning, Diane was trying to unwind over a sketchpad when she heard a knock on her door. It sounded very out of place and frightening. A ring from downstairs would've been startling enough. Coming in, she'd noticed a crazy-looking thing sitting on the steps next to theirs, not even up on the stoop. She'd seen him hanging around a couple of times before with crumpled shirts half out of his pants and dirty pants with the zipper showing. He was usually eating or drinking something out of a paper bag. The possibility that he might not have been too bad-looking if he was clean made him appear that much worse to Diane. She'd practically walk off the curb to stay as far from him as possible.

Having no peephole, she opened the door nervously with the new chain she'd had installed. She unlatched it guiltily when she saw Mrs. Stern outside.

"Hi, hope I'm not disturbing you."

"Not at all, come on in. You're about the only person except Mrs. Kraemer to light here. Delighted to have you."

Diane was about to offer her something to drink when she noticed that she hadn't come all the way in or showed any inclination to sit down. It occurred to her she was overdoing the hospitality bit if all the woman wanted was to borrow an egg or something.

Mrs. Stern didn't keep her dangling. "Ed and I took a place on Fire Island with two other couples this summer. We go alternate weekends and usually drive out with whichever couple we're sharing the house with. We've found keeping a car in the city's a major headache. Anyway, our friend David's come down with something, and rather than risk giving it to the baby, they're not going to come out this weekend. It was too late for our other partners to cancel their plans."

Before she could continue, Diane said, "If you're inviting me, the answer is definitely yes, before you go any further. I've heard of Fire Island, but I've never been, and I'd love to come."

"Well, the point is," she continued a bit impatiently, "we were thinking we might all drive out with you and your friend in his car. He looked like a nice chap. Bob, right? If he can make it, we'd like to leave as early as possible tomorrow afternoon, anytime after two-thirty or three. A regular weekend share for two would be about forty dollars from anytime Friday to Sunday evening. But we could easily work something out if you find you can't stay the full time. Of course, we'll help with the gas, and we can usually get our own ride coming back. What do you think? Would you like to come?"

Diane hoped the expression on her face didn't reveal her amazement at the proposal. It could hardly be called an invitation in the sense that she knew it. It was hard to see herself as anything but an afterthought. A link to Bob, transportation, and shared expenses.

"It was nice of you to think of us," she said in a polite but matter-of-fact way, "only I won't be seeing Bob until tomorrow night, and I'm afraid I can't reach him before then."

"That's a shame. There's no way you can call him?"

"I'm afraid not."

"Well, I guess I'll have to let Dave and Ellen line up one of their friends. They had several people in mind, but they either have small cars or live out on the island, or we weren't that friendly with them. We thought it would be more pleasant and uncomplicated to go out with you two, since we're neighbors and all. It's too bad we're giving up the house after Labor Day, or we'd have you out another time. By the way, what kind of business is your friend in?"

"He runs the New York branch of his family's business. They have headquarters in Switzerland."

"Really, what kind of business is it?"

"Some kind of importing, I believe." She was ashamed to admit how little she knew about him. "He doesn't like to talk about himself much."

She wasn't sure if her answers had anything to do with it or not when Carol said, "You know, if you'd like to come out on Saturday, you could spend the day and we could even put you up overnight if you don't mind sleeping on two couches in the living room. If you give me some paper, I'll write out the directions. We're in Seaview, only two houses from the ocean, and very close to the Seaview ferry."

Carol wrote out instructions, including the name and number of their house. "Here, don't let me forget the ferry schedule," she added, handing Diane a small card she had in her shirt pocket. "Now you can't possibly get lost. Try to make it, we'll be looking for you."

"If you're sure we won't make it too crowded, I'll see what Bob says. I'd love to come if he'll bring me."

"Okay, but with this arrangement, there's no reason you couldn't come alone if he's tied up. Seaview tends to be more families and couples than some of the sections, but we're right beside Ocean Beach, and it's practically all singles. You'd catch the Long Island railroad to Bay Shore and get a cab to the ferry. After that, the directions are the same, and by yourself, you'd only have to go in on the food unless we eat out. We'd all come back on the train if we can't get a ride, but I'm sure we can. We'll be looking for you,'' she told her warmly as she left.

By the time Carol finished, Diane's earlier resentment was completely gone. She realized that most people would jump at the offer, whether it was originally prompted by transportation problems or not, and that the money was probably nothing compared to a resort hotel or motel. Being told she could come alone made her feel best of all, although there was no question of going by herself on the train. She couldn't see any drawbacks to going out with Bob. Although it was only their second date coming up, no one could see anything improper in a weekend sleeping on sofas in a house with two married couples. Since he'd been so outgoing with the Sterns before, she anticipated that they'd all get along easily and he'd get over his periods of awkwardness with her.

When she put the chain back across the door, the prospect of a couple of days when she wouldn't have to worry about such things made her realize how deteriorated her situation had become. She had to concentrate on the immediate weekend plans to keep from becoming depressed. By the next day, she'd succeeded so well she was all keyed up. She was already having trouble concentrating on her work when she received a phone call.

"Miss Keely."

"Hey, baby." Chuck managed to sound as indolent as he had when she'd called him. She hoped he'd used a different voice with the switchboard operator.

"Hi, how're you doing? I've been wondering what you've been up to."

"How about that. Why didn't you call to find out? I didn't give you my number on one of my self-destruct cards, did I? As I recall, you got it on your own."

"Boy-oh-boy, here we go again. It's a shame you're afraid to be civil for any period of time."

"You mean civil or civilized?" He made a funny noise meant to sound like a jungle cry.

Diane laughed. "You're a nut."

"Beautiful, I hope you realize how good for you they are. Very important in your diet."

"I can't believe you roused yourself this early in the morning to talk about my diet. What else is new?" She was wondering why she'd volunteered to give him her number.

"Nothing much. I just wanted to give you my schedule. I'm starting work beginning next week, so you won't be able to reach me at home if you tried to call during the day. I'm getting ready to take off for the weekend now, as soon as I get dressed."

"Okay. Congratulations on the job. Is it in architecture?"

"Yeah, but I didn't call for that. I could've been working all along, but I wasn't about to take the first thing that came along unless it was the right bread. I just wanted to let you know you could reach me either right after work or late at night."

"Okay. I might be a little busier too, though. This weekend I think I'll be going to Fire Island. But thanks for keeping in touch, and I'm glad you're making out so well."

"You'll be at Fire Island?"

"Yeah, I think so, a friend and I were invited out by the couple downstairs from me."

"How about that? I'm heading for Westhampton, but a guy I'm tight with from the Dunes will probably be there with his cruiser. Maybe we could make it over to Ocean Beach Saturday night. Is this famous 'friend' of yours male or female?"

"It's a fellow. He's very nice."

"He must be. I thought I was supposed to be the fast worker. Where're you going to be staying?"

"Seaview."

"Okay, so if we're over that way, maybe I'll run into you. I'm broad-minded. Maybe we can all hang out together. And don't worry, I'll be cool if we do. If I don't see you, have a ball. I've got to split now."

"Okay, maybe we'll see each other. Thanks for calling."

When Diane hung up and returned to her work, she didn't think she'd hear from Chuck again unless she called him first. She couldn't imagine him being in Ocean Beach, either. He sounded too anxious to hang up. She wished he'd acted more flippant, so she wouldn't have felt so rotten.

The next day, when Bob showed up in another of his no-nonsense suits and ties, she wondered what his idea of resort wear would be like. While she didn't anticipate a situation where he and Chuck would have to adapt to each other, she wondered how well he'd fit in with the others they'd be in contact with. It occurred to her that until he acquired some color to his pale complexion, he might look out of place among the regulars. She decided that after they'd worked out the details, they could do some quick shopping if he wasn't sure he had anything appropriate. She hadn't realized she was so superficial, despite her interest in fashion. But part of the problem was that she didn't think she was good enough to pull anyone else up.

"We had an invitation to go to Fire Island this afternoon with my neighbors you met last week," she began.

"We did? That was nice of them. Would you have been willing to go with me?"

"Sure, and we can still go if you want to. I'm really excited about it. Originally, we would've been in the house with only them, because the other couple couldn't go, but when I said I couldn't reach you before tonight, they said they'd let another couple go, but still be glad to put us up on two couches in the living room. So we can go out tomorrow morning if we want to."

Diane was astounded when Bob hesitated awkwardly without agreeing. His response, when it came, wasn't at all what she'd expected.

"I wish I'd known earlier. I can't emphasize enough how pleased I am that you'd like to go with me. But I couldn't possibly stay over Saturday night. I'm sorry."

"Why not? Surely you don't have to work on Sundays. What's so important that you have to be back in the city for it?"

"If it was anything I could get out of, I would. But it's

111

business, and the problem is that there're two other people involved besides me. The reason we've been setting things up regularly for Sundays the last month or so is that one of the parties has another job all week long and has been giving up Sunday mornings as a special favor to me.''

"Well, I suppose we *could* go out on Saturday and come back the same day, but I guess that's silly.''

"I'd do anything to keep you from being disappointed in me, but even leaving quite early in the morning on Saturday, we'd probably spend almost as much time on the road in traffic both ways as we would there. But we could do it if you think it's worth it.''

"I don't know. How long do you think it would take? Even if we only had time enough for lunch and some time on the beach, it might be better than nothing.''

"If you don't mind having so little time to relax, I'll do whatever you want. It'll probably be a beautiful day, and I know I could use some color, but I can't take too much sun at one time. You wouldn't object to my bringing along an umbrella for protection part of the time, would you?'' he asked apologetically.

Diane was finding it increasingly hard to sustain any enthusiasm about the trip. It was almost as if he were deliberately turning up one bothersome detail after another to spoil things. In the dimness of the car, she studied him for clues. It was the first time she'd noticed him smoking heavily. As he squashed out one cigarette in the dashboard ashtry, he nervously lit another.

"There's no point in going if the whole thing's only going to be a strain on you.'' She tried not to sound unreasonable.

"I hate to let you down the first time you tell me something you want me to do,'' he said gloomily, starting up the car.

"Oh, well, *que será, será*, as they say. They won't be able to have us out again before they give up the house Labor Day, but I'm sure I'll see Fire Island one of these days.''

"You know, I've just thought of something. I don't

112

know if it will do any good, but I'm going to see if I can reach both of the people I'm meeting with Sunday morning, and if there's any possibility of canceling our meeting, I'll do it,'' he said eagerly.

"You make me feel like a tyrant. I must really seem selfish. You don't have to go to all of that trouble. It's not your fault you got so little notice.''

"That's all right. Honestly. I want to do it. I'll call as soon as we get to the Oak Room.''

Diane had trouble maintaining her composure when she found herself seated alone in the Plaza's richly paneled, distinguished dining room. It was harder than entering the landmark hotel at Fifth Avenue and Central Park South had been, because Bob had acted so at home. But after he ordered their drinks and excused himself to make his phone call, she had trouble convincing herself she belonged. On the other hand, Bob blended more perfectly into the staid old room than anyplace they'd been before.

His ensuing conversation, however, would've been odd anywhere. It was particularly unreal against the setting in which it occurred.

"Two-four-three-four,'' a woman's voice answered briskly.

"This is Butchie,'' Bob said in a small, high-pitched voice that emulated that of a very young boy.

"What the hell do you want?'' she yelled. "What do you mean calling tonight? No one told you to call!''

"I don't want to make you mad at me, but could I see Miss Vera on Sunday night instead of early Sunday morning, please?''

"You goddamned little fuck, you, you're really asking for it, aren't you? You know damned well you're the only one Miss Vera corrects on her day off. I feel sorry for your poor ass when I tell her you called. She'll take care of you, but good, when she sees you.''

"What do you think she'll do?'' he gasped, beginning to perspire in the closed phone booth, an erection taking shape beneath his well-pressed, conservatively cut trousers.

"How the fuck do I know? Maybe you'll be able to make meat patties out of your friggin' balls when she finishes with you."

"What else?" he begged. He removed a fine linen handkerchief from his inner pocket and unzipped his pants after making sure his jacket and position concealed his actions from any passersby.

"Listen, punk, this call is already going to cost you extra. Don't you think I know what you're doing now? I'm too busy to talk anymore, but Miss Vera will have plenty of time between now and Sunday to decide what special punishment you should get for trying to cancel out. I pity your ass!"

A shudder passed through Bob's body as he heard the phone banged down in his ears. He held his handkerchief close against his throbbing penis and carefully wiped away all the semen as it spurted out. Then he wadded the damp, mushy mass as small as possible and disposed of it in a trash receptacle in the men's room. He also rinsed his hands in cold water and patted his face with a damp paper towel before hurrying to rejoin Diane, still somewhat flushed.

"Please forgive me for being gone so long, but that was quite a scene," he said truthfully. "I could only reach one of my associates, and did I get blasted for trying to make such a last-minute change. I can't say I was too surprised; it wasn't very professional of me. But as soon as possible, I'm going to work something out so you'll have first say about our weekends."

"You're sure you don't have a wife and ten children you have to reserve your Sundays for?" She smiled and tried to sound light.

"I don't consider that funny, Diane. You know I have no family at all anymore. You're the only person I've been close to for a long time. That's why I'm so concerned about doing whatever you want me to. If we started out around six tomorrow morning, we could still go. We'd probably be there by nine or so and could stay till seven or eight. I can take the traffic if you can."

"There's nothing I'd want to do that you have to get up

and be ready at six on a Saturday morning for. I could see going a couple of hours later; otherwise, it's more like work. I guess the traffic gets worse the later you leave.''

"Probably bumper-to-bumper, but you're the boss.''

She didn't know what to say. Knowing he didn't want to go, and with everything already so complicated, she didn't have the nerve to ask him what he'd wear. She had visions of him huddled uncomfortably beneath an umbrella on the beach in some kind of baggy boxer-type trunks, after arriving as if he were going to business on Wall Street. Coming out on a Saturday, there would be the excuse of having no time to change. She couldn't imagine him enjoying himself enough to justify all the driving. But before she answered, he came up with an idea.

"Say,'' he began excitedly, "why don't you go without me? You wouldn't have to leave so early, and you could have a good time, stay over, and come back with your friends on Sunday. Everything would be simplified with me out of the way.''

"Are you kidding? I wouldn't think of going alone. There's no way I could enjoy myself with people I hardly know if you weren't there. And the idea of going out on the train all by myself really turns me off.''

"You can take my car. You drive, don't you?''

"Yeah, since I was sixteen, but I haven't got a New York license and wouldn't even know how to get on the right road if I did. Besides, you can't possibly be serious. What would you use for transportation from now till Sunday night if I stayed over with your car?''

"That would be my problem. I'd deserve whatever inconvenience it caused me for not being able to oblige you in the first place.''

"You're too much. I never saw anyone like you! You sound like you actually mean it.''

"I do. I'd love for you to take the car. But you're right that it wouldn't be practical.'' He reflected a moment. "Perhaps I could hire a driver to take you. Would you go then?''

Diane said she wouldn't want to, and became resigned to forgetting about the trip. It helped to transfer her attention to their immediate surroundings and speculate about who was who. As they ate, she tried to find out if Bob always took his dates to the kinds of places he'd taken her, but she couldn't get a definite answer. He was more interested in talking about what she usually did with *her* dates, and about her routine in general. She parried his questions about her social life before she met him but was honest about only tolerating her job and her studio apartment because of her school ambitions.

"I don't see how you can manage without more help," he suggested.

Afraid she'd overstated her burdens, she assured him she was satisfied and optimistic about her future. After they finished and were returning to the car, he said he wished she'd reconsider his offer about the next day. When she again declined, reminding him they could shop as they planned, he admitted looking forward to it but said he'd feel guilty because she deserved to enjoy herself and the trip was obviously her first choice.

"If you liked me more, I'll bet you'd find it easier to let me take care of your expenses," he concluded, sounding hurt. "Pretty please," he cajoled boyishly when she still hesitated.

"I don't know. It would be kind of nice to see what it's like, and I don't have to stay overnight if I'm uncomfortable alone. I guess I *could* go. . . ." She started to tell him she'd originally planned to pay her expenses there, but realized it was rather silly, since he'd spent over fifty dollars both times he'd taken her out and was far from being a Richard Fenster. As soon as she said she *could* go, he got out his wallet. They were back in the car by then. Although he tried to give her several twenties, she accepted only thirty dollars. He said he'd settle with the driver before he picked her up the next morning.

At her house, he double-parked and appeared prepared to help her out as before, but she turned toward him and put her hand on his arm encouragingly. When he responded by placing it around her shoulders awkwardly, Diane leaned forward until their lips met. Although he put his other arm around her too, his head ended up lying back

116

against his headrest with her face covering his. It created the effect of her kissing him and confirmed her opinion that she'd be in control of their sexual progress or lack of it.

She smiled at him reassuringly as he removed his arms from around her shoulders and lit a cigarette nervously, their dry kiss behind them.

"I guess I disappointed you." He was hardly audible.

"Don't be so modest, you're very gentle and sweet," she countered tactfully, although she wished he'd been more enthusiastic. "Are you sure you won't miss me tomorrow? It's not too late for me to stay in the city."

"You know that's all settled."

"Okay, you can call me at work on Monday to see how everything turned out, unless you'd like me to call you if I come back before."

"I'm sure you'll be enjoying yourself too much for that. I'll call you first thing Monday morning, though, if that's all right."

After he left, she wondered how he could be so accommodating and still retain so much of his privacy. The surprising thing was that it didn't appear to be deliberate. It was as if he were so modest, he couldn't believe she was actually interested in knowing more about him. Like his number. She decided she'd have to be more firm with him to get the information she wanted. Maybe she couldn't find out if he gave everyone who went out with him the same treatment, but her ego required more control than she had.

The next day she overslept and was barely out of the shower when her bell rang. She spoke from the window to the portly uniformed black man below, and almost half an hour later, hurried to the highly polished foreign car with apologies for being late. She waved hello to Mrs. Kraemer when she noticed her near her entrance, but she barely responded.

"I'm Thompson, Miss Diane," he told her as they started out. "I'll make the best time I can, but I hope you're set for a long trip."

She said she was prepared, but thought the situation had

been exaggerated until they'd crossed the Fifty-ninth Street bridge and reached the crawling traffic on the Long Island Expressway.

"Afraid it'll be like this from here on out till we pass Jones Beach, Miss Diane," the driver told her.

"It's Diane Keely," she corrected him politely. "I don't mind your calling me by whichever name you're comfortable with, but I'd rather not be called 'Miss Diane.'"

"That was the only name the gentleman gave us, along with your address and which bell to ring. I don't get as much of that as I use to, but I figure as long as I'm getting paid, I'll call somebody Mr. Charlie and he can call me Doodley Squat as long as they don't expect me to do nothin' but drive. 'Specially when they pay for a Rolls."

Diane had been rushing so much, it never occurred to her that the car Mrs. Kraemer saw her entering was a Rolls-Royce. She thought they were all as large as or larger than Bob's big-model Mercedes. She hoped Mrs. Kraemer didn't think she'd deliberately kept the driver waiting to show off. She didn't worry about it for long, though. She started thinking about the banged-up old cars her father used to drive her to school in. Although it was a good little distance, she would much rather have walked.

Her father was a weekend drinker who drove as crooked as other drinkers walked. All week long he worked hard at the appliance factory, rising early and going to bed practically as soon as dinner was over. He had very little to say to either her or her mother. But as soon as he came home on Friday evening, changed from his work clothes, and had a Hamms beer in front of him, he became another person. Talkative, outgoing, and affectionate. Sometimes Diane didn't see how her mother could survive one more bear hug or slap on her behind. But the only time she winced, instead of smiled indulgently, was when he got particularly carried away and would pinch her too hard someplace. Usually, he was more likely to head out to meet his regular drinking buddies before he was too far along. Although his car might have to be towed out of a ditch or something the next day, it was amazing the way he always managed to make it home in one piece sooner or later.

Diane didn't like to think about it, but it was his drinking, more than the kind of work he did, or the way he went off to Kansas City, that she always felt she had to live down. In fact, even though there would've been more money for her if he hadn't remarried, she was almost relieved when he finally left with his new family. By the time Thompson said they'd reached Bay Shore, she felt she'd come much farther.

After he helped her out with her train case at the ferry, she wanted to give him a nice tip. She opened her bag uncertainly because she wasn't sure if it was expected or not.

He put up his hand firmly. "Everything's taken care of, Miss Keely. Your friend's got plenty of class."

The subject of their admiration was then sitting on a narrow cot in a small, curtainless room with heavy shades and a sisal mat on the floor. He was a deep bruised-looking pink, having just finished showering in an old-fashioned shower with several spouts at torso level in addition to the upper shower head. He liked it so hot it was sometimes almost scalding as he scrubbed himself with a short-handled brush and inhaled the steam with his eyes half-closed. When he finished, the only thing he put on was his glasses.

Before dressing, he always studied his large Staunton chess set alongside his miniature set on a bedside table, while reading the *Times* chess column. The smaller set had magnetic pieces that looked like checkers. He usually carried it with him to the bathroom, or when he was eating and couldn't concentrate well enough to practice moves and variations on both sets the way he preferred. He reverted to playing alone after visiting several chess clubs and becoming infuriated with the single-minded, overly competitive players. That morning he only worked over moves for less than an hour, because it was his custom to go riding in Central Park every Saturday.

He kept his own horse at the last public stable in Manhattan, the Claremont Riding Academy on West

Eighty-ninth Street. The majority of the riders rented their mounts at nine dollars an hour. He always called beforehand so his mare would be ready for him. He didn't like to stand around while other people were getting lessons and practicing in a ring around the floor. They were usually young women and children for the most part, and once they became regulars, they knew he only rode alone. Although he was always anxious to get to the park, he only mounted and took out his prized hunter after examining and smoothing her personally to make sure she was all right.

Bob intensely disliked the ride through the city streets, hot that day, past the vacant lots, run-down tenements, and low-income projects to reach the shaded bridle path in the park. But once there, he entered into such a spiritual and physical union with the animal that nothing else was very real to him. Unless he was jarred too often by the presence of other, less skilled riders and joggers who spoiled everything, he'd ride for hours. Invariably, the horse tired before he did. When he finished with her, her head drooped low, she was slick with sweat and had foam around the mouth. But Bob felt unusually satisfied that day. Not only because he'd been fulfilled by the ride, but because he'd be able to have his session with Miss Vera the next morning, and hadn't had to disappoint Diane to do it.

Chapter 8

The aging ferry to Seaview arrived shortly after Thompson deposited Diane. While some of the passengers headed for the enclosed lower level of the two-deck boat, she was among those who scurried for seats on the unsheltered part of the upper deck. She claimed a spot on one of the short wooden benches, long enough for about three adults, and tied on her scarf. The other weekenders arranged themselves and miscellaneous bags, tennis rackets, children, and pets into all the other available spaces.

She was surprisingly at ease. It helped that there were quite a few people traveling alone, and a healthy percentage of young people mixed in with the more mature majority. Although some of the matrons clutched Vuitton bags or Gucci carryalls, Diane knew the khaki safari suit she'd made inexpensively would fool most people. She figured it looked as acceptable next to the blue jeans and tie-dyed outfits as it did with the white pants and blazers that were almost as popular. With her Dior signature scarf for anyone who took stock of such things, she was sure she was up to snuff. She felt great and was glad she'd had the courage to come by herself, although it would've been nicer if Bob had been able to come along with her.

A couple of sunburned teenagers efficiently unhitched the boat from the pier. In a few minutes it was groaning and chugging across the calm blue water through ribbons of white made by the breeze and a foamy spray created by its passage. Since her instructions mentioned crossing the "bay," she was unprepared for the endlessly stretching expanse of water on all sides and the amount of time that passed before they reached the island.

But while the trip was almost forty-five minutes on the slow boat, and it was at least half an hour before any land was visible, she enjoyed the novelty of peering for land while seagulls flew and swooped about in the distance and of exchanging waves with friendly occupants of small speedboats that passed. It was even fun to shriek with the other upper-upper deckers who fell victim to sudden drenchings from unexpectedly lusty sprays of water.

Her spirits were still high as she stood on line waiting to disembark, studying Carol's directions. Bay Walk was right next to the ferry dock. Quite a few passengers stopped to claim brightly colored children's wagons that were chained down and parked by the dozens like cars in a lot. The dock was crowded with people who'd come down to meet someone. Only a few were leaving. Some of the people who'd been alone had friends waiting. There was a lot of hugging and cheek kissing. There were also a lot of bare feet and legs, and most of the new arrivals looked overdressed by comparison.

Diane turned left and walked along the bay several blocks, as directed. She turned toward the right when she reached the fourth narrow lane. Carol had told her she'd be going toward the ocean when the bay was behind her. The walk was lined by one- and two-story ho houses, mostly shingled and bleached and partially hidden by densely grown pines and other sprawling bushy plants. Although some of the houses looked bigger or better than others, they all looked casual and unpretentious.

Diane saw a few people leaving their cottages with beach towels and lotions, going toward the beach. She met a couple who were pulling their empty wagons behind them, apparently on their way to town to shop or just going to get someone waiting at the ferry. It felt nice when some nodded and spoke, but she wasn't surprised when others observed the no-eye-contact rule of the city.

Within a few minutes she saw the house with the number Carol had told her to look for. She was pleased she'd found it with no complications, but a little apprehensive about arriving without Bob. She went resolutely up the path. She didn't have to knock, though, because she was quickly spotted by an unfamiliar woman inside the screened-in porch. Diane took off her sunglasses and smiled as brightly as possible.

"Hi, you must be a friend of Carol and Ed," she greeted her, opening the door.

"Yeah, I'm Diane Keely. We live in the same house."

"Come on in, I'm Sharon Rosenthal. You must be ready to drop. I'm in awe of anyone who'd venture forth from the city on a Saturday morning. Fridays are enough of a rat race. No one else is here now, they're all at the beach," she continued as she led Diane into a large living room with the promised two sofas and several wicker chairs. It was a shell-type house, with the wooden studs showing, and beamed ceilings.

When Diane said it looked comfortable, she replied, "That's a diplomatic way of describing it. I can take it for a weekend, but with so many lovely places in Seaview, I'm surprised they'd rent one like this. I can't imagine anyone coming here all summer." She looked around, grimacing.

"This is my first time here. I'm from the Midwest. So far, I'm not at all disappointed with anything, but I'm anxious to see all over." She didn't like exposing her skeleton to such a particular person, but she knew she couldn't conceal it for long, with everything so new to her.

"So you'll be wanting to get right to the beach, won't you? You might get your first disappointment."

Her habit of making expressions of distaste had etched fine lines around her eyes and mouth. Her complexion was dry, and she was heavy-hipped beneath the long, coarsely woven djelaba she wore. But skillfully applied makeup flattered her hazel eyes, and her blond shoulder-length hair looked like it was professionally lightened and pampered. She managed to achieve an overall attractive and prosperous look.

"You think so? Why?"

"It's gotten so eroded recently. There's not much of a beach anymore. Practically everyone's huddled together

123

on the dunes. We've been going to Amagansett for the last few years and are moving into our own house as soon as it's finished. So I had no idea how deteriorated the beaches had become here. It's pathetic to see how narrow and crowded it is. That's why I'm spending as little time there as possible. Just enough to keep my tan from fading. Do you want to change now and go?''

Diane guiltily admitted she did.

"All right. I don't know where they plan to put you if you're staying over, since there're only two bedrooms, but I guess you can change in their room. It's over here.''

Diane trooped behind her into a functional, double-bedded room and hurriedly changed into her one-piece maillot. It was a one-shoulder design.

"What a stunning suit," Sharon exclaimed. She sounded unflatteringly surprised. "You'll be the only one of your size around without a bikini. Unfortunately, they're not so uncommon among the Lane Bryant set either.'' She laughed.

"I'm glad you like it. Do you think I'll have much trouble finding the others?''

"I doubt it. They might be about to come back for lunch, though, unless they planned to wait for you before eating. But you'd have to run into them if they were returning, unless they decide to go to town first and go along the beach walk. Carol's wearing a pumpkin-colored bikini, and they have a yellow-and-white beach umbrella for the baby. I think you'll spot them in the mob scene without too much trouble. They can't go but so far, lugging the baby.''

"Okay, thanks, God alone knows what I would've done if you weren't here.'' Diane opened the door to leave.

"Wait! You're not going like that, are you?''

"Like what? What's wrong?''

"No cover. You can't go to the beach without a *cover*. They're very strict about that out here. You could be arrested.''

"Oh," Diane answered in a small, defeated voice, having thought she was finally on her own. She turned around after looking wistfully at the free world. "I suppose I could wear the jacket to my slack suit. My only other tops would look more ridiculous with this."

"Let's see." Sharon hesitated. "I don't really know who belongs to what in these closets. There's a different couple every weekend in one or the other of the bedrooms. I think the safest thing is for me to give you a beach towel."

She came up with a faded blue print one that couldn't have looked uglier with Diane's brown suit.

"I guess that'll have to do for the time being. Carol may find something better for you later. At least, no one will bother you now."

"Okay, thanks again. See you later." With the towel draped around her shoulders, she scurried off, apprehensive of further admonishments. Only when she was several houses away did she slow down to a plod, aware of her tackiness and reluctant to be seen.

She discovered happily that wooden stairs and a fence separated the beach from the public walks. She removed the towel and folded it as inconspicuously as possible before she reached the top of the steps and began looking for her hosts. Sharon hadn't exaggerated about the crowds. But while there was no more than a few feet between most of the groups, it seemed to be largely a matter of choice or convenience. There were unoccupied areas of sand on either side of the spots where everyone was clustered. But although some of it was smooth, creamy-colored, and dry, there was a large part all along the ocean that appeared dark and wet.

The limited amount of flat dry sand was responsible for some people having to sit on or near the mounds of sand along the rear of the beach, among patches of scrubby weeds and bits of driftwood, unless they felt like trudging away from the congested section. Descending the rickety stairs and scanning the crowds, Diane imagined it would be beautiful there during off periods. She was more sympathetic with Bob's lack of enthusiasm for coming, considering all the circumstances, but she wasn't disappointed, as Sharon had predicted.

Diane spotted Carol and the baby easier than she'd

125

expected, and picked her way to them, staying close to the dunes. "Hi, your directions were perfect. Sharon was a lifesaver when I got to the house. She told me you were here and what you were wearing and let me change so I could join you," she rattled off.

"I'm glad you could make it, you look great. Is Bob with you?" she asked after Diane joined her on her towel.

"No, he had a business conference he couldn't get out of, but he insisted on arranging to have me picked up and driven out so I wouldn't have to come alone on the train but still get to see what it was like out here. It's quite a place."

"He must have *some* friends, to find someone who'd drive all the way out here and then turn around and go back again just like that."

"Oh, it wasn't a friend. He hired a chauffeur and, would you believe, a Rolls-Royce to bring me. I still haven't gotten over it!"

"You're kidding. Have you any idea what that must've cost? I never heard of such a thing."

"I think he did it because he felt so bad that he couldn't come with me."

"That's too bad. I know the four of us would've had a good weekend, but I wouldn't have invited you to come by yourself if I didn't think that would be fun too. People don't have to be part of a couple all the time."

Since it was obvious Carol said what she thought, Diane was convinced she was welcome. "Is Sharon's husband out here?"

"Yeah, he and Ed are off somewhere. She sends him along with us whenever we come. I think she hates to put on a swimsuit, but she has so many rationalizations, I'm not sure. We've only met them a couple of times before, and it's hard to know exactly where either one of them is coming from."

Diane had second thoughts about saying anything too critical, since she was everyone's guest and hadn't met Sharon's husband yet. She confined herself to some more comments of gratitude before she set off through the assorted family groups and couples to get her first taste of

126

the ocean. She noticed a tendency of the young men and women to bunch together with their own sex. It reminded her of the awkward high-school dances at home, where both groups knew what they were there for but spent a lot of time showing how self-sufficient they could be. In high school, however, boys weren't so outnumbered.

She waded along the shore, letting the waves wash up to her knees and splash against her thighs. She was just beginning to get used to the cold water when she noticed that Carol had been joined by the two men, and she realized they were probably ready to leave.

Morty turned out to be such a cherubic-faced, potbellied, and seemingly easygoing man in his late forties or early fifties that Diane was more optimistic about getting along with both couples after she met him.

Although the four of them were famished when they got back, no one challenged the spartan lunch of fruit, cottage cheese, and vichyssoise Sharon presented with aplomb. But soon after they sat down, a clash developed between her and Carol that almost caused Diane to leave that afternoon. It was superficially sparked by Carol's breast-feeding at the table. She dropped her bikini strap and made a perfunctory request for permission when the baby cried.

"We're just having a snack, honey, but there's no reason you have to go hungry," she said, lifting her.

Diane was surprised she'd nurse in an outfit like that, with a second man present, but neither man appeared affected by it when Sharon asked, "How much longer before she can use a bottle? Isn't she almost a year old now?"

Carol answered that she had no preconceived timetable and would stop when her daughter was ready. "Judy's the only one we're going to have, so we don't have to take any shortcuts. I decided to do the whole bit before we joined Zero Population growth. I even had a Lamaze delivery because it was safer for her, although, as it worked out, it was a fantastic experience Ed and I could both share. I like the way the nursing's working out, too," she added, patting the busy baby's head.

"You mean you're not among those who believe the

only way men can really *share* in the birth of a child is to become biologically able to experience labor pains? Personally, I was glad to get all the drugs they could give me and have Morty out waiting with all the other old-fashioned pacers when I had the boys. It's humiliating enough to be lying there with your knees a mile apart before a bunch of strangers. But then, *I've* always cherished my privacy.''

"That's why Morty should've been there. So you wouldn't have been all alone, feeling depersonalized. It was altogether different with Ed and me. He helped me relax and breathe right and everything. Of course, I wasn't all strapped down, like you probably were.''

"Did they have you squatting? I understand that's the ideal position. They say the peasants and colored women on farms can deliver like that practically alone, like going to the john or having a litter.''

"I would've been delighted to squat, but most hospitals still have things set up more for the doctor's convenience than the patient's. I envy women who can be that relaxed about a normal function, though, instead of so uptight they're afraid to look at themselves sideways without a doctor's consent.''

"You can keep a little modesty about yourself without going to any extremes. I can't imagine anything more absurd than those groups where women not only dissect each other's private lives but allow a lunatic fringe to examine each other's anatomies with flashlights if they want to. I think even culturally deprived people would be ashamed to put on a show like that.''

"I haven't gotten into that yet, but I'm afraid your hang-ups are showing. Looking inside a healthy vagina shouldn't be any more of a show than looking down someone's throat. There're fewer germs and, the body's the body, whichever end it is.''

"Come off it, Carol. I don't think anyone's all that interested," Ed objected mildly.

"A lot of people are," Carol replied, putting her breast inside her swimsuit top and returning the satisfied baby to her playpen, "and a lot more would be, if they didn't feel

128

so threatened. I don't mean by self-examination specifically, but in letting it all hang out in general. I'll bet if you made a few of our rap sessions, Share, you'd end up organizing all your friends in Larchmont.''

"I don't think there's any hope for me, dear. You have to be dissatisfied about something before you want to get your consciousness raised. Maybe if Morty and I weren't so happy and he didn't keep us so well, it would be different. I'd probably have to have everything raised if I had to worry about things like who'd do how much of the housework if we both worked, and finding a decent day-care center for your children without a bunch of welfare kids in it, and whether they'd make it home in one piece or not. You deserve a medal.''

"You think so? Well, *chacun à son gout*, I think I've got too much on the ball to sit back and let Ed keep me like a courtesan. I guess you didn't read that *Times* article about the women's rap group in Chappaqua, huh? Apparently they're concerned about something, and if it's welfare cases or crime in the streets, it's news to me.''

"What streets? They don't even have *sidewalks* once you leave the village. If you haven't got a car, you'd go lame by the time you went from one estate to another, already,'' Morty added.

"They may have groups there, but I'm sure they wouldn't get into the type of things the women would where Carol is,'' Sharon said patiently.

"They'd have an altogether different outlook from women who might be out fighting with men for jobs, or single and living by themselves in some horrible furnished room. Some of the women there could even be homosexuals, trying to make out with everyone. With all kinds of strangers like that, I'd be scared stiff.''

"I'd like to see something scare you,'' Ed teased. "I've got a court reserved twenty minutes from now, who wants to get beat? Morty?''

Diane kept her eyes on the dishes she'd started wiping with paper napkins and stacking as everyone finished. Until the comments about furnished rooms and scary strangers, she'd remained relatively detached from the conversation, waiting for it to run its course. She could imagine becoming defensive about not having a fairly successful husband as she became older. As it was, she considered herself uninvolved in that aspect of the dialogue too. That was why she was so unprepared for the apparent insult. Not knowing what Sharon knew about her, she had no idea what to say, assuming she had the courage to take her on. The only thing she could think of was to get out and back to the ferry as soon as possible.

Morty told Ed he had some work to do on a brief. "Otherwise, I'd go you a few games, although anyone looking at this"—he rubbed his paunch—"can tell I'm more of a golf man."

Diane rose with her pile of dishes after Morty got up. "I'll do the dishes, and someone will have to tell me what my share of the lunch is. I've never had one quite like it." She figured her sarcasm wouldn't be detected by anyone who wasn't aware she'd been insulted.

Carol didn't appear to notice anything as she answered, "If you're willing to wash and dry, that can be your contribution. And for dinner we'll all be going out. You probably wouldn't know it, but there's plenty of food in the refrigerator, so we won't have to starve till then."

Ed hurried off to change for tennis and look for a partner after he couldn't persuade Carol or Sharon to join him. Sharon said she liked only grass courts. She continued to expound on their advantages when only Carol and Diane remained. "But whatever I play on, I hate to have people breathing down my neck because there aren't enough courts. If Seaview could just keep out the groupers from Ocean Beach better, that would help somewhat."

Carol looked thoughtful. "I wonder how crowded the courts are at Point o' Woods?"

Sharon looked at her oddly. "Who knows? I couldn't care less. With all those ugly Victorian houses and one of the most washed-out beaches on the island, that's the last place I'd want to go."

"I couldn't agree more, but I still like to see everybody's options open."

130

"So why don't you stop being cryptic and make your point?" She sounded more irritated than before.

"It's not that big a deal, really. It just occurs to me that places like that couldn't remain so restrictive if people like you didn't use up all their energy worrying about who they could edge out and look down on. I don't know if you heard about the demonstration we took over there last year, just to hassle them, but you remind me of the Jewish property owners who were more upset by the Harlemites and Village types who were participating in their street clothes than the Woodsies bigots who wouldn't have given any of us the time of day." Looking at Diane, she smiled. "It's kind of analogous to Catholics who spend so much time fighting over some of the old traditions with each other that the people who think they all should go don't even get noticed. It's so silly, because we're all treated as minorities in one way or another. I'm used to crap like yours, Sharon, but when I hear your condescending attitudes about other women, it really gets to me. We're the most oppressed of all, and none of us can afford to feel superior," she concluded intently.

Diane's neck grew hot. She realized she'd been feeling a little smug as the least opinionated female there. The criticism about women not sticking together could apply to her too. But she was pretty sure the discussion was aimed more directly at Sharon. She wanted to hug Carol, although she didn't entirely agree that females were all that bad off.

"Take it easy. I didn't realize you'd had such a hard time. Would you like a Valium if I can find one, or can you take them? That's probably one of the things about nursing, you can't even take a tranquilizer if you want to, not that I need them myself."

It was as if they'd come full circle with nothing changed. Diane couldn't control her laughter. Looking at Carol, she managed to drawl, "Ah think what we've got heah is a little lack of communica-shun."

Both women looked like the wallpaper had spoken. But in a minute, Carol was laughing with her.

"The understatement of the year!"

Unperturbed, Sharon shrugged her shoulders as if they were both to be humored. "I think I'll go back to my needlepoint, if no one minds. I had to stop before, to fix lunch."

"Of course, *all* to do. I'll help Diane finish up; then we can go back to the beach. How's that sound to you, Di?"

"Great." She no longer had any ambivalence about staying. Carol found her a white terry-cloth jacket, and before they left, Sharon volunteered matter-of-factly to watch Judy, who'd fallen asleep. Diane decided to stop thinking she knew what to expect from people. That night she was in for more surprises.

When the five of them began threading along to Ocean Beach for dinner, a few minutes from their house, she realized there was a slim chance of seeing Chuck. She hoped not, as she had no date. But on the other hand, she'd be glad for Carol to see she had a black friend. During their long walk on the beach past the dilapidated wooden fences that closed off Point o' Woods, all the way to picturesque Cherry Grove, where mostly homosexuals stayed, Carol had saturated her with her views on the Establishment and discrimination in all forms. Although Diane didn't agree with everything she said, she was more attuned to her ideas than when Chuck had said some of the same things a few weeks earlier.

As soon as they reached the narrow main street of miscellaneous shops and cafés and large numbers of tanned, mostly young people, Diane spotted Chuck. He was one of the few blacks she'd seen. But he looked typically at home in the ubiquitous ragged-edged Levi's shorts and the faded denim work shirt. He was unbuttoned almost to his waist, exposing a smooth chest with beads hanging against it. He looked so broad-shouldered, small-waisted, and well-proportioned, it was hard to believe he wasn't doing a commercial. He leaned against a shop window laughing with two good-looking girls, one black.

Diane thought seriously of trying to sneak by him, to keep him from appearing so popular. But as her group approached, he and the girls were joined by two white

132

fellows. One was fortyish and the other in his early twenties. They made her less hesitant about speaking, although she still wasn't sure who was with whom. When she said hello to Chuck, he responded warmly, showering everyone with a confident smile and oozing charm. He gave special notice to Ed, though, apparently taking him for Diane's date.

Diane saw no alternative to making introductions and thereby revealing her ignominious position. ''Chuck Johnson, everybody.'' Then, ''These are my friends Ed and Carol Stern and Sharon and Morty Rosenthal.''

When Chuck introduced the girls simply as ''Pat and Barbara,'' and the fellows as ''Steve and Gary,'' she was sorry she hadn't done the same thing. After everyone shook hands and said hello, she was uncertain about what, if anything, should follow.

''We're having dinner at Maguire's,'' Morty told them. ''Have you eaten yet?''

Steve said they'd had a late-afternoon cookout just before coming over from Westhampton on his boat, and Chuck suggested they could join them for drinks after they'd eaten. Pat and Barbara exchanged looks between them, and Diane wondered if she looked as much older than they as she felt, although they were probably the same age.

Pat was completely natural, with straight, extra long brown hair, a ''Smile'' sweat shirt buoyed by her nipples, and short shorts and clogs. Barbara had a fluffy afro type hairstyle, long artificial eyelashes, and an ankle-length T-shirt dress with her towering clogs. With Gary, a lanky blond, acting indifferent, and the two girls acting as enthusiastic as if they'd gotten an invitation to the dentist, Diane thought Chuck's idea would die. But Steve, the deeply browned, salt-and-pepper-haired elder statesman of the group, endorsed his suggestion enthusiastically, and it was settled.

They were having coffee on the deck of the rustic, crowded restaurant when Chuck's party arrived. There wasn't enough room around their umbrella-covered table for everyone until Steve used his influence to get them all seated comfortably together. Chuck pulled his chair in between Diane and Carol.

"Having fun?" he whispered conspiratorially.

"Much more than I expected to when I finally agreed to come, although my friend couldn't finish his business in time to come with me. I had my first ride, though, in a Rolls-Royce he hired to bring me out," she said lowly, ashamed for Carol to hear her still desperately milking that, "and I love the ocean."

"It sounds like you've got yourself a real little sugar daddy. Where'd you meet him?"

Diane didn't want to admit she'd met him leaving Liz's party. For one thing, she didn't want it to look like a pickup, but also she didn't want Chuck to think she was so limited socially that she was unable to meet anyone except through him, even indirectly. When she responded that they were introduced by "someone you don't know," she considered it no great travesty on the truth, since Bob had introduced himself and she was sure he and Chuck had never met. She was learning how easy it was to rationalize small lies.

"Are you enjoying yourself? Is Pat with you?"

"Not especially. You could say we're all platonic."

While they were whispering together, Steve was inviting the others out to his house at Bayberry Dunes. Diane didn't realize Carol was so unenthusiastic about going until just before they were ready to leave, when she insisted that the twelve-year-old baby-sitter was too immature to stay later and persuaded Ed not to go. Sharon appeared impressed by Steve, in spite of his companions, and Morty was glowing like a light bulb as they walked toward the Ocean Beach pier.

Diane tried unsuccessfully to change Carol's mind about the sitter by pointing out that they wouldn't have to stay long. She was surprised when they actually said good-bye and left after seeing Steve's white, teak-trimmed cruiser. He said it had three cabins sleeping six. Diane was ecstatic. After the rest of them were all settled on board, Steve started the engine and they were off, heading through the dark waters toward the Dunes.

A short time later, after passing Lonelyville, Fair Harbor, and Ocean Ridge, Steve cut the engines and docked the boat at the edge of a desolate-looking area with slight resemblance to either Seaview or Ocean Beach. The lights from scattered beach houses were the only signs of life as they disembarked at a dock that appeared to be private.

"Welcome," Steve announced at the path of the large bleached-gray-shingle-and-glass house he waved them to. Inside, there were massive, rough wood-beamed ceilings, unlike the miserly ones at Carol and Ed's, a tremendous stone fireplace, Indian rugs, a sailcloth-covered built-in sofa, Naugahyde chairs, and a hatch-cover table. The smell of the sea came through the open sliding glass windows.

"Very effective. I love your taste. Who was lucky enough to work with you?" Sharon purred.

Steve said he didn't use a decorator because he and the architect, a friend, had arranged it so that much of the furniture was built in, and the rest was whatever appealed to him in his travels. He said he'd be flattered when she asked if he'd mind their stealing some ideas for their house in Amagansett. "We commissioned Barrett, but he encourages you to use a lot of your own ideas."

Among his built-in pieces was a well-stocked, cleverly concealed bar. While he pulled it out, Chuck picked out tapes for the stereo. Steve invited them to try some Cardinal Mendoza, and they all took a little. Although Morty returned to Scotch, Diane and the others continued to sip the rich, ruby-colored Spanish brandy. Although the evening seaside air made the house very cool, the exotic fruity drink gave Diane a warm feeling as she swallowed it.

Pat didn't waste any time before asking Steve for some grass, and Diane was surprised when there were no protests from either of the Rosenthals.

"I'm too old to kick the liquor habit, but it's a hell of a stupid thing to keep the law on the books when this is legal," he said, tapping his glass.

Sharon said she'd tried it once or twice but didn't get much out of it. With surprising candor she added, "Besides, they're good for sharpening your appetite, and that's exactly what I don't need. I'd like to give up smoking altogether, but whenever I do, my clothes start shrinking unless I switch to pills.''

"I've spent a lot of time in the Mediterranean countries, where the men like full-bodied women,'' Steve replied gallantly. "About the worst thing a female can be in Spain, for instance, is *chupada.*'' He sucked in his cheeks to demonstrate. "Only New Yorkers are obsessed with skinniness.''

"Maybe we should be building our house on the Costa del Sol,'' Sharon joked, beaming at Steve, while Pat and Barbara talked with Gary and passed the marijuana among the three of them. Chuck began rolling papers and arranging logs for a fire after he got the music started. When the logs caught on, he suggested they turn down some of the lights so they could enjoy it more. Then he joined Diane.

"Are you okay? Don't worry, there's nothing heavier around.'' He motioned toward the marijuana.

"I'm swell. Don't worry, there's no chance of me rushing out into the night. I still don't care for any myself, but don't let me stop you.''

"I'm cool. I will later. Feel like dancing?''

"I wouldn't mind, but no one else is.''

"Someone has to get it started.'' Then he called to Steve. "Might as well get out the Sousa marches, man. Apparently no one's interested in dancing, anyway.''

Steve got up without further prompting and asked Sharon if she'd like to dance with him. She jumped up immediately.

Chuck turned to Diane. "There goes your excuse.''

When they joined Steve and Sharon on the floor, Morty made a dash for Barbara. She accepted his invitation sulkily, leaving only Gary and Pat sitting.

"I never saw a girl who required so much work to get your arms around her,'' Chuck complained good-humoredly.

"That's because your idea of work is no work,'' Diane retorted amiably. But then she was afraid he might misinterpret her. "I mean, your idea of working on a girl.''

"I know what you mean. I'm not sensitive. Especially with this groovy job I've got now. I'm working for the architect Steve mentioned earlier. Ever since last summer, he kept telling me he was going to put me on to him, but it was still a gas when he actually delivered. It's a fabulous opportunity, and they're going to pay part of my tuition so I can take the last credits I need for my degree. It's a beautiful company."

"Wonderful. You deserve it, after everything that happened before. I wish I was as sure about what I want to do as I was when I first came. Here I'm spending all this money to go to Parsons in a few weeks, and I'm not nearly as certain I'm going into the right field."

She told him how dedicated she was to designing before she left home but how she wasn't as confident of her abilities anymore, and also found it harder to concentrate on her work. "It seems so irrelevant," she concluded.

"What *is* relevant to you these days? I hope it's not that new dude you've met. You really know how to hurt a guy. I'm jealous."

"I don't think it has anything to do with him, and I know you're kidding about being jealous, with all the girls you know. He'd die if he could make out half as well with women as you do. I never met anyone so shy and unassuming."

"You'd be surprised how bashful I could act if I thought it would get me somewhere. Look at your friends—it looks like they're even making out faster than we are."

Diane had already noticed that Steve was still dancing with Sharon, holding her closely. Talking into her ear as she simpered. Morty had switched to Pat. She was bouncing her breasts and doing steamy bumps and dips for him with her hands up in the air. Morty didn't bother to keep time with the music, moving his hips and shoulders energetically and devouring her with his eyes. She appeared to enjoy turning him on. When Gary rose to pour himself more brandy, Barbara stretched out across the sofa where the two of them and Pat had been seated, taking drags from her reefer.

When Pat finished dancing, she tried unsuccessfully to

make Barbara move over, until Morty offered her a seat in his chair near Sharon's and perched himself on the arm. Barbara stretched and yawned conspicuously. Steve continued to talk animatedly to Sharon, and Gary left the room, while Diane and Chuck returned to their spot near the fireplace. Then Steve asked if they'd like to hear some Greek music. Morty was overruled when no one else objected.

"Come on out, Gary," Steve yelled. "Let's show them some real dancing! You too, Chuck."

Gary returned, and the three linked arms and began crossing their legs and dipping in a polished routine with the music. Although Gary and Steve were more proficient, Chuck kept up without any missteps, and Sharon and Morty joined in clapping and calling out. Gary was so agile and enthusiastic, he barely resembled the taciturn person he'd been all evening.

After about fifteen minutes without an interruption, they stopped in exhaustion.

"This brandy's making me sleepy, and you guys could probably use some rest too. Maybe you should run us back to Seaview before we all drop," Sharon suggested.

"Okay, I'll just need a few more minutes to catch my breath," Steve agreed, "but I have two bedrooms upstairs and two down, so there's plenty of room if you'd just as soon stay."

Diane said she was ready to go, since she was still the guest of her neighbors, and Sharon repeated her desire to return.

"You've been complaining since yesterday about how crummy it is at the other house. It's inconsiderate to make Steve take us back when we could just as easily stay over. It makes more sense all around," Morty countered.

Diane expected Sharon to reject his proposal flatly. She was amazed when she only shrugged and deferred to him.

"All right, the defense rests. Do whatever you want to, I'm going to bed. Steve, would you mind pointing me in the right direction?"

138

"By all means." He led her upstairs and came right down again.

Diane was incredulous at the quick turn of events from a casual encounter and visit to an overnight stay. Her immediate thought was of Bob. She could never let him know what happened. She felt irritated and guilty.

Morty suggested they put on some more "soul" before turning in. He wasted no time grabbing Pat for a partner after Chuck obliged. Gary went into one of the ground-floor rooms without saying anything to anyone. When Steve said he was retiring for the night, he told Diane that she and Pat, "or whoever," could have the second upstairs bedroom, and "Chuck and whoever" could have the one downstairs. He got out a cover for Barbara after she said she'd just as soon sleep on the sofa.

"There're towels and washcloths in the closets, and plenty of pajamas and things in the drawers. I don't think you'll have trouble finding anything you need. *Hasta mañana,*" he concluded, winking.

Complaining, "What a drag," to Pat, "I thought you said there'd be something happening out here," Barbara roused herself from the sofa. She padded back later barefoot, in a big man's pajama top, looking like a little kid with her natural braided hair and all her makeup removed. She slung her street clothes she was carrying across the end of the sofa. "You all can keep on a little light if you have to, but this music's gotta go if I'm going to get any sleep around here."

Morty scurried to turn off all the lights except that from a small old Tiffany lamp in the dining area.

"May I tuck you in?" he asked, bending over Barbara.

"Not for a million bucks. Blow!"

He returned sheepishly to where Pat was sitting.

After he spoke with her a few seconds, she went over and spoke quietly to Barbara, who answered loudly enough for everyone to hear. "Fuck off and stop bugging me. That's not my bag."

"Okay, assie." She turned back to the others. "See you tomorrow morning. It's way past my beddie-bye."

After she went upstairs, Morty was next to retire.

"Guess I'll finish my drink and call it a night too." He finished the contents of his glass with a gulp. Climbing up, he called back, "Have fun."

Diane and chuck told him good night and were left standing alone in the soft light from the fireplace.

"Are you going to leave me too?" he asked, taking her hand.

"I'm afraid I have to, Chuck. I had no idea this was going to happen. I never dreamed we'd end up spending the night here. It seems very inappropriate to me. After all, I was invited out by Carol and Ed, and they could be gone by the time we get back tomorrow morning. We wouldn't even be able to ride home together. No telling what they'll think of me."

"Why are you chattering on about those people? They couldn't care less where you spend the night, or who with. What are you so uptight about?"

"I don't think I am, but if you don't understand, there's no point in my trying to explain it. You see things one way, and I see them another. I guess that's all there is to it."

"You talk too much." He pulled her to him and tried to put his arms around her.

"Please, Chuck." She resisted. "I mean it. I'll admit I'm attracted to you, but that's not enough. I'm going to go up and go to bed."

"Well, go then! I've never had to beg anybody yet, and I'm not about to start now. Sleep tight." He left Diane standing there and walked into the bedroom, closing the door behind him. Diane looked at it apologetically before climbing up to find the bedroom assigned to her and Pat. She opened the door and entered, locating the light switch beside the door in the darkness. She was sure Sharon had turned to the other side, but she was quiet just the same, because, unlike Pat, she would've had time to go to sleep.

When the light went on, she saw Pat and Morty heaving and grunting together on the bed. Pat was on top, with Morty beneath her in a reversed position. Her head was facing the door, but despite seeing Diane as soon as the light went on, she never lifted her head from between his

140

fat thighs or stopped sucking his penis noisily. Morty was equally single-minded as he squeezed and clutched Pat's rapidly moving buttocks with his hands and pressed her sex hungrily to his wet face.

Diane closed the door hard behind her, leaving the light on and wondering why they'd bothered to turn it out in the first place, since neither appeared concerned about being seen. She hesitated in the hallway outside the door. Obviously, there was no place to go but back downstairs. She tiptoed down, hoping not to attract anyone else's attention. She succeeded in returning unobserved to the living room, where she'd have to remain long enough for Morty to get enough of Pat before going to his wife's bed.

There was absolutely no way she could reconcile the sordid scene above with the enviable marriage Sharon tried to depict. Her husband would hardly behave so flagrantly without her tacit approval. Perhaps she resented him but tolerated it as long as he met her financial requirements. Her hypocrisy was almost as disgusting as his behavior. Diane speculated about how much Carol knew or had heard about them. Some of her earlier comments and unwillingness to accompany them could have come from an awareness of the arrangement. It was ironic that for all her blunt and liberated rhetoric, Carol was apparently more conventional than Sharon.

As for Pat, Diane imagined she was probably available to anyone for the right price. She doubted if a mere swinger would bed down with a Morty type for the fun of it. But she wasn't absolutely certain. She looked very enthusiastic. She wondered how soon they'd be through, grimacing at the idea of having to sleep in that crumpled, disheveled bed. Perhaps she could lie on the spread or find some fresh linen. She'd give them no more than fifteen or twenty minutes before returning. If they weren't finished with each other by then, they could move out on the beach or into Sharon's room for all she cared. She certainly had a right to go to bed.

The nearest bedroom door opened, and Chuck came out in brief undershorts, headed for the bathroom. The light in the dining section of the room was still on, and Diane was also reflected in the dying coals that remained from the fire.

"What are you doing here? Don't tell me Patty tried to molest you," he said sarcastically when he saw her.

"No, she and Morty were too busy to worry about me."

"How about that. So here you are, poor little Alice in Wonderland. What're you going to do, sit here all night and pray on your rosary?"

"I'm okay. I don't think they'll be there much longer. At the rate they were going, I don't think Morty could hold up too long."

Chuck laughed. "You know, you're really a good sport tonight. I would've thought something like this would have you out on the warpath, rushing in to wake up Sharon and show her how dirty and filthy men are. . . . I'm sorry I said that about the rosary."

"That's okay, I'm not a practicing Catholic anyway." It wasn't often she told anyone that.

Chuck sensed that they were closer. "Why don't you at least get into a robe or some pajamas so you can be more comfortable until you can get to bed? There're some in my room. You can change while I'm in the john."

Diane hesitated. She knew she wasn't that uncomfortable as she was. If he'd come out half an hour later, she would've been back upstairs. She'd been against staying in the first place. But, with so much phoniness around her, why should she refuse his well-meaning offer? She could hardly pretend any surprise, though, when Chuck returned to his bedroom shortly after she went in, allowing her just enough time to get out of most of her clothes. She was down to her bra and panties.

"I'm not finished changing," she announced mechanically as he closed and locked the door behind him and switched off the ceiling light, to leave only a small lamp beside the bed. "You know this isn't right and I can't stay," she protested weakly as he gently drew her to him.

He unfastened her brassiere with one hand while pressing her to him and taking possession of her mouth, sucking her lips and pushing his tongue deep inside her mouth,

142

then moving it in and out against hers in a throbbing rhythm. He didn't seem to mind that her arms were hanging limp beside her. She recalled the sensation of power Bob's passivity once generated in her, and hoped Chuck might feel the same for a while. She was too weakened by anticipation and suppressed desire to try to stop him, but still unable to respond uninhibitedly.

Still kissing her, Chuck pushed both brassiere straps from her shoulders and removed it. Then he stopped, took her hand, and led her like a docile child to sit on one of the narrow twin beds. As he laid her down, gently pushing back her shoulders and lifting her legs onto the bed, she remained in her submissive role, deeply ashamed of what was happening but desperate for it to continue as a force beyond her control.

Sitting beside her on the bed, Chuck removed her panties, but not his shorts. He bent over and began kissing her eyes, nose, and throat. Then he bit her earlobes lightly and put his tongue into her ears with the same increasing and decreasing pressure he'd used in her mouth. She finally wrapped her arms around him passionately, whispering, "You don't know what you're doing to me."

"I know how you feel, baby. I only want to make sure you want me as much as I want you, so you won't be sorry later. I don't want to rush you, I think I'm beginning to dig you too much."

Keeping his tongue in her ear, Chuck lowered his hand and touched the lips of her vagina for the first time. But instead of forcing his finger deep inside as Lester usually did, he rubbed her clitoris between his fingers, squeezing it and manipulating it as his head moved down to her breasts. He made circles around first one nipple, then the other with his tongue before he finally touched one directly. When he did, he flicked the tip of his tongue back and forth over it until she writhed and moaned uncontrollably.

He sucked and tickled her taut nipples while squeezing her breasts with one hand and working steadily on her vagina with the other. Then he lowered himself and commenced to lick the underside of her clitoris and suck her

143

sex until she was almost senseless, sure she would reach a climax momentarily.

She wouldn't know till much later whether she was confusing love with passion when she murmured, "I love you so much, darling, please take me," because he made a horrible, irrevocable mistake. He removed his shorts, but instead of mounting and penetrating her as she wished, he resumed tonguing her and lifted his legs from the floor to arrange himself parallel to her, upside down, so she could reciprocate in his oral lovemaking. Suddenly, she was confronted by a twitchy, veiny penis almost touching her face. She was stunned and crushed that he didn't want what she was so anxious to give him, and she remembered what Tony had told her. Her shock was magnified by the fact that Chuck, unknowingly, had almost duplicated the crude, commercial-looking scene she'd seen earlier.

She shoved him back and sat up with such force that he was knocked to the floor with a loud thud. It brought a rapping on the wall and a call from Steve next door.

"What's going on over there? Sounds like it's getting wild."

"Nothing's happening, man," Chuck answered, getting up off the floor and putting his shorts on. "Nothing at all."

"I didn't mean to make you fall. I'm sorry. I've never done that before."

"Get out of my bed, bitch," he hissed. "You'd better get out of here early tomorrow morning and keep your smelly, ass out of my way from now on, or I'll kick the shit out of it!"

Diane didn't try to talk any more after that. She held her head so he couldn't see her tears and gathered her things up as quickly as possible. She didn't stop to put anything back on until she was outside his closed door. She crept through the house and back upstairs, trembling and crying softly. Once again the lights were out, but she only had to switch them on and off to see that Pat was alone. Though it was very possible she was still awake, Diane was grateful she didn't speak. She might have wanted to compare notes. Diane laid her things over a chair and retreated to the

144

bathroom in a man's robe she'd found before Chuck's return.

Washing her face and body in the basin to avoid the noise of a shower or bath, she tried to convince herself that maybe the way things had worked out was for the best. But tears kept finding a way to brim over in her eyes, no matter how many times she thought she had them stopped. She hadn't cried since she'd been in New York. But she did that night. Uncontrollably, to the background of the lapping surf. Frustrated, hurt, disappointed as she was, she never imagined that the pain of that night was minor compared to that which was still ahead.

The next day Diane had no problem rallying either Sharon or Morty to her proposal to skip coffee so they could leave without delay as soon as they were all up and dressed. With Chuck and Gary remaining in their rooms and the two girls dawdling, in no rush to go, Steve cheerfully delivered the tense and awkward trio back to Seaview. He carefully maintained the demeanor of genial host through the last wave before he turned back to the Dunes.

The group's effort to pretend Ed and Carol had missed a "charming evening," in Sharon's words, didn't go over as well as Diane had hoped. Carol didn't bother to conceal her skepticism. It was revealed more in the way she looked at them than by anything she said. After a light breakfast, there was agreement that they'd prepare to leave on the next ferry. Carol declined Diane's attempt to contribute ten or fifteen dollars for her share of the weekend.

"How can you owe anything? You would only have been sleeping on an unused sofa in the living room, and you didn't even need that, as things worked out."

Diane felt so shoddy, she was glad she wouldn't have to face Bob until the next day at the earliest. She had no way of knowing it, but he wouldn't have wanted to face her then either. Actually, in the position he was in, it would've been impossible for him to face any upright adult if he'd wanted to.

Chapter 9

Bob was moving around on all fours in much the same way the horses circled around the Claremont stable. He was in a gaudy old house, nude and neighing to the best of his ability in between his ear-splitting cries of pain. Straddling his back was a sharp-eyed, long-limbed woman who appeared to be in her late forties. There was little softness to her body; her breasts were firm-nippled little knots. Her long thin hair was tightly pulled back and dyed dark, the gray part looking purplish. She was also unclothed except for black-leather knee-high boots, a black jockey cap, and a riding crop in her hands.

As Bob crawled around increasingly laboriously, she kicked or lashed his body in random parts, periodically connecting with his inflamed, badly bruised genitals.

"Giddy-up! Faster, you scummy fucking animal . . . don't you dare let me catch you trying to look at me again. Move!" She kept shouting commands fiercely until he finally collapsed to the floor with her still astride him. In that position, she hastily shifted her grasp on the riding crop and rammed the firm leather handle between his buttocks and deep into his anus. A final scream erupted from Bob, and a convulsive tremor shook his limbs. She withdrew the sticky handle from his rectum and got up stiffly from his limp body.

"That's the second time you've soiled yourself. You've been disciplined enough for today." Wiping perspiration from her face and armpits, she looked at him in disgust. She loathed a client like him, who required constant innovations in the routine to keep him satisfied, and also liked to stay so long.

It was only by accident that she discovered she could give him his first orgasm immediately by letting him wait for her a humiliating amount of time in a closet of a room. It happened at his first visit to Madam Georgette about six months before, when a new maid got confused about who was waiting for whom. Bob was overlooked for almost an hour, but when he was discovered and she began to apologize, her experience made her spot the special excitement in his face even before she saw his erection.

Although she knew he was embarrassed, she deliberately examined him critically from top to bottom, focusing on his bulging undershorts. The maid had removed his other clothes to a nearby closet. "How dare you present yourself to me in that condition?" she demanded angrily. "I don't like wise guys, butch, so I'm going to teach you some manners right away." Moving decisively, she snatched up an umbrella someone had left and rapped it sharply against his penis. He cried out in shock, but ejaculated instantly.

After that he bypassed the other prostitutes and became a steady Saturday-night customer of hers, always seeking punishment. But Madam Georgette didn't specialize in the M&S trade, and some of her other customers were distracted or turned off by the cries of customers like "Butchie." That was why, for the last couple of months, she'd agreed to see him on Sunday mornings at unflexible seven-thirty appointments at her house. She'd have him put in a closet with handcuffs and ropes and some umbrellas or a whip until she was ready for him two or three hours later.

Bob looked at his fourteen-karat Rolex when he was able to rise. Eleven-fifteen. The woman had outdone herself, thanks to the call Diane was responsible for. He never would've thought he could withstand such severe pain, let alone enjoy it so exquisitely. He'd be sore for a good part of the week and might require Band-Aids for the rest of the day to keep the lacerations from staining his clothes or becoming more irritated.

Driving home would be unusually hard, but the tire-shaped cushion he'd obtained would keep his weight off his bruises. He'd considered giving the woman a tip, over her standard one hundred and seventy-five dollars, but decided not to because of the money he'd spent on Diane. Not that he regretted it. He was proud he'd thought of such a perfect solution to keep from displeasing her and still be taken care of by Miss Vera.

After nearly a year of going to prostitutes, he'd found it increasingly difficult to be satisfied by them. He was getting to be almost as disillusioned as he'd become from his limited experiences with nonprofessionals when he discovered her. Finding unfailing gratification through pain and humiliation was frightening at first. But he loved the highly personalized aspects of it. The close involvement. After a while he'd come to regard it as something offbeat that he was fortunately able to afford, and which hurt no one. As far as any physical harm to himself was concerned, he embraced it unequivocally as long as it was temporary and self-healing.

As he dressed painfully, he enjoyed visualizing Diane somewhere on a Fire Island beach, thanks to him. He couldn't entirely account for his continued attraction to her, apart from his unbelievable visceral response to her at the party. The only reason he'd gone was because he expected to find a lot of call girls there like the one who told him about it. He knew he should've stayed home as soon as he walked in. But when he saw Chuck and Diane, he thought Chuck might be her pimp. After he saw she wasn't what he hoped, he was surprised he could proceed at all.

He gained confidence from the discovery that Diane valued material things more than many of her contemporaries and also had the requisite assertive personality. Even her name did something for him. He thought of her as Diana, the Roman hunting goddess, and fantasized about being her helpless quarry. He met her at a time when

148

he had no illusion left about other women. Outside of business affairs, he had no regular contacts with men. When he came home each evening, he felt no identity to the exacting money manager he had been all day for the old, family-controlled investment business. The days between his Sunday sessions were becoming interminable. The Saturday rides weren't enough. He felt so rootless, lonely, and unappreciated, he could hardly stand it.

When Bob was laboriously entering his car for the trip home from Riverdale, Diane was trying to convince a driver to take her and the Sterns home from Bay Shore even though he'd have to return from the city without a fare. Although both Sterns thought it would be simpler to take a train, Ed said it was a "nice treat" once they settled into an oversized old Buick limo Diane got for thirty-five dollars. Diane snapped that she was slumming when Carol said it was a comedown for her. She expected either a completely glacial trip or open hostilities after that.

She was confused when Carol said, "I'm beginning to see why Mrs. Kraemer didn't get her clutches into you."

"What do you mean?"

"You're not the typical little Uriah Heep she likes to befriend. How much is Hannah charging you, if you don't mind my asking?"

"Don't worry about us mentioning it," Ed interjected. "We know he overcharges us."

"I don't mind telling you. I have a two-year lease for one-fifty a month. Why?"

"She never would've persuaded him to hold it if she'd thought you'd be so self-sufficient. Her only daughter was found dead when she was just a few months old, and apparently healthy. She never got over it. I'm no psychiatrist, but I think she's been looking for substitutes ever since," Ed suggested.

"How did the baby die?"

"It must have been crib death, but at the time, they thought she might've been smothered accidentally," Carol answered.

"God, that's terrible. If my aunt had told me, I

would've gone out of my way to make her like me. For some reason, we haven't hit it off too well, but maybe it's not too late for me to try to be friends with her.''

"Don't get me wrong," Carol said quickly. "We're not suggesting you try to become closer to her. It's probably good you didn't. I was just explaining her background to you, because it wouldn't surprise me if she tries to make you move. Especially if she gets the idea you're getting too . . . uh, popular.''

"I'm safe if that's all she'd worry about, although I can't see why she'd care. Until I met Bob, I'd had so few dates it was ridiculous. You saw how nice he was. But I don't think she's ever seen me with him, or anyone else for that matter. You're the only ones he's ever met, and I've only seen Chuck a couple of times. He's just a friend from around the neighborhood," she added guiltily.

"Don't fool yourself. There's very little she misses that happens anywhere around that house. I hadn't been seeing her hardly at all, and she knew I was pregnant before I was into maternity clothes! Luckily, we'd just signed our second two-year lease before she got the word to Hannah.''

"Yeah," Ed agreed, "we were sure she wished he could break it, but he'd upped our rent to five hundred dollars, and he'd rather have a couple than two singles sharing the duplex. He probably realized any couple paying that kind of rent might have children. But she was determined to try to keep the building just like it was.''

"Wow, whoever would've thought you paid that much! He'd be crazy to want you out. Besides, if she liked children so much when she was younger, I'd think she'd enjoy a baby around the house. Especially after you had a girl.''

"Babies probably make her uncomfortable now. She's never said anything to us about any of this, but according to the doorman in three-seventeen, who's been there for years, she was always interested in children or girls old enough to influence. Babies are too unmanageable, I guess.''

"If it weren't for some of her arguments with Bernard

before the last girl moved, we'd think the doorman was exaggerating.''

"Who's Bernard?''

"Her son. You haven't met him yet?'' Carol asked.

"No.''

"Just as well, he's rather an oddball. But considering the way he's apparently been treated since his baby sister died, it's a wonder he's not worse than he is. Still, if I were you, I'd go on keeping my distance from them both.''

Their conversation was interrupted by sudden violent honking and cursing as another car attempted to switch lanes in front of them. After that they became aware of the driver's competitive driving style. When they resumed talking, it was mostly in whispers about whether or not they'd make it home in one piece. When they arrived, they scurried out eagerly to escape the driver's grumblings about the hot, slow-moving trip. He emptied their overnight cases from the trunk, accepted Diane's forty dollars sullenly, and departed.

"Be sure and thank Bob for our trip back, and let's see if we can't get together sometime soon,'' Carol said. "After Labor Day we'll be around every weekend. Ed and I both have a couple of specialties we make. Maybe you'd like to come for dinner.''

"Great, anytime you say. I'd love to see your place, too. I'll be sure and tell him.''

"Okay, but you don't have to have a formal invitation for that. It's hard to keep things the way I'd like with the baby, but you're welcome to drop in if you'd like. Try to call before, though, because otherwise we might not open the door.''

That evening, although not as disconsolate as the night before, Diane was still depressed. Cleaning the room, shampooing her hair, and giving herself a manicure didn't help. She was compelled to go back over all the things that had led to the disastrous night before, to see if there were signs of a serious defect in her own character that led to scenes such as that one and the misunderstanding with Richard. She'd heard of mixed-up girls who enjoyed

151

"leading men on" by suggestive behavior when they had no intentions of having sex with them. Could she be one of these? With as much candor as possible, she tried to examine her behavior with Chuck.

There was no question that she would have had intercourse with him. Not only *would* have, which implied a certain amount of submissiveness, but passionately *wanted* to have. But what bothered her most was her uncertainty about whether she actually loved him, as she'd said, or only wanted to believe she did, to make her desire more respectable. While he never mentioned "love" to her, his tender and unselfish lovemaking could be considered more significant than her words, with nothing to back them up. Without remembering exactly what he said, she knew there'd been an overall tone and attitude very different from his customary breeziness.

It was depressing to have no one close to talk with, to help her understand what had happened and why. After the Dunes episode, she doubted that she had the same "sisterhood" rapport with Carol. Yet, she'd acted reserved all evening, while Sharon was more congenial than she'd been all day. Assuming her liberality didn't stop with the black female activists like Shirley Chisholm and the black lawyer she kept quoting, it could've been the makeup of Chuck's group she didn't like, and the surprising way the Rosenthals responded to them.

What merits could she possibly find in the conspicuously groupie girls; Steve and Chuck, whom she probably tagged as classic chauvinists; or the unfriendly Gary, who only bloomed when he had Steve's full attention? Diane's own role couldn't have helped, either. There on one man's money and going off into the night with another she "ran into." That would hardly be Carol's idea of being "liberated." A scorned sex object was more like it. And referring to Chuck as a neighborhood pal must've sounded completely phony. Diane's head spun from the many imponderables. One of the most obvious things was Carol's preference for Bob without knowing too much about him or Chuck. She wasn't sure how to interpret it, and wondered how Jacky would compare them if Bob's

152

marital status wasn't at issue. But then she caught herself. Even if there were no Bob, or anyone else, what could possibly be salvaged with Chuck?

She could understand his threat to hurt her, because he was so hurt and angry when he said it. But he'd called her a "smelly bitch." She struggled to push that from her mind. If he meant it literally, it meant there'd been limited pleasure and mostly sacrifice for him during their intimacy. If she'd been at all sensitive, she could have concealed her sharp disappointment in him and the sixty-nine position better. She was sure she would've been incapable of doing the things he'd done for her, just like that, but she could have stroked him with her hands or kissed his smooth tan thighs as a prelude to intercourse.

If they loved each other, she believed they could have resolved that problem. But Tony's story about what Chuck expected of all his white girlfriends shouldn't have stuck in her mind so much. She still could've been special to him. She hated to think she was so preoccupied about the category someone like Tony might put her into. But if she couldn't overcome it in such an intimate moment, regardless of the feelings between her and Chuck, then the whole affair was doomed. In that case, it was just as well he wanted nothing further to do with her. Apparently her background and concern for conventional opinion would make any future with him impossible. She was sure it would never happen, but she wondered what she'd say or do if he had second thoughts about what happened. . . . A part of her wished he didn't live so close.

Bob called her on schedule the next morning, greeting her buoyantly. "Hi, this is Smitty, am I in the doghouse, or was the weekend a success?"

"Hi. Carol and Ed were very disappointed you didn't come, and I would've had a much better time if you'd been there, but I still haven't gotten over the Rolls you sent, and they said to be sure and thank you for our trip back yesterday. We all left on the twelve-o'clock ferry, and they want us to have dinner with them some night soon."

"That's fine with me. It sounds like you were worried unnecessarily about not hitting it off with them."

"I guess so. They were very nice."

A brief silence followed. She waited for him to say when he wanted to see her. When he didn't, she asked, "When're we getting together again?"

"I'm free anytime. You're the boss."

"Um-hum, famous last words. Do you like to go out only on weekends, or shall we do something sooner?"

"If you feel like seeing me every day, it's all right with me," he answered stoutly.

After nothing but disappointing, transient relationships since she'd arrived, Diane was surprised that, as reassuring as his words were, they were slightly disappointing. It was a little like he'd be doing command performances instead of something he wanted to do for his own enjoyment. But she was too grateful to mention it except humorously.

"Okay, your first assignment's Wednesday after work. We can eat someplace simple and see a movie afterward. You can report at quarter to seven."

He liked her joke so much it became standard. That Saturday she "instructed" him to meet her at Bloomingdale's to shop. They'd considered several all-men's stores, but she decided she'd be more comfortable in a store she was familiar with. Their major purchase was to be slacks and a sports jacket or a medium-weight casual suit wearable until later in the season.

After he told their salesman he was a forty long, there was an awkward period when the man asked what style or color he had in mind. Diane didn't want to act like she was in charge, but when Bob told him, "I'm accustomed to buying the type of suit I have on now," and looked at Diane for direction, she understood that he expected her to take the initiative.

From then on, things went smoothly. She suggested they be shown where the casual things in his size were, and said they'd let the salesman know when they needed him. There was no problem in finding things she liked, but the price tags made her hesitant about asking him to try them on. She admitted the problem as he stood patiently beside her, slightly toward her rear.

"I think they have a budget shop downstairs. These prices are outrageous. Let's see what they have down there."

"Have you found anything here you like if I don't mind the price?"

She pointed out a couple of blazers, a toast-colored hopsacking suit, and a checked double-knit tan suit. When he tried on the deeply vented, more shaped jackets, he took on an entirely different look.

"You look great in everything. You could be a model if the pants fit you as perfectly as the jackets. But I still think a hundred and twenty-five dollars is too much to pay for a sports jacket, or a hundred and ninety-five dollars for a suit."

"If I were a forty regular it might pay to look at reduced merchandise, but if there are any good buys in longs, they're usually in limited supply and go pretty fast. Besides, we still want to check Sills, and it's definitely more expensive, so don't worry about the prices. Tell me which jacket and suit you like me best in."

When she settled on the hopsacking suit and one of the blazers as her preferences, she asked him what he thought.

"Mother used to tell me I wasn't paid to think when she'd take me shopping or tell me to do something she wanted me to when I was younger." He laughed.

"But that was different, and you weren't paying the bills then," she reminded him.

"True, but she usually knew what was right for me, and I trust you too. Besides, I'll still have my old wardrobe for business, and my new look for you. Your taste is very moderate. I thought I might wind up looking like Super Fly."

They had such a good laugh about it, a few people noticed them and smiled. When he left her to have the trousers fitted in the dressing room, Diane thought what it might've been like shopping with Chuck, and accidentally drawing attention to themselves as she and Bob had. Although interracial couples weren't as common in that area as where she lived, they weren't too unusual and

155

acted just as comfortable. But her face grew warm just thinking about being there with Chuck.

It was stupid to keep thinking about him. Bad enough when she was alone. But to be reminded of him when she was out with Bob was inexcusable. She blamed the "forbidden-fruit" adage for a large part of her problem and returned her thoughts to Bob. When he was through, she insisted on walking to Sills on East Forty-eighth when he started looking for a cab. It was the first time they'd been out without his car.

He held her stiffly by the elbow crossing the streets, and she was surprised to find she wasn't entirely at ease with him. Turning up Fifty-seventh Street, she reached for his hand after he shifted the box with the jacket and hastily switched to her curb side. Momentarily, she'd forgotten how wet they were from perspiration once or twice when she'd held them briefly before. She'd heard that was often a sign of nervousness, and she didn't want to embarrass him again. But on this humid day, his hand was completely free of moisture. He grasped hers eagerly and held it tightly as they proceeded.

Grinning broadly, he told her, "This is a wonderful afternoon. It's been a long time since anyone's taken so much interest in me."

"It's fun for me too. I can't wait to see you in your new outfits. Maybe I should specialize in men's wear."

Hand in hand and relaxed, they walked west on Fifty-seventh Street enjoying the elegant shops and art galleries along with the other strollers before proceeding south more briskly down Madison Avenue. At Sills, a small second-floor shop, easily missed by all but the cognoscenti, a female cashier-clerk, a black tailor, and the friendly diminutive owner himself quickly dispelled Diane's fears of being out of place in a snobbish all-male sanctuary. After they selected checked slacks and a couple of sports shirts, Bob showed amusement that some of the imported turtlenecks labeled medium looked small enough to fit a girl when Diane held them up to him.

"They stretch when you put them on, but if you've got any bulges around the midriff, even the larges wouldn't hide them. The only reason you'd need a large, though, is for the length. But you're right about them fitting girls. They buy quite a few. We also make up tailored pants suits for women, in case you're ever interested," he added, turning to Diane.

She definitely wasn't, considering his prices and her own novice's skills. She was murmuring something polite when Bob spoke up with considerable interest, seeking further information. After he got answers about materials, styles, length of time, and number of fittings required, he said they'd probably be interested in a dark velvet and a leather suit for Diane a little later in the fall. In the meantime he bought himself a couple of the turtlenecks Diane liked, and a small one for her, over her protests. They were twenty-five dollars each.

When they were downstairs with their new purchases, Diane admonished him about his extravagant impulses. "I can see where I'm going to have to watch you like a hawk to keep you from going overboard. I'll be embarrassed if you keep trying to do so many things for me."

"I haven't done anything very consequential that I can think of. There're any number of men who'd be able to do much more than I could if you gave them the chance. But they might not enjoy it as much as I would. You know how happy I am when I'm able to please you."

"I know, and I appreciate it, but you can do that without coming up with ideas about ordering me custom-made suits that could easily run a good two or three hundred dollars apiece. Especially leather. It's expensive anywhere."

"We don't have to come back here if you don't want to. I was just excited by the idea of seeing you in the kind of beautifully tailored suits they'd probably make up. That's all." He sounded apologetic.

"How come you always make me feel like a spoilsport in the end, when I'm trying to look out for you? Don't forget, I *am* a design student. It's usually been too warm for a jacket recently, but I think I can make up a couple of fairly professional-looking suits for later on. The one at the party didn't look too homemade, did it?"

"Oh, no, not at all, but I'll bet it's a lot more work on heavier materials."

"Wool and velvet, or more likely velveteen, aren't that hard. I probably couldn't manage leather or suede, but maybe I can pick up something reasonable on sale. That way, I could afford it."

"We'll see. Maybe you'll change your mind later if I'm careful not to make too many demands on you to do everything you want me to do."

She shook her head back and forth and sighed. "You're lucky I'm not a city slicker. It's a good thing I found you before you were waylaid like a baby lamb."

He laughed and gleefully repeated "waylaid like a baby lamb." "My fate's in your hands, then. That settles that. Am I allowed to suggest someplace to eat now? You must be hungry?"

"I could eat, but I just got an idea—how'd you like for me to fix something at my house?" The thought was very impulsive, as a way of doing something for him for a change. But after she apologized in advance for the size and furnishings of her studio apartment and the lack of air-conditioning, she wasn't surprised when he didn't jump at the offer.

"I didn't know you liked to cook."

He looked relieved when she admitted she didn't relish it and described her miserable wall niche that posed as a kitchen. "Let's go to La Goulue then. There's no point in your cooking when you don't have to." He hurried to Fifth Avenue for a cab, as if he were afraid she'd change her mind if there were more discussion.

After they'd checked their packages and been served, Diane noticed his picking at his entrée. "What's wrong, don't you like your mushrooms?"

"I can get it down, but it hasn't nearly enough wine."

"Mine tastes delicious to me. Good thing I didn't try to cook for you. I forgot you were such a gourmet."

"Come on, you know I'd eat anything you set in front of me, if you'd made it, but you're not supposed to be professional. This is altogether different. I could make better coq au vin than this."

158

"You cook?"

"Perhaps I should say I enjoy it. I don't want to sound too immodest. But I really do love it, especially for someone else. I almost asked you to my house so I could prepare a meal for you today, but I thought it might look contrived after I discouraged you from cooking."

"Really?"

"Naturally, I know how devious women expect most men to be. I didn't want to risk spoiling things after such a nice day," he said simply.

She couldn't help it. There was no way to avoid comparing him with Chuck. Chuck had kissed her in public when she barely knew him, and expected her to go home with him before they could get through their first dinner alone. He'd had the nerve to get angry when she didn't. Bob was completely deferential after all he'd done.

"You're beautiful, in a way. But promise me you'll invite me another afternoon. I think I'm a little mad at you for not letting me know what you were thinking about before it was too late." She couldn't think of any reason why she would be hesitant to go and see how he lived and all.

"I promise. And I won't try to make any decisions like that on my own anymore." He reached across the table and grasped her hand excitedly. "If I try to, you have every right to let me have it. Okay?"

"Okay, honey," she replied. But her smile was forced. She was growing somewhat tired of their joke and his childishness, although she still enjoyed being in control of things.

When he dropped her off later, she told him to call her that Thursday, and looked forward to a day to herself the next day, since she knew it was a matter of choice. She missed the park and thought it might be pleasant to take her sketchpad to see what ideas she might come up with. Normally, she would've gone around one or two o'clock to be there when the sun was hottest. But she was afraid of seeing Chuck if she waited too late and he was in town. If she was to go at all, she decided it had to be before he was likely to be up and about.

159

When she got there shortly before nine, she found few people. But as they were mostly dog walkers, she worried that Chuck might follow their routine. Looking for a more secluded spot away from the main walk, she noticed a small dog yapping and fussing about a tree and heard a man's sharp command.

"Sit, Mia, sit, damn you."

She looked as she passed about twenty feet away, and saw a young man with his back against a tree zipping his trousers while another one kneeling on the grass facing him tried to shift into a more natural position. The standing man showed more irritation than anything else at Diane's intrusion, while his friend's face was as embarrassed as Diane's when their eyes met for a flush-faced second before she could turn away. Both men looked very "normal."

Mostly because it was post-Fire Island, Diane was more saddened than shocked by what she saw. The park had represented a daytime haven for her. It had survived despite her after-dark fear of it and the uneasiness she'd developed about the neighborhood in general. Although she recognized that the men posed no threat to her personal safety, unlike the well-publicized predators of Central Park and Morningside Park, it hardly comforted her.

She forced herself to stay out awhile on a bench near the busy Seventy-second Street highway exit she usually avoided, but she couldn't sketch. She was too preoccupied with watching for any sign of Chuck in the distance and wishing everything wasn't being spoiled for her. Between her fear of the transients and her disgust for the wide assortment of types who shared the Riverside Park, Diane began to wonder what someone like her was doing in the middle of them. This was on Sunday, August 12.

The next morning, Diane lined up Jacky for lunch determinedly. Feeling increasingly trapped where she was, she couldn't rely solely on Bob anymore. She'd decided it was time to stop humoring Mona. She softened the switch by saying she'd be doing some shopping with Jacky. A fundamental cheapness had emerged as a major factor in Mona's dated appearance and family living arrangement. Recognizing this, Diane gambled safely that she wouldn't offer to join them. After her experiences on Fire Island, she had the idea she'd be able to hold her own much better with Jacky than before. She found, however, that little had changed.

Jacky was very animated. She'd had it out with her engineer. "He was getting too serious. Starting to act like he thought he was my old man. Even Gabe doesn't come on like that. That's the main reason we still get along so well."

Diane had barely touched on Chuck and Fire Island before Jacky lost interest. Although she said Chuck sounded like a "groove," she appeared too distracted for Diane to get to any of the details of their misunderstanding or discuss any of her other conflicts. She wasn't sure she wanted to anyway. Jacky was less attentive than the last time they'd lunched together, when she'd had Bob to mull over and dissect. On the way back to the office, she told Diane she'd be away the following weekend, but would try to see her again for lunch before then. The only call Diane received all week, however, was Bob's. Until she spoke with him, there wasn't even anyone to tell she'd be getting her phone the following week.

"I almost hate to go to the expense. Except for you, it'll probably be the most unused phone in the city," she told him Saturday night. "But that's all right," she added, afraid she might sound petty after all the money he'd spent on their dates. She was still impressed, but it was getting a little demoralizing having such a stiff relationship with the only person she was seeing regularly. After nothing but fiascos, she didn't feel very desirable. She decided to invite Bob in after their date. He parked with a compliant attitude.

As soon as they were inside, she saw it was a mistake. After the places he'd taken her, her studio room was grubbier than ever. She fixed him a drink with some bourbon she'd bought. He declined the tin of peanuts she opened. Neither one of them could think of much to say.

161

"Do you mind having to do your own housework?" he asked timidly.

"Not especially, but I think I keep things in pretty good shape, considering what I've got to work with."

He didn't say anything else, and she misunderstood his question at the time. As a result, they became more strained. When he was ready to leave, eyes averted, she softened toward him and told him when to call her at work for her new number.

"Of course. Thank you, Diane." He brightened so quickly, she envied him his simplicity. She was sorry they were further apart than ever when he hadn't even picked up the clothes she'd had him buy.

She remained brooding and perplexed after he left. Not only about him, but about Chuck and all her aborted relationships. She felt much better about things when Jacky finally called her for lunch that Wednesday.

They did some shopping and decided to continue after work. Diane was having trouble finding shoes, while Jacky, already slightly taller, didn't care how high they were if she liked them otherwise. She was so willowy and stylish, Jacky had something of a complex about her. With her flair, she could've carried off some of Diane's designs that hung in her closets because Diane was self-conscious about wearing them herself.

When she suggested dinner at Maxwell's Plum after they'd finished, Diane was very enthusiastic because it was so well-known. It was so ornate when they got inside, it was more like somewhere Bob would take her than the other singles places. Although Friday's had its hanging plants outside, and some stained glass and Tiffany lamps inside, it took the sawdust-floor route and was by no means in competition with Maxwell's Plum. You could've picked up both the bars she'd visited before and set them easily inside.

Jacky chose the upper level, where the bar was, instead of the glass-enclosed terrace, which was handiest. Diane could hardly read the menu for speculating about the cost of the enormous tulip-shaped Tiffany chandeliers, the ornate mirrors and stained-glass panels, and the heavy brass banister with figurines that separated the restaurant into its two levels.

She curtailed all the looking when she found she kept meeting the eyes of a lean Madison Avenue type at a nearby table with a friend.

"There's a guy who keeps looking at me," she confided to Jacky.

"Yeah, attractive?"

"Uh-huh, he's in the denim suit at a table to your right, with a fellow who looks kind of short and baldish. But I don't think there's any way you could see him without it being too obvious."

She could have been talking to the wall. Jacky did her famous flipped-hair number and turned immediately. She gave them the type of smile and nod customary among people who've met before. The tall one immediately stood and came over to them. "I'm Ted Abrams. Can we join you after we finish our dessert?"

The question was aimed at both of them, but Jacky answered as Diane pretended she was transparent behind the menu. A short while later, the two men were transferred to their table, with no one showing much interest. Once they were there, Diane was flattered when the good-looking one centered his attention on her; however, she was still uptight.

"Why don't you try the chateaubriand," he suggested in the same tone Bob might use.

"Okay" She wanted her voice to get stronger before she had to use it too much.

"Is this your first time here?"

"Yes. . . . do you come often?" She wished she could act more natural. With Jacky doing her routine for his receptive friend, she could see she was on her own.

"Ummm, fairly often, but not enough to be due for something like you."

"Thanks, but you're embarrassing me."

"I don't believe it. You sound like you don't know how fantastic-looking you are. What do you do?"

"I'm . . . about to become a fashion designer. I'm going to be at Parsons."

"That's beautiful. I had no idea you'd be talented as well as beautiful. I'm doing some publicity for a textile account. I'll bet you could give me some help."

It did her good to be seen as a young woman with a purpose for a change and find someone interested in her ideas. Having such rapport with Ted, she didn't make a fuss over the check, although she imagined most pickups came after expensive gourmet meals. On the other hand, both men had expense accounts. When Ted said he'd brought his car, she was happy for Jacky's sake. Standing, she towered over his friend Lenny.

Ted's Jaguar had a parking ticket on it at a nearby meter. However, he promptly tore it up, with only limited curses. "That's what happens when you lose your head over beautiful girls."

If he was divorced, as he said, he was nice but almost too smooth. Diane had told him how he could reach her, but she wasn't going much further until she knew if he were legitimate or not. She didn't know her plan was in jeopardy until they were at First Avenue and Eightieth, near Jacky's residence, and Lenny said, gesturing, "That looks like a parking space you could fit into, Ted."

When he couldn't fit and found no convenient garage space, he agreed with Diane that one ticket was enough for the day. She didn't know what to think when Lenny trotted off with Jacky into her luxurious high-rise.

Diane complained about how terrible her place was all the way there and also got it in that Jacky had a roommate. Just before they turned into her street, however, a car pulled out of its spot, and Ted got it. "Our luck is changing."

If she'd had an apartment she was proud of, Diane suspected she might've had a different attitude. Even with someone like him, whom she had no intention of sleeping with right away. He'd be nothing like Richard.

"Are you in town weekends?" If she could show an interest in another date, perhaps they could end the evening on a promising note in the car. It could also resolve some of her dubiousness about him.

"I may be on Shelter Island part of the time, but I'm

sure we can spend some time together this weekend if you want to. Let's talk about it upstairs.''

"You've been so sweet, I'd love to see you again, but I haven't got the kind of place I can invite company to. Not even girls. I'm sorry.''

"Come over here.'' He put his arm around her and pulled her around to face him. "What's the matter, honey, don't you want to get it on?'' He didn't try to kiss her, cupping her breasts together and bending to put his mouth there. "A lovely body like this, I could swallow whole.''

She stopped him reluctantly. "One of my neighbors might see me.''

"So, let's go in, then, unless you'd rather go to a good hotel. I'm not obsessed with the idea of making love in cars either.'' Diane almost laughed at that. When she wasn't satisfying herself, cars had provided her most erotic experiences, and still could. But not with someone who was interested only in a one-night stand.

"Why does everything have to happen tonight if we're going to see each other again?'' Pockmarks on his sun-tanned face gave it a masculine look. His dark hair was thick and carefully styled. She put her hand to it affectionately.

"Careful!''

You could see he wanted to get the word back. Looking at him, she was absolutely certain that he was married.

"You'd better be getting home before it gets too late.''

"Too bad you didn't think of that before. Maybe I wouldn't have gotten the ticket.'' He leaned across, opened the door, and said, "See you around.''

She was becoming so disappointed with the so-called "singles scene,'' she hoped Jacky would forget their lunchtime plans to get together again that Friday. Maybe she'd go if Bob went. She didn't know.

The next day, Diane's situation deteriorated further. Her fragile relations with Mrs. Kraemer collapsed entirely when the telephone man came. Before Diane could get down to admit him, Mrs. Kraemer was up the stairs to see if he belonged there.

"I've got the order for a Miss Diane Keely, three

165

forty-one West Seventy-sixth Street, top floor. Why, what's the problem?'' The pimply-faced youth brushed his long bangs back to look inquisitively as Diane rushed to see what was wrong.

"Miss Keely," she demanded before Diane could speak, "would you mind telling me why you're having a telephone installed when you're not able to pay your rent?"

"Not pay my rent? I've paid my rent on time every single month I've been here. And even if I hadn't, it's none of your business. You only live here, the same as I do."

"Look, ladies," the installer interrupted, "I've still got a lot of other stops to make. Do I put in the phone or don't I?"

"By all means. As the young woman points out, I'm not the owner. I'm just a person who recommended her for an apartment she never would've gotten if I'd known more about her. If she doesn't mind having a phone and no place to use it because she's been evicted, I shouldn't object. Go ahead with your work."

"I'll be ready to get started as soon as I get the rest of my stuff out of the truck, miss. You'll just have to show me where you want the phone," he told Diane in a sympathetic tone.

When he left, Diane tried to find out what Mrs. Kraemer meant. "I don't know why we were yelling at each other before. I'm sorry. But I've no idea what you're talking about. Mr. Hannah hasn't said anything to me about anything. What did he tell you?"

"That you gave him a bad check that he's mailing back to you. I was waiting for you to go out this morning to speak to you then. Instead, I saw the man from the telephone company."

"A bad check! I don't see how that's possible." She tried to think. "I changed banks recently, because the lines were so long at my old one. . . . I hope I didn't accidentally mail him one of my old checks! But that must be it. I'll send him the right one today. I must've had something else on my mind to do a stupid thing like that."

"It doesn't surprise me. I wouldn't have believed Elizabeth would've put up with such an ungrateful niece. You came here under the pretense of being a poor struggling student, and right away you have the attitude that you know everything and don't need anyone to help you. Working God knows where. Running around with every variety of man. No wonder you're all mixed up."

"I'm sorry you feel that way about me. When I came here, I assumed you'd have a life of your own. If my aunt had told me more about you, I could've told you I was still going to school in September and come down to keep you company sometimes. I know how lonely—"

"Lonely?" she sputtered. "Lonely! Of all the presumptuous little nobodies. After I saw what you were like, do you think I would've wasted my efforts on you? If I were Mr. Hannah, I wouldn't take your check when you send it."

"Well, don't worry about it, because I've been miserable ever since I've been here, and after this, I won't be here any longer than I have to. I'm glad to know I can count on you to get Mr. Hannah to let me break my lease. When I find something, you'll be the first to know, but until I do, I'm afraid you'll just have to put up with me." Diane turned to leave, but Mrs. Kraemer called after her.

"Really, after all the years I've lived here and had who I wanted upstairs? We'll see how long I'll have to put up with you and your men while you take your time moving. You may find that just as easily as I got you in here, I can get you out."

After all the trouble it had caused, Diane thought it was a little late to cancel the phone. She also realized it might make it harder to get one the next time. But before the phone was in, Mrs. Kraemer had an urgent call of her own to make. The phone rang over and over again on a littered table beside a dirty unmade bed in a Lower East Side furnished room. A crumpled pajama bottom lay on the floor. A roach crept across some orange peels that had fallen nearby. More peels were on the night table, along with the skeletons of some grapes and an empty carton of papaya juice. Piles of newspapers, torn news clippings, and hard-backed books were strewn everywhere. Favorite topics were World War II, philosophy, and primitive tribes and their customs.

There was no inside toilet in the room, but hairs and yellow droplets in the sink showed that it often doubled. Whenever Bernard wanted a shower, he'd hang around the West Side Y until he could sneak in or use someone else's registration card. He was ambling that way when his mother called. He'd just run the reservoir after completing his dips and chins and hanging from the monkey bars at the Central Park playground. He'd become restless after no one replaced the little girl he watched on a nearby swing until her mother took her away.

In his torn Adidas sneakers and loose-crotched khaki work pants, he didn't look like anyone who could run the reservoir once, let alone twice, as he'd just done. His back was so humped over that his boxer shorts showed between his pants and his hiked up T-shirt from the back. Everything was so soiled, he could run in the shorts without fear of missing anything when he finished. If he could clean up a little at the Y, he'd go over to the Fifth Avenue bookstores to see what he could pick up when the guards weren't looking. Maybe he'd sell something afterward. He didn't usually do that, but if he could get an extra three dollars, he could get the bus to Jones Beach the next morning. He was tired of little kids, he wasn't sure how much he could pull off around his mother's, and needed some full-grown ass to get his rocks off with.

Mrs. Kraemer hung up angrily when there was no answer at her son's. But she would call again.

Although the worker finished before noon, Diane was in no mood to go to work after he left. He said he'd mail her rent check for her. She took a couple of aspirin, pulled the shades all the way down, and went to bed heavily. She first considered going down to talk with Carol, if she was there. But if she was in, she'd heard everything and could come up and sympathize if she wanted to. Otherwise, either she wasn't in or didn't want to get involved. After all, they'd still be neighbors with Mrs. Kraemer after she was gone.

Diane listened hopefully for a knock on her door, but none came. She felt isolated. So tired of being alone when she needed someone to talk to. But she willed herself not to cry, and managed to fall asleep in the warm room, uncharacteristically darkened to shut out the afternoon's brightness.

The next morning at work, her supervisor told her she'd expected her to call if she wasn't coming in all day. Although Diane understood she had permission to take the day off but could come in in the afternoon if she wanted to, she probably would've called in as a matter of course if she hadn't gone back to bed because she was so upset. Diane told her it was fairly late before the phone was in and she didn't think there was any point in calling.

"I see. I'm sure you'll be more conscientious in the future. I've been very pleased with your on-the-job performance, but it's just as important for you to have the same sense of responsibility toward the company when no one's looking over your shoulder."

Diane was in no mood for either a lecture or an argument. She suspected a broader criticism in her supervisor's words, but had no desire to probe into it. She wouldn't be there much longer, and was certain personnel would call her in and dismiss her forthwith if she tried to give any advance notice. She'd stick to her plan to request leave for an emergency at home and say she didn't expect them to keep the job open for her when she didn't know how long she'd be gone.

If she ran into anyone later or wanted to be in touch with Jacky, she could say things had worked out at home and her family was helping her through school. If she managed to avoid any more incidents or controversy, she might be able to give the firm as a reference to get a job the following summer. She made a difficult apology that appeared to more than satisfy her boss.

"So give me your new number so I can give it to personnel. With so many things happening all over the city, I'm glad you took care of this."

A little later, Bob called, and Diane gave him the number too. "There was a little trouble over it," she

169

added, and promised to tell him all about it when she saw him.

"I promised Jacky I'd go to Wednesday's with her tonight, and until I reach her, I'm not sure if I can get out of it. Would you like to go? She says it's really different and has dancing, and little shops and things."

"I don't dance."

"I don't know all the latest steps myself. I don't think that makes any difference, if you think you'd enjoy yourself. I'd just as soon not go without a date."

"You know I'll do anything you tell me to. It's up to you."

She'd grown accustomed to taking charge of their dates, but when he wasn't invited in the first place, she didn't want him to come if he was going to act like he was completely out of it. "Bob, it's not up to me, you have to take me because you want to. Otherwise there's no point in your going."

When a few seconds passed and he hadn't answered, she told him she'd probably go with Jacky and see him either Saturday or Sunday. "Call me tomorrow afternoon."

"You're not looking for a new job just because Mrs. Morganlander chewed you out, are you?" Mona caught her by surprise when she remained longer than usual at her desk that noon, studying the *Times* ads. Although Mona had become less disagreeable after Diane's friendship with Jacky, Diane still hadn't forgotten some of the things she'd told her.

"No, just the real-estate section," she replied, closing the paper. "Who told you she got on me this morning? I didn't know it was that noticeable."

"No one had to. She was fuming around late yesterday afternoon, asking different people if you'd called in or given them any message for her. So I knew she'd speak to you about it today, but everyone knows it's not that big a deal. They never like it when people take off a day near the weekend, even when they've got a good reason like you did."

"God, what did this office do before I came? I can't

even get a phone in peace. I used to count the days before I'd be leaving my old job because everybody was so out of it. But at least there, there was never any maliciousness. Here, they're like a pack of vultures waiting to pounce on you."

"No they're not, don't be so sensitive. Come on, let's go to lunch. You can't afford to shop with Jacky every day."

Mona was curious about Diane's sudden apartment hunting but was afraid to push Brooklyn anymore. Without giving a reason, Diane couldn't even admit she planned to move as soon as she did. Although she knew it wouldn't be anyplace near where she was, she didn't know where she'd end up. She still liked the East Side, but had mixed feelings about the parts catering to singles crowds.

It was her growing ambivalence about that whole scene that made her ask Bob to come with her that evening. She saw no obligation to be his Siamese twin when he was so obtuse and trying at times, besides being such a prude. She still wanted to meet new people. Yet, it bothered her to go places where it was so obvious you were available. Women often outnumbered the men and appeared to have far fewer alternatives. Some of the least attractive men acted like talent scouts.

The other thing was that, while Jacky and Rita were close, she always felt like an afterthought and a tag-along with them. Maybe this was inevitable as a newcomer. But whereas Rita was the kind who could get along with anyone, Diane preferred to have her own identity as much as possible. With Jacky, it was a little hard to maintain it. She was still indecisive about what to do when Jacky called her back later that afternoon. If she'd been indifferent, as she sometimes was, Diane might not have gone out again that night.

She passed right by Wednesday's at first. She reached Second Avenue and had to ask someone where it was before she located it back near Third. When she found it was down a flight of stairs behind an inconspicuous entrance, she decided they were either very cheap or very cocky. No comparison to the other places she'd visited, it was also less visible than most of the other restaurants in the vicinity.

Downstairs, there was the additional surprise of an admission charge. Jacky hadn't mentioned it when she'd urged Diane to come, and added that Paul Slattery would be there. Diane's interest in seeing him again was accompanied by disappointment that he hadn't called her himself if he wanted to see her. She would've been more disturbed if she hadn't wanted to be as inconspicuous as possible until she could move. Alone, she'd been able to creep out of the house silently, much as an intruder might. Her preoccupation with stealth made her forget her after-dark jitters enough to catch a bus and save on cab fare. Not in the class of Mona, she was always conscious of money changing hands, even when others were spending it.

Apparently all who wanted to find Wednesday's had. With the dancing right alongside the wrought-iron tables, it reminded her most of a large traffic jam. Light cobblestone floors contributed to the idea of people dancing in the streets. Making her way through the main thoroughfare, it was interesting to see how some people were grinning and laughing as they danced, while others tried to look nonchalant or had those faraway blanked-out expressions, as if they didn't have any partners.

She was jarred seeing a tall, composed young black man between two smiling white girls. From a distance, he looked like Chuck. But Chuck would never have worn such a wide belt or bright-orange, clinging shirt. Pinpointing other ways Chuck was better, she almost collided with a skinny young man with a smirk on his long, rice-grain face. It took a few minutes to convince him she wasn't looking for someone just like him. Then she saw Jacky, dancing.

Wednesday's wasn't the kind of place where one could easily be the center of attention. But Jacky was a heavy contender. She had a repertoire of movements, sounds, and facial expressions that could've resulted in an indecency charge for a more voluptuous girl. It didn't surprise Diane when she spotted Paul, turned toward the bar, with his back to the dancers.

"How's it coming?"

"Much better now." He turned and smiled, eyes nearly as dreamy as before, and greener than she'd first thought. "Jacky said she'd spoken with you, but wasn't sure you'd show up. I'm glad you did."

From his words, Diane couldn't tell if he was there as part of a group again, or because he specifically wanted to see her, as she'd believed that afternoon. To cover herself, she was about to launch into a report about Bob. Before she could start, he continued.

"I've thought about you a lot since I met you before. I have a feeling we're both looking for something more consequential than you usually find at places like this. Wasn't there anyone you cared about in Iowa?"

"Not really. There was this one fellow I saw from when I was about fifteen till I decided to come here. But it was mostly habit. He mentioned marriage just before I left, but mainly because he thought it was what I wanted to hear. What about you—have you been married?" With him, she didn't hesitate to ask something like that.

"No, but I've thought more about it recently than I ever did. The trouble is, I'm still a half-assed Catholic and I'm not sure if I'm ready for a family yet."

"I know what you mean, they're a big responsibility. My dad remarried when my mother died, and I ended up with my mother's sister after he had such a hard time supporting my stepmother's two sons and me."

"I've been pretty lucky. Besides being a consultant, I write manuals that do fairly well. If we didn't go over three or four kids, I'd be all right. It's the commitment more than the money that worries me. Nowadays, women can be as afraid of it as men."

"What's going on over here? Been here long, Diane?"

"Oh, no, just a little while . . . you were busy dancing, and I didn't see Rita." It was unfortunate. When they weren't leaving her, she was forgetting them. To compensate, she decided she'd better compliment Jacky on her dancing. "You were really something else," was the best she could do.

Happily, Jacky's loose-jointed partner was with her,

anxious to resume their show. Although Diane normally found slender men attractive, he looked a little too fragile in her opinion. Part of it was probably the contrast with Paul. He was like the fullbacks she'd mostly observed from a distance. Surrounded by girls. When they were alone again, they couldn't pick up where they'd left off.

"They're supposed to have some kind of cheese shop here. Are you interested?"

"Not unless you are. We never went in for it that much at home. I'm a little past the American and Swiss stage now, but I'll never be a connoisseur. What about you?

"No way. I can take it or leave it. How's your drink?"

It was obvious that his mood had changed, but not back to the awkwardness of their first meeting. Now, he was clearly angry and trying ineffectively not to show it. Diane had found it hard not to draw any inferences from the type of conversation they'd been holding. But seeing how upset he was at having it interrupted, she let her fantasies run wild. The more he snarled at a bartender or glowered at the dance area, the more excited she became. Apart from being a practicing Catholic, he was the type she'd always wanted. Physically and sexually attractive, yet serious and substantial.

A slow number she liked had started. "Want to dance?"

"Sure, come on."

Diane nestled against him like she used to see the short, cuddly girls do. He wasn't especially "light on his feet," but maybe that was an attribute of some fat men, not big ones. It didn't matter, in any case. Bob didn't dance at all. She tried not to feel guilty about him. He'd been a savior, but he'd had every chance to pick up where Lester left off, and he hadn't done it. Paul was such a comfortable type, it might even be all right with him in her apartment until she moved. It depended.

"Do you live in the city, Paul?"

"Yeah, Fifty-seventh and Sixth."

"I love it around there." It was only a couple of blocks from Central Park South, probably her all-time favorite street from the day she'd arrived.

174

When the number ended, she and Paul continued holding hands. They were returning to the bar area when Jacky waved to them. She was standing next to a table where Rita was seated next to another young woman. Rita was as sunny as before, and Jacky also looked cheery.

"In case one of us leaves before the other one, I wanted to tell you you should ask Diane to your company picnic, Paul. I definitely can't make it tomorrow."

At least they were no longer holding hands.

"Don't get me involved, Bob's getting so ridiculous, we had a big fight about my coming here tonight without him. I don't want him to get mad at me again," Diane babbled.

It was hard to remember Paul as the gentle giant, seeing the big hands clenched at his sides, eyes narrowed, and the pulse jumping in his temples. He looked so menacing, Diane could never have stood there as calmly as Jacky did.

"You can go and fuck yourself," he finally hissed through his mustache.

Jacky shook her head and shrugged as he turned and stomped off. Rita and the other girl squirmed. "You just can't win," Jacky declared.

Diane felt caved in on the inside. "You could've told me Paul was your boyfriend."

"But he's not. There was nothing to tell. I told you, I didn't want to get too tight with anyone."

Diane remembered something she'd all but forgotten. "What kind of a consultant is Paul?"

"He's in structural engineering. Why?"

"I just wanted to be sure who he was. I might not know that many people in New York, but I'm not desperate enough for your rejects!"

Paul was waiting for her as she moved hurriedly down the main "street."

"I must look like a real ass, getting hung up on a bitch like that. I shouldn't have let you get caught in the middle, but she actually goes in for all that switching back and forth. One of these days I'm going to lose all my patience with her. It's not right. . . . What can I say?"

"Don't apologize, Paul. Maybe we'll both get lucky yet."

"Can I take you home?"

She looked at her watch and shook her head. "The phones must be over there. It's not that late, I think I'll let this guy I date pick me up. He's not too far from here, and knowing him, he'll be outside almost as soon as I get upstairs."

If he knew she was lying, he was sensitive enough not to say so.

Chapter 10

At least, whatever she had wasn't fatal. It was a legacy from her aunt. It wasn't much, but it was the best Diane could come up with to get her through the night and the next day. There was one other thing that helped a little. What happened to ugly girls who came to New York? The reason it didn't help more was that she was afraid they might've been better off than someone like her who had such high expectations. She didn't know if Jacky had deliberately made a fool of her or not. Perhaps she'd considered Diane more self-satisfied and competitive than Diane thought she was. Whatever it was, it would've been far crueler if she'd permitted her to become more involved with Paul than she did. . . . The less she thought about him, the better. There was no point in doing reruns on someone who hadn't ever been available to you. It was humiliating to think how ready she was to become intimate with him because of all he represented to her. In a way, it was almost funny. His eyes were sexy, but she didn't even know what his mouth looked like, let alone how he'd be to kiss.

When Bob called, she told him she disliked Wednesday's, couldn't keep up with Jacky or her girlfriend, and left almost as soon as she arrived. She was tempted to take his number for future situations like that, but she was afraid of letting him lose the little initiative he had.

"Are you going to see me tonight?"

It was the kind of gray, overcast day she would've just as soon spent at home. Especially after her rough night. But she detected a slight edge to Bob's tone that made her reluctant to say no to him. The last thing she wanted was to make him less secure about her, when no one else in the city wanted any part of her. She told him to double-park a little way up the street and stay in the car until she came.

As soon as he saw her, he apologized for not picking up the new pants he'd left for alterations. Although a little disappointed that he didn't have on any of his new clothes, Diane found she was much happier to see him than she'd expected to be. In spite of his peculiarities, she didn't know what she would've done or said if she'd slept with someone else the night before.

"It seems like a long time since I saw you, so much has happened. Let's get away from here."

"All right," he replied, starting the car. "What's wrong, does it have anything to do with me?" he asked anxiously.

"Oh, no, honey. I just quarreled with my aunt's screwball friend downstairs, and I've decided to move." She told him all about what happened and threw in the lecture at her office for good measure.

His heated reaction surprised her. "Who the hell do they think they are, treating you like that? You don't have to take that. If this woman's so preoccupied with what the other tenants do, she should buy her own brownstone and keep it for her private guests. She obviously can't afford that, so what she ends up is nothing more than a frustrated super! It sounds like you were too restrained. I wish you would've put both her and that supervisor in their places so they'd know who they were dealing with in the future."

Diane looked at his angry profile with amazement. His eyes were narrowed, staring at the road, his lips thinned and taut as he spoke. She was so moved by his resentment, it was almost as hard not to cry as it was two mornings before when she thought no one cared about her problems. She'd never brought out the protective side of people before, starting with her father. Bob's being such an easygoing person normally made his attitude that much sweeter.

He got out a cigarette and pressed the lighter knob with a

trembling hand. She patted his knee. "Don't worry about it. The job business is nothing. I'll be quitting in a couple of weeks anyway, so there was no point in blowing up when I might need a reference later on. I shouldn't have mentioned it. As far as my moving, I was liking the neighborhood less and less, and you saw how I was almost ashamed to entertain there."

He ran through a light that was turning red as they reached Central Park West. Another driver honked at him to assert his right-of-way, but braked as Bob sped through recklessly.

"Be careful, you could've wrecked your car if the other driver hadn't stopped. We're not in any hurry now. I just wanted to get away from in front of the house before. By the way, your hair's growing nicely." She'd intentionally changed the subject. "When you start wearing the new things, no one's going to recognize you as the same person."

"I know you're looking forward to it. I tried on the blazer and checked shirt this evening, but I wasn't sure if they looked right without the proper slacks, so I decided to wait until I have everything. You're not mad, are you?"

" 'Course not. Don't forget, you looked the same way you did now when I let you pick me up, didn't you? So you couldn't have been so bad."

"Were the others more your type from the start?" he asked, not looking at her and driving with excessive concentration on the road through the park.

"What do you mean, what others?"

"The different men your neighbor's seen you with."

Diane was sorry she'd been so specific about Mrs. Kraemer's accusations. She was pretty sure she hadn't repeated being called a "nobody," but in emphasizing how crazy the woman was, she might've said something worse. Since Bob hadn't focused on it right away, she assumed he hadn't blamed her for anything.

"She's crazy. Before you, I only went out twice with a fellow from my job and a couple of times with one other fellow from the neighborhood. That's it. Period."

"What about the good-looking black one you were kissing at the party—are you still seeing him?" he pressed on doggedly.

"Look, what's this all about? I said I went out with two fellows. He's one of the two. I haven't been seeing anyone but you since our first couple of dates, and nothing of consequence happened between me and anyone in New York before I met you."

Her first inclination was to go into more detail about the past week. Then she determined that she'd have to take the offensive if she were to regain control of the situation. She suspected he was probably more upset all along about her seeing other people than the reasons he first gave. But she also knew he respected her more when she acted like a strong, forceful person.

"You'd better cut out this third-degree business before it's too late. I can have affairs all over the city if I want to. You don't own me. You can turn around and take me home right now if you don't trust me and think you can do any better!"

Her stomach was nervous as she finished. She prayed she hadn't overdone it. When he pulled the car over to the curb and parked, she didn't know what to expect. She needn't have worried. She'd met his needs.

Bob looked at her adoringly. His eyes were moist and warm. The tension was gone from his mouth. It looked soft, almost sensuous. His voice was filled with emotion when he spoke to her, taking both her hands in his.

"Please don't threaten to leave me. You know I couldn't stand it. I like having you all to myself, but you could go out with other people too, as long as you told me. I'm afraid of what will happen to me if I have to go back to the way it was before I met you. I know you can help me. I—"

Diane tried to interrupt him, to say something reassuring. "I won't—" she began, intending to say she wouldn't leave him. But he stopped her.

"Please, this isn't easy. Tonight I've realized I'd even marry you if you said so. You probably wouldn't want to, though. I know you prefer more attractive men, but I'm willing to do anything you say. Whatever you think will make you happy.''

"You're not serious, you don't know what you're saying. You never acted like you thought of me on those terms before. I know you're fairly comfortable with me and all that, but there's a big difference between wanting to see someone more or less exclusively and being ready to get married. Don't you think you should feel something more for a girl before you think about marriage?''

"What do you mean?''

"Don't you think of me more like a sister or something than a potential wife?'' she finally asked.

"I don't think so. May I show you something?''

"What?'' she asked, curious.

Nervously he lifted one of her hands from the seat, where he'd been holding them to his, in his lap. He guided it to his right thigh, close enough to his groin that she could feel the stiffness beside her hand without having it placed directly on top of the erection. She didn't know it had somewhat diminished since reaching its peak when she'd threatened to go home. It reminded her of her earlier notion that he might be a very sensual person who held it in. But whereas the idea excited her before, she now found his immaturity embarrassing.

"Now what do you think? Am I behaving disgustingly? Have I shocked you? Don't worry about hurting my feelings, you can be honest with me,'' he said expectantly.

"I guess I asked for it,'' she replied, adding laughingly, "but you are a little sneaky behind that serious surface of yours, aren't you?''

"Sneaky,'' he repeated gleefully. "You really think so? How close am I to getting my face slapped? I'm so excited. Please don't be cross with me,'' he begged. May I undo my zipper?'' he asked, looking like a child expecting to be chastised. He was barely tender from the Sunday before, as his genitals hadn't been hurt like the time Diane went to Fire Island. "If you say no, we'll leave right away. I know you're not obligated to do anything just because I said I'd marry you. But I wish you'd just touch me. I don't want you to do anything else. Just squeeze it a little.''

181

Diane looked around. People were occasionally walking by, and cars were passing in the street.

"I'd rather not, we don't have much privacy here. It's not that dark, either."

"It's dark enough inside. I promise I won't do it again. Pretty please, Miss Diana," he cajoled in a playful, babyish voice.

"Okay."

He quickly unzipped his trousers. Diane slipped her hand inside, tentatively taking hold of his organ. Its size and hardness surprised her. She'd never seen anything like it, and it certainly contradicted the old story about the larger dimensions of black men. At least, as far as Chuck was concerned. But she was far from aroused as she held him.

"Harder. Please squeeze harder. You won't hurt me."

When she put more pressure on it, looking around uncomfortably to see who might be curious about what they were doing, he began moving and groaning. Then he pulled out a clean white handkerchief before closing his hand around hers inside his trousers and lifting her hand and his penis outside his pants. Squeezing her hand so tightly it was hard for Diane not to protest, he masturbated himself with her hand with a few hard strokes until he ejaculated in a final spasm.

Although he immediately released her hand and cupped the handkerchief around himself, some of the semen still got on her palm. With no water around, it was messy and unpleasant. It looked like he was finally going to cure her of anything she'd had about cars. Actually, there'd never been any specific attraction to cars anyway, only the extensive foreplay she associated with them. There were no cars on Fire Island. . . .

Bob immediately noticed her discomfort. "I'm sorry," he apologized, stopping his own project to remove his breast handkerchief and wipe her hand as clean as possible. Then he kissed it several times on both sides. "I was selfish and terrible. I don't blame you if you're mad at me."

"You don't have to apologize. I'm an adult. I wouldn't have done it if I didn't want to. But I'd feel better if we left here as soon as possible."

"Right away, Diana." He gave a final wipe before crumpling the wetter handkerchief up and putting it into the glove compartment. The less soiled one, he folded neatly and put into his breast pocket with a pat before starting the car.

Diane was still very uncomfortable, but was determined to act natural. She suggested the Library. She'd heard that Tuesday Weld and some of the Knicks basketball players ate there. "Go back to Broadway." She thought of the old song, "East Side, West Side, all around the town . . ." The story of her life.

"Whatever you say, ma'am."

For the first time since she'd known him, he hummed a tune and tapped out the beat on the steering wheel as he drove. She was glad to see him so happy. But between the semipublic masturbation and the odd marriage offer, she couldn't share his mood. There was an average-looking crowd at the glassed-in restaurant of private booths and endless shelves of books covering the walls. The dishes they offered weren't pretentious, but Bob didn't complain. He didn't mention marriage anymore, either. But he did talk about how he didn't mind grocery shopping and cleaning and doing the laundry after being so inactive at work.

"I get so tired of sitting in my office all day making decisions and trying to get them carried out right, it's a relief to do something altogether different afterward. If you don't like housekeeping any better than you do cooking, I'd get a kick out of helping you out. There'll be a lot to do if you have to get settled in a new apartment while you're still working or getting started at school."

"That's nice of you to offer. I admit I don't have any lost love for anything connected with the house, outside of decorating. Who knows, maybe I'll take you up on it." She was careful to be as noncommittal as possible, because she didn't want him to think she wanted to pin him down on marriage. She was sure she didn't love him and that he didn't love her either. Thinking the way she did, she felt funny about what happened a little later.

As they walked out of the restaurant, they ran into Tony coming in with another fellow. Both were in high-heeled shoes and open-chested body shirts under their jackets. Although she was restrained in her greeting to him, Tony kissed her on the cheek and acted so friendly, she introduced Bob as her "fiancé" so he wouldn't think Tony was a boyfriend.

"You're a lucky dude," he told him, shaking hands and slapping him on his shoulder.

She braced herself for questions about him from Bob, but he didn't show any concern about him before they said good night. When the phone rang less than an hour after he left, she was afraid Bob was calling to relieve his curiosity. He wasn't supposed to call till the next day.

"Hi, honey," she answered expectantly on the first ring.

There was no response or dial tone either. She was sure someone was there but figured her phone wasn't properly connected after she asked, "Is that you, Bob?" a couple of times and no one answered. She hung up, disappointed. When it rang again a while later and there was still silence, she said, "I don't think my phone's working right yet. I don't know if you can hear me, but I can't hear you at all. I'm sorry." The operator gave her the number of the repair service when she angrily reported her new phone wasn't working right. However, with that office closed for the weekend, the operator agreed to test it to make sure there was a problem.

"It's working all right now, miss."

Diane agreed after she called her back a second time and they could still hear each other. There were no more calls until the next day.

"Did you call me last night?" she asked as soon as she heard Bob's voice.

"No, you told me to call you today, why?"

"The phone rang twice, but no one answered either time. I had it checked by the phone company afterward, and it was all right. I don't know why I couldn't hear whoever it was last night, but you were the only one I thought it could possibly be."

"It must have been someone else you gave your number to. Does your friend Tony have it?"

"He doesn't know I have a phone, let alone the number. And even if he did, there wouldn't be any reason for him to call. I barely know him, and you're the only one besides my job that knows my number. I guess it must have been a wrong number or something."

"If he's the guy you said works with you, he could know about it easily enough, I'd imagine." He made the suggestion casually.

"You thought that character worked with me? Uh-uh, he's a friend of Liz Carpenter. I'm surprised you two didn't recognize each other from the party. He was trying to co-host."

"I didn't notice him. Until I saw you, I was still looking for the young lady who'd told me to come. And he doesn't look like the sort of guy who'd notice anyone as square-looking as me. He and his friend looked like real swingers."

"Could be. All I know about him is that he dates black girls exclusively." She didn't like sounding prejudiced, but she was glad to throw that in to end any speculations he might have about the two of them.

"The way he acted, I have a hunch he'd make an exception in your case if he thought you were still available. I'll bet he wondered what you were doing engaged to me." He chuckled.

"You shouldn't put yourself down like that. If you ever do become seriously engaged to someone, I'm sure whoever it is will be very proud. By the way, who was the girl you said you were waiting for when you met me?" Diane was pleased with the diplomatic way she'd handled the fiancé business. Asking about the other girl, however, was as much genuine interest as a device to change the subject to his other friendships.

"Just an acquaintance. No one of consequence," he answered evasively.

"You must have liked her to keep looking for her when you saw all those fabulous girls at Liz's party. I'm not jealous, what's she like?"

"I'm not sure what you mean. I only saw her once. She said she did some modeling. Even if she'd shown up at the party, we never would have dated like you and I do. I think she had . . . uh, quite a few friends. The main reason I didn't talk to anyone else there is because most of them didn't appeal to me very much. And besides, I find it very difficult to approach a regular girl or hold a conversation with her—you know, I told you that."

"I'm not a regular girl?"

"Not to me, unless you're pretending. Most girls as popular as you were would've lost interest in me a long time ago."

"Maybe I should be flattered when people get the idea I'm such a social success. But the truth is, I'm probably not that much better at making friends than you are. I was never close to many people at home, including my aunt I told you about. At least you were close to your mother. And since I've been here, I've probably alienated more people than I've made friends with. I used to think New York was waiting for me. But you're the exception rather than the rule. Hope I haven't disappointed you."

"I know you're trying to be nice. Do you want to see me tonight?"

She said she was going to work on some design ideas she had but told him when to pick her up the next day. When she hung up, she realized it was the first time she'd spoken about herself and her New York expectations so honestly to anyone. But instead of being embarrassed, as she would've expected, she liked the idea that she was becoming a little more down-to-earth.

When Chuck used to zero in on her adjustment problems, she'd resented it terribly. But it was increasingly obvious that going someplace new couldn't immediately perfect her old personality or assure her of instant success. If that had happened, it would've proved conclusively that she'd been too good for Newton all along. That it hadn't

186

stimulated her properly, or recognized her potential, probably because of her father.

Although she'd come up with a fairly practical reason for escaping to New York, she suspected she was actually as starry-eyed as the most obvious dreamers who set out. She'd also discovered that the same big-city characteristics that attracted people like her could make them feel less significant than they did previously. It was easy to understand how some would give up and go home. Or stay and become cynical. She'd been disappointed, but not enough to see herself in either category.

Stoically fixing an omelet on her toylike stove, she accepted the possibility that it might have been better to arrive closer to the beginning of school. Then she might have been too busy to notice her social deficiencies. As it was, she'd hardly thought of anything else. It was hard to see how Bob and Mrs. Kraemer didn't realize what an unsuccessful candidate she was for the playgirl image they had of her. She thought of how there were local organizations for women, ethnic and racial groups, divorced people, alcoholics, and even mothers who beat their children. She wondered why she hadn't heard of one for recent small-town transplants. It couldn't have had all the answers, but at least it could've prepared you for the problems. If it only helped young women become reasonably self-sufficient and comfortable being alone, it would've been a blessing to her.

After her experiences with the swingers, Diane wasn't nearly as fearful of being alone anymore. Knowing she had Bob to fall back on, and the prospect of starting classes soon, both helped. There wasn't much question that she'd become involved with people more quickly and less discriminately than she would have if loneliness hadn't been a factor. Not only with men, but with women too.

Jacky, with her show-off sophistication, wasn't much more likable than Mona with her biases and admonitions. Dating a co-worker with as little going for him as Richard Fenster was destined to fail. Building up fantasies about someone as moody and unpredictable as Paul was childish, and speaking of love to Chuck, totally irresponsible. Bob was always good for her ego, but anyone could see he was too dependent and immature for his age. Knowing he was available shouldn't stop her from going to museums, movies, or theater matinees, or conceivably women's activities, where escorts obviously weren't needed. Maybe Carol Stern would have some ideas.

Diane couldn't have been prouder of herself as she finished in the kitchen and laid out the fabric for a three-piece skirt and pants suit she'd put off working on for weeks. In a larger apartment, she was sure she'd be in a creative mood more often. She was starting to cut when the phone interrupted her.

She said hello only twice before hanging up impatiently when no one answered. When it rang about half an hour later and the same thing happened, she was sure it was Mrs. Kraemer. "Drop dead," she said, and hung up. Half an hour after that, she was ready with, "I'm sorry you're so lonely down there you have to hear my voice all night."

That time, however, a muffled male voice spoke. "How's your cunt?"

Diane banged the phone down viciously. But her hands were trembling, and she was very shaken for the first time since the calls began. The masculine voice and crude language were totally unexpected. If it wasn't Mrs. Kraemer, then who?

Unless Jacky had told Paul Slattery, Richard Fenster was the only person other than Bob who probably knew she had a phone. She couldn't remember whether she'd told Ted Abrams she was getting one or not. Since she didn't have an unlisted number, no one would have a problem getting it. She couldn't see why anyone would want to be bothered, though, and she couldn't imagine Richard being sick enough to carry any grudge to that extent. But she'd try to catch the inflections to see if it sounded like him if the man called again. She continued to work on the outfit, distracted by the silent phone.

Shortly before eleven, she turned off the lights and the radio and went to bed. Apparently the caller was through for the night. But before she'd fallen asleep, her doorbell

188

rang twice sharply. It startled her so, she was almost afraid to look out of the window to see who was below. She got up fearfully. Approaching the window stealthily from the side, she peeped out as inconspiciously as possible from behind the edge of the curtain.

No one was there. The doorway was empty. She looked out the open window. Cautiously at first. Then craned her neck in both directions. Apart from an unfamiliar girl walking several buildings away toward West End, no one was in sight. She drew her head inside and stood quivering with anger in the darkness.

There was no longer any question in her mind about the caller or the mysterious night visitor. She didn't know why she hadn't remembered Mrs. Kraemer's son sooner. She'd forgotten his name, but it wasn't important. She returned to her bed and sat on the side debating what to do. She could call the police, but she had no proof of anything. Telephone harassment was taken seriously by the telephone company but she knew no one would get overly concerned about two evenings of calls and one obscene one.

An idea came to her that made her smile. She turned on the light and found her address book. Dialing excitedly, she heard the phone being picked up after a few rings. But it was an operator.

"What number are you calling?"

She gave them Mrs. Kraemer's.

There were more rings before a voice announced, "This is a recorded announcement. The number you are calling is no longer in service."

She hung up and quickly called information. "Do you have a new listing for Mrs. Kraemer at three forty-one West Seventy-sixth Street?"

"I'm sorry, there is a phone, but at the party's request, it doesn't appear in our records."

That was final proof if Diane needed any. Mrs. Kraemer and her nutty son were united in an effort to drive her out. Knowing positively who it was made her lose her fear, although they were so close. She only regarded them as harmless pranksters. As little trick-or-treaters. Get out or get harassed. She turned the phone down as low as it would go and wrapped it up with towels. She'd accelerate her efforts to move, if possible, but in the meantime she'd keep on getting a good night's sleep.

She'd started picking up the *Times* religiously, the first thing in the morning. The next few days, she checked for new ads at her desk. She'd decided it wasn't too early to prepare them that she might be leaving soon, so any criticism would've been almost welcome. If she'd had it to do over again, she'd have quit at the time of her other reprimand. It would've been a good excuse, and she wouldn't have had the problem of making up a story. The next summer, she'd look for a temporary job. If none was available, she could probably find something with or without a reference. But she still hated to quit with no good reason. She didn't want it to reflect on the judgment of the interviewer she'd persuaded to hire her.

The Thursday ad section was small. Some of the brokers' listings weren't bad, but then there'd be their fee added to the month's rent and security in advance. That could take almost eight hundred dollars if it was a "good address" in Manhattan. It definitely wasn't going to be easy. She went over the ads a second time. When she finished again without her supervisor's objecting, she decided to go in and give her the story she'd prepared and get it over with. Without offering any details, she told her she might have to leave suddenly within the next few days.

"Why, what on earth for?" she asked.

"I'd rather not go into the details. There's illness in Iowa."

"What a shame. I hope it's nothing serious. How long do you think you'll be gone?"

"Indefinitely," she answered solemnly.

"If it's that bad, I think we'd better let personnel know. I'll call and let them know you'll be up to speak with them."

When she left, she was pleased. She'd managed to convey the unavoidable impression she was returning home due to family illness without actually saying so.

After her personnel visit, her conscience was completely clear.

"You understand you haven't been with us long enough to have any vacation time accrued yet, or to be considered for a leave of absence, don't you?" she was asked.

"Yes, I know," she said pitifully.

"All right, then, call Mrs. Morganlander if you have to leave anytime outside of office hours. You won't be on the payroll, but we won't look for a replacement for at least a week. Good luck. Let's hope everything works out better than you anticipate."

The remainder of the day, Diane was besieged with questions and condolences, although she consistently said she didn't want to talk about it, even to Mona. She shouldn't have been so shocked when Richard Fenster approached her when no one was near, toward the end of the day, saying, "Tough luck, your aunt's dying with the Big C."

"What on earth are you talking about? I never told anyone my aunt was dying of anything. I don't even know what the big C is. Surely you don't mean cancer?"

"Oh no, everybody knows that stands for chest colds. Sorry I mentioned it. For a while there, I was so busy feeling sorry for you, I forgot what a phony cunt you were. You deserve whatever happens," he said angrily, turning to walk away.

"What did you call me?" she asked excitedly.

"You heard me," he said, turning back to face her defiantly.

"Have you been calling my house?" she demanded.

"Why would I do that? What's the matter, someone you messed over's been calling up just to bug you?"

"I didn't say that. I only asked you a simple question, but I shouldn't have expected a decent answer. Not if you're the type of person who'd make those kinds of calls. It's not important, though. I won't have that phone much longer anyway."

"You'd better watch your step. They say people who make dirty phone calls are sick. Sometimes they get themselves so worked up they end up molesting the woman. I'd hate to see something like that happen to such a nice girl like you.'' He left smirking.

Diane stared after him. She was sorry she'd mentioned the calls to him. Most likely it was a coincidence that he'd used the same word the caller had. He'd used it in a different way, too. And to ring her bell in the middle of the night, she decided he'd have to be completely crazy. It would have meant coming all the way down from upper Manhattan. Or hanging around downtown till then. The only thing she credited him with was confusing her just enough that she wasn't sure whether to tell the Sterns what was happening. After Bob's reaction, she'd decided not to mention the telephone-installation scene unless they did.

When she arrived home, she hesitated at their door and decided not to knock. She was anxious to get out of her clothes and shower. New York was in the middle of a raging heat wave. In the office she used a sweater to keep from getting a chill from the air-conditioning. So the heat outdoors was a relief when it first hit her. But by the time she reached home, she could hardly remember having been too cold a short time before. She'd turned on her fan and undressed to shower when her first call came. The anticipation of fresh clues kept her from being too upset.

At first there was no sound, like the earlier calls. Then the person began sucking in air and making moans and guttural sounds. She replaced the receiver quietly, to appear unperturbed. In the bathroom again, she tried to dismiss the caller. Of all the unimaginative things, breathing into someone's phone was the worst. But when she reached for the soap after she was underneath the shower, it slipped from her hands. Picking it up from the tub, she saw that her hands were trembling slightly.

It was hard to understand why the breathing bothered her so much. Perhaps because she'd braced herself for any spoken obscenity. It might have been the surprise of the unexpected. She hoped the calls weren't getting to her so soon. Especially since she hadn't gotten any closer to the man's identity. If that was to be his new pattern, she decided she might as well report it to the telephone company right away. They could advise her about the police. She completed her shower hurriedly, hoping it might not be too late.

"What's the procedure for reporting indecent phone calls?" she asked information.

"One minute, please."

She waited as sounds in the background made her think she was being connected to someone else. But when the woman returned she said, "You'll have to notify the business office. Eight-one-one. The hours are nine to five."

Diane thanked her and hung up. It was just as well that she'd agreed to go to the theater with Bob that night before her resolve to be a little more independent. With the phone-calls still unresolved, she wouldn't have been able to relax anyway. The only positive thing about them was that she no longer had to worry about keeping a low profile. She didn't want Mrs. Kraemer to think she was upsetting her in case she was responsible. She kept the phone off the hook until Bob arrived. It was funny how she'd gotten it to feel more comfortable and secure. The antidote had turned out worse than the poison.

Chapter 11

When Diane saw Bob, the awkwardness of their last date receded from her thoughts, and she became more confident of her fashion judgment than ever. Although the heat lingered on into the evening, he had on his new blazer as well as the checked pants and solid-colored sport shirt they'd bought. Several buttons were surprisingly left unfastened, in the Chuck and Tony tradition. Unlike the time he'd unzipped his pants, he wore no serious white undershirt. His chest was hairier than she would've thought she'd like, but on him it looked good.

"Hey, you look sensational." It wasn't only his clothes. It was his hair, too. For a quick second she thought it could be a wig. It looked altogether different from his old straight brushed-down look. "What did you do to your hair? It's so long."

"I went to a different barber on Lexington Avenue. I knew if I went to my regular man he'd expect me to get a haircut too, but I missed my regular shampoos and massages. The new place turned out to have only 'stylists,' and the one I got insisted my hair would look longer if I let him 'shape' it and dry it with a blower. He had to show me pictures of some of his other customers before I agreed. I told him my fiancée liked it long."

Hearing him speak in his same humble way while looking so much more desirable made Diane pretty much forget her ideas about cutting the umbilical cord. She also felt much better about the Paul Slattery embarrassment and would've been delighted to produce him for both Paul and Jacky to see. The only thing that nagged her was regret

194

that they hadn't run into Tony after Bob's metamorphosis, since he was bound to tell Chuck she was engaged. It wouldn't have looked like she was marrying the first safe white businessman who'd presented himself. One with all the flair of an embalmer. She knew it shouldn't have mattered, but she hated Chuck to think she was so shallow. Sometimes she wondered if she was more shallow than other girls her age, or just more insecure about what other people thought of her.

Bob surprised her with tickets for *The Prisoner of Second Avenue*, after she'd mentioned in passing that she'd never gone to a Broadway play or show. Although he tried to play down his accomplishment, she realized what a coup he'd pulled getting tickets so quickly for such a popular hit. When they wcre ushered to third-row orchestra seats in the crowded Eugene O'Neill Theater, she was even more surprised. What pleased her most as the comedy progressed was that she considered herself as attuned to the inside jokes for New Yorkers, about the harried Manhattanite, as most of those in the audience. Probably more than the commuters from the suburbs.

Although Bob was generally straightfaced and solemn throughout, when he wasn't staring around icily at a man who sometimes laughed too loudly, he told her he enjoyed the show when it was over. They were among the first to reach the lobby, because he didn't want to be jammed in with everyone. However, he told her they could see anything she wanted to see in the future, and he'd buy her tickets to go alone if she wanted to do that. He may have sensed he made her somewhat uncomfortable. However, when they finished up the evening with a late supper including some black caviar and Dom Perignon at the Russian Tea Room, she considered the evening one of the nicest since she'd been in New York.

At the end of the next day, she congratulated herself on having reached the point where she could do something without reporting it in full to the girls she'd soon be saying good-bye to. She arrived home after stopping to pick up a few things from Food Mart. She opened the street door and had stopped to check her mailbox when a gloved hand was shoved roughly over her mouth. What felt like a knife point was placed against her neck.

"Don't fight. Open the door quickly or I'll kill you!" The voice sounded familiar, but the words were whispered, almost hissed, and she was too terrified to think clearly. She did exactly as she was told.

When they were inside the hall in front of the stairs leading to her apartment, she looked desperately at the Sterns' door.

"Get up the steps and don't try anything."

She was held closely against the man as they climbed the stairs. Several times she stumbled. Her legs were weak. She felt chilled, dizzy, and nauseated. If only her mouth weren't covered, she could have tried to reason with the person. She didn't think she'd scream with the knife sticking in her neck. At her door, she hesitated.

"Unlock it. Fast!" He held the point against her throat, pressing ever so slightly. She unlocked the door. He pushed her through and closed it behind them. He removed the knife long enough to stuff a handkerchief into her mouth. Then he gripped her around her neck with one arm and forced her to the bed, the knife back at her neck. He shoved her down, face first, and climbed on her. His knees were pressed close against her waist. He held her head firmly when she began struggling and trying to turn. She was panicking. He could easily smother her to death if she didn't resist.

"Hold still if you wanna live," he rasped, placing a wide strip of adhesive tape over her eyes, beginning it at the back of her head and wrapping it twice. Then he put a smaller piece over her mouth, with the large handkerchief inside.

"Won't be needing that right away," he said in the same whispering voice, attaching her hands at the wrist with the same adhesive, then lifting his weight from her body and rising. Diane immediately rose too, jumping off the bed and stumbling into the coffee table.

She heard the radio begin to play, and ran toward where the door should be. The hand that grabbed her no longer wore a glove.

"Relax," he whispered, pulling her back to the bed. Face up this time.

Then he began removing her clothes. He unbuttoned her blouse slowly. It reminded her a little of Chuck when they'd been at Fire Island. But then she was submissive and expectant. Not struggling in fear with her legs pinned down and a strange body straddling her. She was encouraged when he didn't tear the blouse off. He said "shit" when it caught on her hands but left it intact. He undid her brassiere and pushed it up above her breasts as she struggled uselessly. He didn't act like anyone planning to kill her. If he was Mrs. Kraemer's son, he might not even rape her. But if he was only there to scare her, he didn't have to go any further.

"Nice tits," he whispered, playing with her breasts briefly while holding her wrists with one hand. Then he began unfastening her skirt. She kicked so violently he could hardly pull it below her thighs. But in a little while he had it over her ankles. She heard him breathing harder as he started on her bikini panties with both hands. They tore as she pressed her arms to her protectively and tried to hold them. A few pubic hairs were pulled out painfully in the struggle. Then his hand was on her crotch.

She was jolted by fury when his finger was forced into her rectal opening the same time his thumb entered her vagina.

"Ummm." He sucked air while pushing his fingers in and out exploratively. "You're lucky I don't fuck you in your asshole."

Diane was driven to a plan. She'd act subdued and pray he tried to remove her heavy platform shoes. If he did, she was going to kick him senseless, whoever he might be. He rose but didn't touch her shoes as she waited tensely. When she heard a muffled, metallic thud on the floor, she realized he was taking off his clothes. It sounded like his belt buckle dropping on the floor with his trousers.

Then the telephone rang! It was right beside her on the end table. Before he could stop her, she knocked the table over violently, crashing the phone to the floor, and snatched the tape and handkerchief from her mouth with

197

one of her attached hands. She screamed with all the power of her lungs until a swift blow to her chin stunned her briefly into unconsciousness.

When her head cleared, she didn't hear anything. She appeared to be alone. She placed both hands behind her head and was finally able to unstick the edge of the adhesive band and begin unwinding it. When it was completely torn off, with hair from her head, eyebrows, and lashes sticking to it, her assailant was nowhere in sight. Her door was ajar. The phone was sprawled in the distance. Torn from the wall. It was hard to refrain from screaming for help out the window or running downstairs to bang on Ed and Carol's door. But she calmed herself enough to know she didn't want to run around naked.

She got up unsteadily and got a butcher knife from the kitchen. Wedging the handle between her knees, she rubbed the adhesive against the blade until it was frayed enough for her to yank her wrists apart. Then she put on a robe and peered down the stairs. She decided to carry the knife with her just in case. At the Sterns' door she pounded and called out, but no one was home. Confused and sore, she began to cry. There was no question of going to Mrs. Kraemer's.

She stuck the knife in the door so it wouldn't lock behind her and opened the outside door. A woman was walking her dog across the street. Diane called "Miss" a couple of times and waved to get her attention. The woman approached hesitantly as Diane kept beckoning to her, going out on the stoop.

"I'm sorry to bother you, but a man just attacked me upstairs and broke my phone. Would you be able to call the police for me, please, and tell them to come to this address right away?"

"How horrible. Certainly, I'll call at once. Will you be all right until they come?"

Diane said yes, and the woman rushed back across the street and into a nearby building. Diane climbed wearily back up the steps and took two aspirin as she waited. She wanted to make some coffee, but instead stood by the window and left everything as it was. Her torn clothing and the overturned end table were on the floor; the adhesive on each wrist and the strip from her eyes, on the sofa. Looking at the scene sickened her. It was more humiliating thinking about others seeing it.

In unbelievably few minutes, she saw the police car turning the corner. The woman who'd called was outside her building with a stocky man watching as they arrived. When the two patrolmen got out and approached the door, Diane spoke to them through the window. "I'm on the top floor. I'll drop my keys down so I don't have to climb up and down again. It's the silver one."

"Okay, miss, drop 'em down," the older one said.

When they were upstairs, she gave them her name and told them what had happened. The younger one took down everything in a book, shaking his head and making disgusted expressions on his pockmarked but pleasant face. The gray-haired, solidly built older man walked around, inspecting things as she spoke. He looked in the kitchen, the bathroom, and the closets.

"Mind if I look in the drawers?" he asked.

"Not if you think it's necessary, but I'm sure he didn't have time to do anything with them." He was looking anyway when she told the other one she believed she knew who'd attacked her.

"You said you never saw who did it before. Didn't know if he was colored, white, or Puerto Rican when you brought him up to your room. Now you admit you knew him," he barked accusingly.

"I didn't say I knew him," she snapped back. "I said I think I know who it was. I think it was my neighbor's son. I've never seen him, but I've heard he's somewhat off, and she threatened to force me to move before my lease is up a few days ago. We had a quarrel about my getting the phone that's now been ripped out. I also started getting a lot of dirty phone calls as soon as I got the phone."

"Why didn't you say so before? I could tell right off this wasn't a regular mugging or attempted rape. The guy knew your habits, and he didn't hurt you or take anything.

199

Where's this woman and her son? If people would give us the story straight in the first place, it would make our job a whole lot easier."

"I assumed I had to tell you what happened first. I'm new at this. Her name's Kraemer. There're steps to her apartment downstairs. Outside, her door's the one below the street."

"If there's anything to tie them to it after all this time, it'll be a miracle. What's the son's name?"

"I don't remember, I only heard it once."

"And no description at all." He shook his head. "Come on, Freckles, let's go see the landlady. We'll be back. We'll need you if she's home."

"I'd like to get cleaned up and straighten the place out. Would you mind taking the key again so you can let yourself in when you need me?"

"Okay, but you shouldn't make a habit of handing your keys around like you do. By the way, what's your line of work?"

Diane looked at "Freckles" and back at the big officer. "I'm a bookkeeper at an insurance company." She motioned toward the keys on the dinette table, and the young one picked them up. He acted embarrassed. It was a few minutes before seven. Bob would be there at seven-thirty. She prayed he wouldn't come early and find the police still there. But if they were delayed because they found Mrs. Kraemer's son and were arresting him, she didn't care if it took all night.

She looked out the window to see if they got in. When they gave up ringing the bell and calling Mrs. Kraemer's name loudly, Freckles started back upstairs. A couple of doormen and other neighbors besides the first were looking on from different spots up and down the block. The big officer started talking to some of them.

"Here're your keys, Miss Keely. No one answers downstairs. We'll report this to the detective squad. They'll probably ask you if you want to come down and sign a formal complaint. But with so little proof to go on, it'll probably be hard to make any arrest unless something more turns up. I could tell the phone company to get

200

someone out to fix your phone as soon as possible, unless you plan on staying someplace else until we can reach that neighbor of yours."

"Maybe I'll go to a hotel. I don't know."

"All right. We're from the Twentieth Precinct. Here's our address and number of the detective squad. I'm Patrolman Reardon. When you decide when you want them to come, tell the phone company. We'll verify you need emergency service. Can we call you at work if anything comes up?"

"Yes. And thanks for everything."

"That's okay. Take care of yourself."

It was almost seven-fifteen. She had to shower and find the strength to get herself together. Fortunately, she was still tanned enough that all she had to use was eye makeup. That took only a second. There was a slight swelling in her jaw. But unless you looked for it, it was barely noticeable. She pulled her hair back and put on seldom-used gold-hoop earrings as a distraction. Her face looked pretty good.

Bob was double-parked the next time she looked out. She pulled on the matching cowl-necked top to her reptile-print pants, and stuffed a change of underclothes and toilet articles into her handbag. She would have carried her train case, but the other was quicker. It wasn't as conspicuous, either, that that evening was different.

"Let's go someplace quiet where we can talk," she told him quickly. She knew she sounded mysterious but was glad he said "all right," without questioning her. As much as she wished she could keep the attack a secret from him, she saw no way to tell him she couldn't go home that night without telling him some of what had happened.

They were unusually quiet as they waited for their drinks in La Petite Marmite. When they came, she understood what people meant when they talked about having a few belts to give them courage. After her second gulp, she said, "A man tried to mug me when I came home from work tonight."

"Tried to mug you? Christ, what happened? What did he do?"

201

"It was pretty horrible. I'm still a little shaky. He grabbed hold of my neck inside the foyer and threatened to kill me if I screamed. He stuffed a handkerchief in my mouth, but I managed to get it out and scream as loud as I could. No one was in the house, but it scared him away, and a woman across the street called the police. He was gone before they got there, but still I was very lucky it wasn't worse."

"Why didn't you tell me right away? Are you sure he didn't hurt you? Is that all that happened?"

"Well"—she hesitated, wishing she could tell him more—"he did punch me on the cheek to stop me from screaming anymore before he could get away."

"Where? Is that it, where there's a little swelling there?"

"Ouch! You pressed it too hard. Don't touch it anymore, it's gotten tender. Is it very noticeable?"

"No. I'm sorry, I didn't mean to hurt you. What was the man like? What race? Was he very strong?"

"I don't know. He was behind me all the time and wore gloves. He didn't hit me with all his might, I know that. But I'm not going to take any more chances. Tonight I think I'll stay at the Y, and I'm not going to stay there anymore if I can help it."

"Why don't you go to the Barbizon?"

"Too expensive, for one thing."

"Don't worry about it, I'll take care of it."

"No you won't. Thanks. Under any other circumstances, I'd really go for it, but as much of a thing as I have for Central Park South, I'm afraid I'd feel funny as a lone female with nothing but my handbag for luggage."

"You're thinking of the Barbizon-Plaza. I meant the Barbizon for Women, but they're both good, and I think you'd be comfortable at either place. The one for women's on Lexington."

"Oh," she answered apologetically. "Well, maybe it would be all right if I treated myself tonight, and tomorrow I can go to the Y if I can't find anyplace to move to. On top of everything else, I just remembered, the landlord's got a month's rent and security of mine. Technically, I'd have to stay till the first of November if he insisted I live out the security now that Mrs. Kraemer knows I want to move."

"I don't think he'd do that. They probably wouldn't want any more trouble. Did the police say anyone else had been bothered there recently?"

"No, but I told them it could be her son trying to scare me out," she decided to admit.

"I'm getting confused. You never mentioned a son before. Did you recognize him as he ran away?"

"I wouldn't know him if I saw him. He doesn't live there, the Sterns told me about him. But whoever it was was completely out of sight by the time I looked out. I was stunned by the blow, and everything was one big blur for a while. The only thing I know is that he was fairly tall. But it's so disgusting, I don't want to talk about it anymore. Unless the police can prove it was Mrs. Kraemer's son, whoever did it might never be caught."

"If you're that sure he's the one, I hope they nail him. Whoever it was shouldn't get away with it. That's the important thing."

Diane was reassured by his words, but a little surprised he hadn't asked her if she'd like to stay in his apartment. At least overnight. Since he'd talked about marriage so recently, she thought the gesture wouldn't have been inappropriate. She would've liked the idea she was still making decisions. Instead she felt her position was shifting because of the attack. It made her uncomfortable.

The strained meal was finally over. When they were leaving, he said he had something for her. Walking to the car, she wondered if it would conceivably be an engagement ring. Not that she wanted to marry him.

"Hope you like it," he said, unenthusiastically handing her the large flat box he removed from the trunk. He stood beside her on the sidewalk as she sat sideways on the car seat and opened it with appropriate protests.

When she finally reached the tissue paper inside the gift-wrapped box, she discovered a very dark, sable-brown leather suit and matching hat. She lifted the jacket out carefully. It was supple, beautifully lined, and elegantly tailored.

"This is the most fabulous thing I've ever owned," she told him sincerely. "It's a good thing you don't pay me any mind when I tell you not to do something. I'll die if it doesn't fit."

"You can exchange it for another size if it doesn't. They found someone to try it on who looked like your height and size, but since its not custom-made, there shouldn't be any trouble. It's from Miller's Country Store."

"They have beautiful things. I can't wait to try it on and let you see how it looks on me, but I guess you'll have to wait a few weeks at the least before I can possibly wear it."

His flat "There's no rush" showed her he'd either overlooked or ignored her opening.

When Bob took her to the Barbizon-Plaza, she was surprised, thinking they'd settled on the women's hotel. Looking at the marquee, she had mixed feelings. Driving past on her first day in the city, she never would've imagined staying there could be under such depressing circumstances.

"It's probably better if you pay," Bob said, getting out his wallet.

"Oh, no you don't! You've done me a big enough favor by talking me out of the Y. Tomorrow morning when I tell the police where I spent the night, I won't feel so pitiful."

"You're going to see the police tomorrow?" he asked, brightening.

"Of course, the detectives who'll be in charge of the investigation."

"I didn't know that. May I pick you up and go with you?"

"You don't need to do that, but we could meet afterward for lunch before I start looking for somewhere to move to, if you want to."

"Why can't I come? I won't bother anyone. Besides, you'll probably want to pick up some of your belongings from your apartment. You might need help."

"All right. You can come tomorrow around eleven."

She knew he couldn't accompany her to the precinct or

204

come up to help with her luggage either, with her room in such a telltale condition. But there was no point in arguing once he started wheedling. And he was right—she could use some help. She only wondered briefly when it occurred to him. Primarily, she focused on how she could keep him in the car without making him too disappointed. She decided to call the precinct and make an appointment for later in the day. Then she could go alone. Before the time came, she'd think of a logical reason to keep him from coming up to her room with her.

Looking out of her window at the bright lights of traffic and nearby buildings was a new experience for her. After a long hot bath she sat looking out with a towel wrapped around her, appreciating Bob's taste and wishing she'd never gone much farther uptown or west of Central Park. When she went to bed, she'd made up her mind that it was well worth it to pay what was necessary to be in the area of her choice. She'd still be alone, but at least she'd be with a more predictable class of people.

Diane fell asleep easily in the air-conditioned room once her thoughts were sorted out. The next morning she awoke refreshed until she sat up. Then she felt painful salutes from her rectum and jaw. Her spirits dropped lower when she found her jaw had become purplish and more noticeable overnight. She could hardly wait to speak with the police, but she decided to check out first and call from the lobby so Bob wouldn't have to call for her at the desk. With no luggage and the bruise, she wanted to be as inconspicuous as possible.

When she reached the detective familiar with her case, she was pleasantly surprised when he told her he'd already spoken with Mrs. Kraemer that morning.

"Was her son there? What did she say, did she deny threatening me?" she asked excitedly.

"The son wasn't there. She gave us his address but said she hasn't seen him for the last couple of months and told me to warn you that she was contacting her lawyer about a slander action against you if you made any more accusations about either one of them. Sounded like she meant it."

"How can she have an action against me? The telephone man was there when she attacked me, and she was one of only two or three people in the whole city who knew my number when I started getting the obscene telephone calls. They couldn't have been a coincidence, and neither could the attack. Whoever it was knew what time I got home from work and that the other couple would probably be away for the weekend. It definitely wasn't a stranger.''

"She didn't think so either," he said dryly, "but she had a different theory about it."

"And what was that?" She was growing angrier by the moment.

"If you've had run-ins with her before, you should have a pretty good idea of what she'd say. She didn't deny encouraging you to leave because she didn't like your . . . uh, habits. Her story's that you probably invited one of your acquaintances up and got the idea of blaming her son after things got out of hand and your friend got too rough. Don't think I'm agreeing with her, there's no way for me to know what happened. I'm not a magician."

"No, and I'm not going to be put on the defensive either. So what are you going to do next? Talk to her son or see where he was when I was attacked or whether anyone in the neighborhood saw him leave the house?"

"That's already been done. The only fellow anyone could remember around was a tall, slim guy with a big afro and large dark glasses, going toward the Drive. A light black or Puerto Rican. But he wasn't actually seen leaving your house. Just walking away. Sound like anyone you know?"

Diane was completely silent. Looking for an answer. Could Chuck possibly have tried to rape her at knife point? Was that remotely possible? Cool Chuck, with so many white girls at his beck and call? She was incapable of believing it was he. "How do I know? A lot of people around there fit that description, and no one can say he was the one anyway. This Bernard could have been hiding in his mother's until way after the police left. If you could search both places, you might find the glove or handkerchief he used, with my lipstick on it," she suggested desperately. "Besides, if he has no alibi, he might confess if you acted like you really believed he did it."

"Frankly, miss, I don't think we have enough evidence to get a search warrant, and if we had one, I doubt he'd be crazy enough to keep the stuff around once his mother tells him we're looking for him. I'm a little busy right now, but if you want to come in and make out a complaint, be my guest. We'll talk to the son, but without more to go on, don't expect any arrests. And don't forget the woman's threats. She blew her top about your charges on top of having the police looking for her and talking to her neighbors yesterday. She talked like she had connections and might make trouble as it is."

"So as far as you're concerned, I guess that's that," she said bitterly.

"It's up to you, honey. I'm neutral. Afraid I've got to go now. The next move's up to you. So long."

"So long," Diane repeated into the mouthpiece with no one on the other end of the line. Thanks a lot. Neutral, she thought. Thanks for not hanging up on me sooner, "honey."

Diane felt defeated as she waited for Bob. She didn't know who to blame for her situation. Perhaps she should tell the police about Chuck. But she was ashamed to admit how close they'd been. Besides, with a fresh start and no forwarding address, whoever it was couldn't bother her anymore. When Bob arrived, she went proudly to meet him. In his tapered sport shirt and well-fitted slacks, he had a much better build than anyone would have suspected before. He was looking better every day. On the other hand, she was self-conscious in her second-day clothes with her mental as well as physical bruises.

He looked disappointed when she told him the detective wanted to delay their meeting till after he reached Bernard. When she made him park on Riverside Drive, he accepted it stoically. She returned resolutely to the house, disgusted that there was so much truth in the reason she gave him. That she didn't want anyone to be able to say she was going off with a man. On top of everything else, Mrs. Kraemer could give such a report to her aunt.

She was so angry, she didn't have time to become apprehensive until she entered the foyer. But she became very frightened unlocking the door and rushing up the stairs to her room. Once inside, she ran to the windows and raised them and the shades very high. She made a victory sign to Bob before locking and chaining her door. There wasn't that much to do, actually. She retrieved her torn clothes from the wastebasket and put them in a corner of the closet in a plastic bag along with the tape and its bits of her hair. The way things were turning out, she might use more for her own defense than anybody else's prosecution.

After everything was in order, she threw out all the food in the refrigerator that could spoil and started selecting the things she'd need for at least a week. She packed them into her smaller piece of luggage and changed into a fresh white linen pants and midriff-top set. In the bathroom she discovered a coverup makeup she'd forgotten. It covered her bruise amazingly well. She stuck it in her handbag and was about to leave. Then she remembered it was Labor Day weekend and school wasn't far off. She decided to use her train case for her catalog and a couple of books she fitted in with her scissors and a few other small sewing accessories.

All finished, she waved she was leaving to Bob, very glad he'd insisted on coming. She closed the window except for a little at the top, left the blinds halfway opened, and locked up behind her. Although she was sure they were away, she paused and knocked on the Sterns' door just in case. With the city still struggling under the persistent heat, she barely waited for a response. They'd never be in town in that steambath.

Leaving, she had the sensation of being watched. But when she was back inside Bob's cool Mercedes, she felt better. She was relieved to be getting away. She looked with pity at the people crowded in the park. She'd come a long way since the Fourth of July.

"Is there anyplace special you'd like me to take you for lunch?"

She had a suggestion she thought might appeal to him and restore his normal mood and attitude.

"How'd you like it if I cashed in my rain check for a meal fixed by you?"

"At my house?"

"I don't know. It's up to you. It was just a thought. Maybe I could phone about apartments afterward if that's okay."

"I don't mind."

It wasn't the grateful reaction she would've expected a few days before. But her curiosity about his residence kept her from withdrawing the proposal. She had him pick up a paper at Seventy-ninth and Broadway so she'd be able to check the ads. His attitude was dutiful but unenthusiastic. There were lively crowds all around Central Park, but after they passed the Fifth Avenue side, the streets in the East Eighties were very still, like inside the car.

The street was deserted by the time they pulled up before a small brownstone between Madison and Park. As Bob parked, a car entered the block behind them but stopped near the corner some distance away. No one got out. The houses were similar to but more individualized than the ones around Mrs. Kraemer's. A variety of lacquered or carved doors, shutters, and carefully planted greenery marked the difference.

"This is it," he said, opening Diane's door from the inside and leading the way to the upper entrance.

She'd assumed he lived in a very good apartment building. Someplace old and prestigious, with an elderly doorman and an elevator operator. She'd anticipated being a little self-conscious in front of them, but not overly so. If it turned out that he had something similar to hers with only a better address, she didn't think she'd be able to take it. She was beginning to be sorry she'd come as he unlocked the door. But she waited anxiously. At least she'd know one way or the other.

When the street door was opened, she wasn't in a tiny vestibule with a narrow stairway facing her, as she had expected. Instead they were in the marble-floored

209

entranceway to a quietly rich and dignified living room. A slender oak staircase curved upstairs to the rear on one side of her. On the other side, a carved stone fireplace and authentic-looking Chinese Chippendale mirror were the focal point with a sofa and several silk, apparently eighteenth-century French armchairs grouped around it. They sat on an unusually muted rug with a deeper colored floral pattern in the middle and on the border, which had to be a Savonnerie.

The rest of the floor beyond the foyer was bare, a dark, intricately parqueted, highly polished oak. Walls covered in an ocher silk twill added to the tawny monotone look of the room, but there were a few lighter areas where large pictures had been removed. She assumed the remaining smaller ones were originals and the miscellaneous porcelain vases and other accessories were genuine collector's items. Although she had only her *House Beautiful*s and *House and Garden*s as references, she'd studied them almost as much as the fashion magazines whenever she felt extravagant enough to buy them.

Diane breathed deeply and tried to think of the right compromise between being completely overwhelmed and too nonchalant. It seemed funny that she'd once taken Bob as much for granted as she had. "I wish you'd never seen my poor studio room. I never dreamed you had a duplex like this," she finally confessed.

"You probably find it rather old-fashioned. I haven't changed anything since Mother left, but the last time she was in town they decided to stay at a hotel. She said it was too dated here except for some modern art she'd acquired. Her suite at the Carlyle didn't look much different from our house to me, but in Switzerland she's replaced many of her antiques with contemporary pieces."

"I guess you get used to things after a while, no matter how beautiful they look to someone seeing them for the first time," she philosophized, walking through to the dining room. "Do you eat here when you're by yourself?" She touched the edge of the dark, oval-shaped dining table with seating for eight, wondering if it was just waxed. She could see the reflection of the crystal chandelier above in it.

"Never, not even when we used to entertain, as a rule. The downstairs is much more comfortable unless *you* prefer this."

She quickly straightened that misconception out and quietly digested the fact that he owned the garden floor too. A door near the compact stainless-steel kitchen opened unexpectedly to a miniature elevator. Downstairs she was relieved to find a relatively casual area of terrazo-tiled floors, birch-paneled and paisley-printed walls, and several round paisley-covered tables and banquettes. The low-ceilinged room had a publike atmosphere. A butcher-block countertop divided a well-equipped kitchen from the rest of the room and also functioned as a kind of bar.

Bob opened a kitchen closet and hesitated over a denim apron inside.

"That's snazzy. Do I get one too, or shall I just fasten yours for you and let you spoil me?" she joked with an effort.

"You won't need one. I'll have everything ready shortly."

Working without the apron, he deftly prepared their meal. From the fresh pineapple through the lobster tails, cheese, and demitasse he served outside on the cobbled patio, Bob was a flawless host. Diane praised him endlessly.

"I can't get over this! Who needs the Lutèce garden with a chef like you? I'm surprised you're not black as coal, though, with a terrace like this."

She regretted the remark when he replied uncomfortably, "I used to have a beautiful tan all summer, but I've been taking some medicine recently that seems to react negatively if I'm in the sun too long. I'm always under the umbrella whenever I'm out here."

"Oh, I'm sorry. Lying around tanning yourself is phony anyway, and they say people are more prone to skin cancer who bake themselves all the time."

When he didn't answer, she added, "If I had my choice

211

between a house on a beach somewhere that was always hot or one in the mountains with a lot of shady evergreens and a lake or something for when you wanted to swim, I'd take the mountains any day. The beach could get very boring, I bet.''

Diane happily found that her contrived sentiments had finally struck the right note.

''You really think so?'' Bob beamed. ''That's precisely what Mother says. Her chalet in Gstaad is unquestionably her favorite spot in the world. She swears by the dry cold in the Alps, and claims she catches colds and loses all her vitality if she's stuck someplace like Palm Springs for more than a few days. A lot of people can't understand that.''

''Well, I'm in complete agreement. We might as well go in. On a day like today, this umbrella's not much help, and I can start checking some ads while I cool off. Okay?''

Bob agreed eagerly, saying there was a den on the top floor with a desk and plenty of paper that might be more convenient than the other phones. When they reached the top floor on the elevator, after stopping for the *Times*, he showed her to an ornately paneled room with a leather-inlaid Louis XIV or XV desk and leather sofa against the dark oak *boiserie*. Almost two whole walls were lined with books. It, too, had a fireplace and adjoined a cheery, chintz-printed bedroom.

''If you don't mind, I'll go back down and start cleaning up while you phone. I only have a girl in two days a week.'' He barely paused for her answer before hurrying off.

It occurred to her that he didn't want her to suspect any hidden motive for suggesting that particular phone. She never expected to see a man so puritanical. But remembering the car incident, as she turned to the real-estate pages, she decided that was an out-of-character fluke. There were disappointingly few ads in the Saturday paper. She circled less than half a dozen, and no one answered at the two nonbroker numbers. The answers she got from brokers about the size or furnishings of their listings remotely in her price range were very discouraging.

She was looking for the telephone directory for the nearest YWCA when she found a thick, leather-bound photo album. Opening it, she found single eight-by-ten or eleven-by-fourteen color photographs on each cellophaned page. Nothing like the haphazard arrangement of small prints she was used to, held by white triangles at the corners. Besides the imaginative wintry pictures she took to be of the Alps were some of brilliant autumn leaves, wonderful sunsets, covered bridges, and other rustic scenes. Some strong sex shots were hidden.

When she went downstairs, she took the album with her. She was a little embarrassed after peeking inside a closed door and finding an antiseptically neat but dismal room with a very narrow cot, drab floors, and only dark shades at the window. She hated to think of such terrible servants' quarters. But she was glad to have evidence that any extra time she'd spent was in admiring the pictures, not poking around.

Chapter 12

Bob was almost through fastidiously putting things in order when she returned.

"There's nothing in the way of apartments today. Tomorrow should have a lot, though, unless no one's advertising because it's a holiday weekend." Then she told him how she'd found the album and asked who'd taken the pictures. Bob said he had. She unintentionally tweaked his ego with her indication of surprise that they looked so professional.

"I don't do photography for a living, of course, but a lot of professionals use the same Nikon F-2 I do, and I have a fairly good selection of lenses."

He sounded like another person as he began selecting various pictures as examples of his wide-angle, telephoto, and macro-lens shots. Some of the terms were so technical it was as if he chose them mainly to convey his knowledge. But his pride was obviously genuine. He told Diane it had taken several years to accumulate the country shots taken around the family's cabin in the Catskills.

She tried not to react. A triplex off Madison. A "cabin" in the mountains, and even if they weren't solely his, his mother appeared too attached to Switzerland to make any claims on the New York properties. Diane couldn't say if she was more annoyed or more hurt that the old available Bob appeared to be gone. She did know, without satisfaction, that she was embarrassingly dazzled by his successor. Hiding it was increasingly difficult. But she tried to gamely.

"Most out-of-towners would never associate pictures

like these with New York. All they usually think of is Times Square and Coney Island. My aunt thinks I'm living in a jungle. She wouldn't dream there were places like this anywhere near Manhattan. It's really a shame. How far is it?''

"Only a couple of hours."

Speaking of her aunt made Diane so conscious of how she'd react to someone like Bob, she hardly noticed his first words.

"You know, I have a new zoom lens I haven't had a chance to use much. I wouldn't mind taking a run up to try it out, and if you wanted a few shots of yourself to send home to show the civilized side of New York, it would be fine with me.''

Although it wasn't easy, Diane managed to accept without fawning over the invitation. Bob noted that it wasn't quite one-thirty and they'd have time for him to shoot a few rolls of color and have dinner at a good restaurant he knew before returning to the city.

"We'll get back early enough for you to get settled with your things at whichever Y you've decided on."

It was like a gratuitous reminder that she'd be going back to the other side of the tracks at the evening's end, but she no longer had the confidence to say anything sarcastic.

In a few minutes he was locking up behind them with a large black camera case on his shoulder, a folded-up metal tripod, a shirt, tie, and one of his original type suits on a hanger across his arm. After Diane made a gesture to help with the case, she didn't argue when he confirmed her discovery that it was too heavy.

"How does your mother manage to carry it?" she asked as he set it on the back seat.

"It's mine. What makes you think it's Mother's?"

"The initials. F. R. Smith."

"Oh, that. I finally decided to stop using my first name, Francis, except for business and people who've known me too long to change. My full name is Francis Robert Smith, Jr. I went through a Frank stage first, and I'm still not entirely comfortable with Bob.''

"I don't suppose anyone's called you Junior lately," she ventured, in the name of humor.

"Sometimes Mother did if she was in a kidding mood. But Francis was mainly her idea. Father had always hated it too. Although, unfortunately, it was a case of misery loves company. She went through too many scenes making me answer to it to call me anything else very often. It'll be ironic if I end up going back to it. But it's beginning to look as if I might." He laughed.

As soon as they entered the West Side Highway at Ninety-sixth Street, they found traffic barely moving on the uptown side. Bob was astonished that so many people would wait until a Saturday afternoon to start out.

"Presumably, we'll lose most of them to places like Bear Mountain and Lake Sebago. Any rational person planning to go any distance for the weekend would've left by Friday, I'd think. I'll get on the throughway as soon as I can."

Just before they reached the George Washington Bridge, the Hundred and Fifty-fifth Street parking area was so jammed with motorists who'd decided not to join the exodus, Diane was encouraged. It looked like half of Harlem had come with their blankets and coolers to the sweltering park beside the highway. But there was a surprisingly festive mood. There were many more family groups than at Riverside Park. When they finally got across the bridge onto the Palisades Parkway, overheated cars were scattered along the scenic road, and no one was smiling anymore.

By the time they reached the turnoff to the New York State Thruway, Bob was very disgusted. He said it had taken the time it usually took to be twice that far. "It'll have to be all right after Harriman. That's where most of the borscht-circuit set turns off."

"What's that?"

"The Jewish resort crowd. They're mostly in Sullivan County. We're in Ulster."

"Oh." She wondered if Ulster was comparable to Point o' Woods.

Although traffic moved better after Harriman and the

farther they got from the city, it was nearly five when they left the throughway at Kingston for Route 28 north. In a little while they turned off onto a gravel road.

"At last," he muttered as they jogged along the narrow, curving road of evergreens and overhanging pines until they reached a turnoff road marked "Private" by both a small wooden sign and "No Trespassing" posting signs. A painted milk-can mailbox with an American eagle emblem sat beside the entrance. They entered between a piled-stone fence that started out crisply on either side but gradually began to meander into tall shrubs and dense pines Bob called hemlock.

"I'm increasingly convinced this trip wasn't really worth it," Bob announced crossly after some bent branches scratched at the car and a loose stone bounced up against the bottom.

"I wasn't driving, so I shouldn't talk, but it would be worth it to me to come to a spot like this even if a house wasn't on it. Especially when I think of all those people crowded beside the highway. At home, we don't have any mountains at all. This is beautiful."

They drove maybe five minutes more before crossing a trout stream and narrow bridge, as creaky as it was picturesque, before reaching the house. It was a minimally landscaped weathered-brown retreat that could've been a shingled, slightly renovated barn. However, with two stories, it wasn't quite Diane's idea of a "cabin." When Bob found he didn't have the keys in the glove compartment, he asked her if she wanted to ride up the road with him to get the other set from the farmer who acted as caretaker. Diane decided to wait while he sped back toward the main road, making a cloud of dust.

Except for spotting a couple of chipmunks and a gray squirrel, she was alone. Although she enjoyed the country around her, thoroughly relaxed at first, occasional unfamiliar sounds made her nervous when Bob was gone longer than she expected. Beyond the immediate area of cut grass and scattered white birch trees, the hemlock rose abundantly on several sides. Their shadowy density revived apprehensions Diane thought she'd left behind in the city. She was fine when she saw Bob returning. But he was in a rage because neither the man nor his wife was at home. He said everything was closed up so tightly it looked like they'd probably gone to visit their grandchildren in Delhi.

"They're not good for a goddamned thing when you need them. I'm paying him every year for nothing. Instead of money, what he needs is a two-by-four against the big fat dentures he's so proud of, knocking them right down his skinny throat. If there's anything I won't take, it's someone who thinks I'm a fool!"

"For Pete's sake, Bob, no one knew you were coming or anything. You act like they're gone on purpose. Stop getting so wound up and acting like a spoiled brat. The worst thing that can happen is we'll take a few pictures and I'll miss seeing the inside of the house. We'll survive."

Bob looked at her angrily for a minute. Then he became more calm. "I'm sorry. It's just that we're wasting so much time, but I'll find a way to get us in."

After checking all the windows, he selected a small one on the side of the house to remove the storm window and screen from. He succeeded with a screwdriver from the car trunk and boosted Diane in. She opened the front door and admitted him.

"God, I've got to rest a minute." He collapsed in a large rush-bottomed chair. "Would you believe it's past five already?"

Diane wasn't concerned about things like that. She found this house as comfortable as the townhouse had seemed formal. The exterior was deceiving, although the inside was still basically rustic. It's beamed ceilings looked more craggy and aged than the ones at Fire Island. The fireplace was a cavernous fieldstone one with a crane for cooking inside. The stuffed deer heads looked as right to her as the pine gun rack or the hurricane lamps on the walls. The contrasts were what made the house most appealing to her. Crude homemade chairs alongside an antique colonial table. Handwoven rugs and a squashy-cushioned crewel-embroidered sofa with needlepoint pillows on polished barn plank floors. An extensive collection of pewter and some antique china looked unselfconscious on old pine sideboards. Diane kept thinking of the term "throwaway elegance."

Bob was receptive to her suggestion to show herself around while he unwound. Besides the downstairs bedroom she found three upstairs. She was relieved she didn't have to worry about whether Bob would be uncomfortable or not. There was a wonderful old four-poster in the master bedroom upstairs, in addition to the smaller one below. She recognized that resentment was mingling with appreciation as she moved about. It seemed such a waste having beautiful possessions that were rarely enjoyed. Fashionable clothes would always be important to her. Designing them had given her more self-esteem. Now she aspired for the status of fine homes and furnishings, which had seemed so remote before that she never gave them much thought. People like Bob and his mother didn't deserve such things any more than she or her poor mother.

Bob was still resting when she returned downstairs. Although he appeared expectant, she avoided further comments on the house.

"Would you care for something to drink?" he asked when he saw nothing was forthcoming. "There's a pretty good selection in the sideboard."

"I wouldn't mind some fresh juice, if you could make some. Otherwise, I'm ready when you are. Sometime before we leave for good, though, you should put out something for the mice. I've seen a few signs."

Diane was rewarded by Bob's quizzical, deflated expression. "They're only field mice. It's practically impossible to keep them out of an old house that's used so little," he explained, getting up to see about drinks.

"They got at some Indian corn you had hanging up," she continued reprovingly.

"That sounds like one of the Tates' tricks. They know how much they like grain. We only keep garlic bulbs and herbs from Mother's garden out as a rule. Martha and Evan will probably have nothing but weeds in it before long." He smiled nervously when Diane didn't answer, and slunk into the unfairly maligned kitchen. It was

remodeled so perfectly, Diane felt guilty about knocking
it.

"Frozen orange juice okay?" He handed her the glass
on a pewter tray.

"Uh-huh."

"I'm tremendously excited about my new zoom. I got a
good buy on it, too." He was getting out some of his
impressive equipment as Diane concentrated on her drink.

"It lists for about six hundred dollars."

"Good," she said dryly.

"Is something wrong?"

"Why? *Should* something be wrong?"

"I don't know, I hope not." He paused uncomfortably.
"Do you know what you've forgotten," he suddenly
blurted out.

"No, what?"

"Your suit I gave you!"

Her forgetfulness wasn't part of her new act. "I must be
flipping out. How could I have forgotten it all day? You
still have it in the trunk, don't you?"

"Yes, shall I bring it in?"

Diane retired to the downstairs bedroom and hurriedly
changed. The trousers were a little snug but would be the
right size after they gave a little. Best of all, they were
almost too long. The jacket, with a deep center vent and
patch pockets, fit too. The shoulders could've been a bit
narrower, but with a regular long-sleeved blouse or
sweater instead of the sleeveless midriff she wore, it
might be all right too. She rushed out so Bob could see
her.

"Fantastic! Absolutely fantastic! It looks like it was
made for you," he cried, circling around her. "Let me get
the hat. I'm anxious to see how it looks on you." He
returned promptly and watched approvingly as she gave it
a Garboesque dip over her eye. She thought it was a bit too
much, but he loved it. He'd almost bought her boots, but
was afraid of looking foolish with no idea at all of her size.
He'd decided to get her several pairs later.

"I can't believe how terrific you look. Is it too hot to
keep it on for a few pictures?"

"It's pretty hot, but I think I can manage. Models do all the time."

A few pictures became over a dozen careful studies. He shot her in various standing positions he arranged. Standing with legs straddled. Or with hands on hips, or pocketed. Or stepping up and leaning on one knee. But whatever the pose, he discouraged her from smiling. "Look superior" and "Act like you're completely cold and unapproachable" were key instructions. Diane followed them enthusiastically. She'd never been relaxed before a camera, but his leads made her pretend she was the cool and scornful mistress of all she surveyed. Although they didn't go very far into the more open land rising behind the house, he said there were thirty-five acres.

Bob touched her with increasing frequency. Adjusting her legs. Smoothing her lapels. Patting her damp brow. And finally asking if he could tuck in her hair. She let him, but the hat didn't fit down on her head the way it had before. Not the way he liked it.

"I wish your hair were a little shorter. The man who did mine said a number of his most fashionable women customers were cutting theirs because long hair is becoming *démodé*."

"He's right. I wouldn't mind having a shorter style, but I'm not ready for anything extreme yet."

"Only a couple of inches would make a big difference. You'd probably be afraid to trust me, but if you looked in the mirror all the time, couldn't I trim it just a little? I'd be careful."

Diane rejected the idea as ridiculous, telling him she didn't even venture to cut her hair herself. But Bob insisted he was capable. "I promise I'll be careful. Mother used to let me cut hers sometimes, and wash it too," he argued.

She agreed with reluctance. "Okay, but you can only cut a little off the back, and very slowly. No big hunks at a time."

"I promise I'll be careful. You'll see. Shall we do it in the bathroom?"

"We might as well use the bedroom. I noticed there's a bench in front of the dresser, and I have some scissors in my little case in there. Probably you should get a towel, though, for my shoulders, and some paper for the floor, although there shouldn't be that much if you hold on to what you cut."

"Okay." He rushed off to get the towel and some old newspapers.

When she sat down in front of the mirror, she was glad she'd consented to his request. It was hard to remember his pompous moments. Even the old Bob could've taken reverence lessons from him. He handled her hair so gently and made each cut so cautiously, he might've been working on a shrine. She was almost embarrassed by the expression she saw in the mirror as he worked. His eyes shone and his face radiated immense joy. He lost all sense of time, and she hadn't the heart to tell him there wasn't going to be much time for more picture taking if he continued. After nearly twenty minutes and perhaps two inches of carefully cut hair, she leaned back, wearied of her position.

He blushed deep red and dropped the scissors on the floor when she bumped into an unexpected bulge in his pants. "I'm sorry," he stammered, turning his back to hide his embarrassment while Diane flushed too. She couldn't think of anything to say, she was caught so completely by surprise. But she knew she didn't want him to think she was angry at him. He might get moody again.

"I always suspected I had sexy hair. How about that! Here, take the towel carefully so you don't get any more hair on the floor or let any fall down my back. I want to comb it and see how it looks. Looks like you've done a good job."

Combing her hair, she still felt awkward about what happened, but was determined to minimize it. She picked up the scissors and clipped a little more from the sides and some from the front to leave a sort of brushed-back look distinctive from her old hairstyle and not bad until she could get to a beauty shop.

She gathered up the paper and asked if it was all right to put it in the fireplace.

"It's all right," he said, staring out the window, avoiding looking at her. "I'll burn it before we leave. Do you feel like eating before I take some more pictures, or do you want to leave as soon as possible?" he asked dispiritedly.

"Let's take some more pictures of me, unless you think you hacked up my hair so badly I don't inspire you anymore. Then I can get out of this outfit for good and you can shoot whatever else you want."

"I like the way your hair turned out," he said, looking at her for the first time since leaving the bedroom. "Do you?"

"Yeah, it's nice. Come on, let's get going, so I can get out of this."

When she nearly fell trying to strike a statuesque pose on top of some rocks near the trout stream, Bob decided he'd taken enough pictures of her. "I haven't been very thoughtful today. Hiking boots would've been more comfortable than what you're wearing. We could've climbed up on the meadow and seen the view. I should've gotten out the jeep, but I never think of it, because we always like the exercise unless we have the horses out."

"Where do you keep them?"

"Over at the Tate's. We're not here often enough to take care of them ourselves, and we don't have any retaining fences, either. Do you ride. . . . are you all right?"

"Yeah, I'll be okay once I get inside and change and all. I'm just too hot."

He took her arm solicitously. "I'll bet you could eat something, too. I'll fix something to hold us till dinner. If we don't eat something soon, we'll ruin our appetites."

"Will your pictures be spoiled if you postpone them until after we eat?"

"Heavens no. There'll be plenty of light, but I could shoot in near-darkness if I had to."

"Okay." She took a quick rinse-off and put her white pants back on while Bob produced fresh salad greens, tomatoes, and scallions and made an antipasto with canned anchovies, olives, and imagination. He apologized for not thinking to get anything out of the oversized freezer when they first came.

"That was just right. But I still feel kind of icky, because I didn't want to make you wait for me too long. I'd like to shower and change now, while you finish shooting. Okay? I notice you brought along a suit. Is this restaurant of yours fancy?"

"Not really, it's an old inn, but some people dress. I suppose it could be considered formal, but not phony."

After he left, and she finished dressing, she saw it was almost seven-thirty already. She turned on the shortwave radio to see if it was any cooler in the city. She'd changed into an ankle-length jersey dress after first putting on the pants suit she'd worn when they met. But thinking about the earlier bedroom incident, she decided she didn't want to look like she was trying to "turn him on" again. He might really get overbearing if he thought she was trying to trap him like that. Besides, even when she thought of being married to him, she couldn't stir up much enthusiasm for him as a lover. Despite his ample equipment, he seemed limited to letting it jut into her back or sticking it into her hands.

When Bob returned almost half an hour later, she told him about a three-car throughway collision just reported, marveling that there weren't any fatalities. She'd proceeded to tell him the temperature when he interrupted to find out what the traffic conditions were. She hadn't noticed. He started changing stations anxiously. Finally he got the full story. The accident was near Harriman. Only one lane of traffic was open for several miles while they cleared the wreckage. Traffic was practically at a standstill from New Paltz.

"It will be backed up to Kingston before we could get there. This means another four-hour trip minimum, not including dinner. I wish I'd known sooner."

"There must be an alternate route we could take."

"Yes, Nine-W, but everyone will have the same idea."

"I'm sorry I don't have my license so I could help drive, but if we wait and go later, it's all right with me. Even if we got back around one or one-thirty or so, at least I have luggage tonight so I won't look like a complete gypsy checking into the Y.''

"But suppose the desk's closed. I wish you'd stayed at the Barbizon a few more days. That way you'd at least be sure you have someplace definite. I didn't mind paying. As it is, I feel I'm responsible for you.''

Diane shoved her chair back as she angrily got to her feet. "Listen, Bob, or Francis, or Junior, or whatever you want to call yourself, you don't have to feel responsible for me. I'm free, white, and twenty-one. I'm not an albatross or a leech, so if you're afraid I'm going to try to trick my way into your precious townhouse or something, you've got another thought coming. You could have fifty brownstones and a hundred country houses, and you still wouldn't be anyone I'd want. I'm not finished yet!'' She raised her voice louder when he tried to say something.

"I feel sorry for you,'' she continued. "All you can do for me right now is take me to the nearest train or bus station, and I'll be only too happy to be off your hands for good.''

"Don't say that!'' He scuffled to his feet and caught her hands as she tried to pull away. "Please don't threaten to leave me like that. I forget how frightened I am at being alone again until I'm actually faced with it. I know I'm nothing. Not good enough for you or anyone else. But I'm willing to do whatever you even *think* you want me to do. I wish you'd believe me and give me a chance instead of keeping me so uncertain about what you want. I thought you were going to be different. You know how I want it to be with us.''

Diane didn't quibble about exactly what he meant. "*I* haven't changed. *You're* the one. You've acted so funny since I had to leave my building, I thought you'd decided I wasn't good enough or something. You shouldn't put yourself down, any girl would like you the way you used to be. At least you never seemed snobbish before.''

"I didn't mean to. No wonder you finally blew up just now, if that's what you thought. I probably should've told you what was bothering me. I was all mixed up, but it won't happen anymore.''

225

"What was bothering you?"

"Nothing. The main thing is that you have to tell me when you want something, not ask me to do it."

"As a rule, I have no complaints. I'd let you know in a minute if I did. But you usually go all out to make sure I have a fabulous time with you."

"I'm not talking about taking you places. There're all kinds of other things I could do. Like cooking for you more often or doing work you don't want to do, like taking care of your laundry and shopping. Or cleaning up for you." He sounded quite animated.

"Well, if you're serious, you sure won't have to twist my arm. We'll see what happens once I'm out of the Y."

Bob fidgeted awhile, then blurted, "Do you think you could live with someone like me?"

Diane wasn't sure how he meant it. "Got any more good jokes?"

"Maybe it's not as crazy as it sounds. You'd probably be bored if you didn't go to school like you've planned, but outside of that, you wouldn't have to lift a finger. I'd do everything. I'd lie down and let you use me for a foot rest if you wanted to." He flushed, aware he might've gone too far. Then, confused, he tried to sound light and humorous. "No one could blame you if you didn't want a weakling like me for a husband."

Somewhere during the summer Diane had lost her optimism about making it alone in New York. She'd been terrified when she'd demanded that Bob take her to the nearest train or bus. It was nothing like it was with Lester. She hadn't expected the city to take away what little self-sufficiency she'd had. Her recent experiences had convinced her she could never enjoy the city without someone she could count on. Both embarrassed and flattered by Bob's statements, she was more grateful than anything else considering his circumstances in contrast to her own.

Still, when she answered, she didn't understand all her conscious and unconscious needs involved much better than Bob understood his. "Why not?"

Bob looked at her uncertainly. "You mean it?"

"Of course. Would I joke about something like that?"

A big grin moved across Bob's anxious face. He began kissing her hands emotionally on both sides. Then he swung around in circles with her. It looked more and more like a scene of children at play than two healthy adults approaching marriage. But it matched Diane's mood as well as it suited Bob's. It wasn't as thrilling as *The Graduate* or as poignant as *Picnic* on the late show, but she told herself they too could Live Happily Ever After. . . .

Instead, Bob excused himself to get something from upstairs. Actually, he had to make a phone call. He dialed a number and reached the same female he'd last called from the Plaza phone booth. But his tone was noticeably different. "Butch here," he said firmly.

"What do you want, creep?"

"Look, I can't talk long. Could you put Vera on the phone?"

"You know goddamned well she's too busy to talk to you. Stop trying to get your rocks off by bugging me."

"If she's really busy, I'll give you the message. Otherwise, please call her. I'll pay you both for the inconvenience."

"Well, I'll see."

It seemed like a long time before she came. "What's this about your wanting to speak with *Vera*? You know how you're supposed to address me, and that this is my biggest night. You're so fucking out of line, I'm really going to enjoy kicking your ass tomorrow."

"Listen a minute, that's why I'm calling. I'm stuck in the country and definitely can't make it in the morning."

"Don't tell me your problems. Get your ass down to your session, or you're finished."

"I honestly can't, but I'll send you the money."

"All right this time, but don't get the idea you're going to start doing things your way. I'll take care of you next week."

Bob realized he was getting on very touchy grounds, but he knew he'd have to have things a little more flexible than they had been. He was sweating nervously. "I'm not trying to be disobedient, Miss Vera, but I'd appreciate it very much if I could let you know next week whether I can come or not. There's a possibility I'll be getting married. She'll definitely be moving in right away, and I'm not quite sure what's going to happen afterward.''

There was a burst of derisive laughter from the woman. When she finished she said, ''Just send me a money order for what you owe me tomorrow. I'm too busy to be your fuckin' marriage counselor. Let your old lady beat your balls awhile. Maybe she won't find it so disgusting.''

''You're saying I disgusted you,'' he sputtered, ''you second-rate whore degenerate? You'd better be damned glad you never said anything like that to my face. It's too bad you were too stupid to know you were the real slave. Garbage I paid to do exactly what I wanted, when I wanted. Hired scum. But I'm going to do you a favor, I'm not going to pay you for tomorrow, but I'm going to let you stay in business.''

''Suck off, penny-ante motherfucker, pigs don't scare me.''

''Police weren't the ones who put Carletta in the hospital—'' He was cut off by a loud-banging receiver. His hands shook badly as he hung up. He got out a cigarette and smoked, with his left hand supporting his head. He'd left his strong tranquilizers at home. He hadn't had anything since his ten milligrams of Thorazine in the morning. He missed his afternoon pill and would have to get through the night and next morning without either of the prescribed dosages. Usually, he was more likely to exceed than take less than the doctor prescribed. Skin eruptions from too much sunshine were the only side effect he admitted to.

He hated the power of psychiatrists. After his mother remarried, all the things that made him a unique son became increasingly unhealthy. Having few male friends. Rarely dating girls unless someone pushed it. Being unusually attentive and compliant at home and overly demanding at work. When she learned he'd gone out with several call girls, that was additional proof he needed help. He resisted and began moving more toward his stepfather.

228

Soon after that, they decided to move to Europe. Among other things, it was supposed to be for his own good.

After such stubborn resistance, he ended up seeing a psychiatrist anyway. But never to talk to him and let him be superior and condescending. Just to get something to make him sleep. And be less shaky. And less angry and devastated after his mother left him. He believed he'd gotten over his real father's abandonment soon after it happened during his grammar school. He wanted to believe it would work with Diane, but wished things weren't happening so fast. He was still ambivalent about letting down more of his defenses and trusting her completely. He'd always lived with suspicion.

Bob thawed venison steaks and served them with mushrooms and organically grown vegetables for a candlelit dinner. Diane made no move to help. Both were comfortable in their roles. Afterward it was cool enough for a modest fire in the fireplace. They sat and made wedding plans compatibly. He was glad she wasn't a practicing Catholic. A Protestant judge he knew would marry them civilly. An old Yale rooomate would probably be his best man. Mona Chernock her maid of honor. She only briefly considered Carol Stern. He'd tell his mother after the ceremony. She'd do the same with her family, though she could hardly wait.

He liked her first honeymoon choice, Acapulco. She love his selection of Las Brisas, the city's unusual mountainside hotel with completely private bungalows and pools overlooking the sea. Although Bob felt more natural with her than he had in the city earlier, he began tensing up as the hour grew later. The fire was almost out. He suggested a toast in heirloom goblets. Then he didn't know what to do. Brandy was a poor substitute for Thorazine.

He cleared his throat. Diane smiled at him encouragingly.

"Do you usually sleep late?" he asked.

"That depends on what time I go to bed, honey. I'm usually up by ten-thirty or eleven, I guess. Why?"

"I was just wondering. At home I often fall asleep in my chair as soon as I finish dinner, around seven or so. By the time I get up and get undressed, I'm usually so wide-awake I have trouble getting back to sleep. But no matter how late I finally fall asleep, I always wake up at about six in the morning."

"Man, that's wild," she said cheerily. She assumed he was trying to tell her something about sleeping arrangements. She waited anxiously to see what.

Unfortunately, since he'd first met her, Bob had assumed Diane was much more experienced than she was. When he first approached her, he had the idea she could be a very particular hooker. Although he no longer entertained that idea after the first evening, he thought she'd slept with a number of men and expected to do so with him that night. He was desperately afraid of failure if he tried to make love to her under normal conditions. He was also afraid of what she'd think if he waited until he had more confidence in her willingness to stimulate him properly. In the past, she'd aroused him, but only by accident.

In the mornings he usually awoke with a strong erection. Having become conditioned to sexual release every Sunday morning in recent months, he believed he could satisfy Diane and himself both if he waited. "If I let you go to bed early and get a good night's sleep, would it be all right if I came in early in the morning to see if you feel like taking the horses out with me, or . . . uh, anything?"

Diane was surprised he wanted to wait until the next morning for "the anything," but she answered, "Sure, but don't come in with an alarm clock or a breakfast gong."

"I won't." He held her to him outside the downstairs bedroom door and said good night with a dry, perfunctory kiss on the lips. Before going upstairs, he bolted the front door at Diane's request. Normally, it was unlatched.

It was barely eleven. Neither of them could sleep. Diane could barely wait for the morning to come. Although he hadn't said it, she was sure he'd make love to her when he came, with the slightest encouragement. Whatever else he was, she knew he'd be gentle and considerate. She was also confident that anyone who talked so much about being her servant would never expect her to do what Chuck had.

She wondered if he'd want to kiss her body. If he did, in time she'd probably reciprocate. For one thing, he wasn't sleeping all over town. For another, she owed him a lot. He had so much to offer, marrying him would be a real coup. As she lay nearly asleep, the stunned reaction of people like Lester and Mona and Mrs. Kraemer and Jacky pushed almost everything else from her mind.

It was shortly past five when Bob finally tired of tossing and turning. It was still quiet and dark outside. He awoke, as he expected, with a monstrous erection. Meticulously clean normally, he only brushed his teeth and put on fresh undershorts in order not to disturb it. He took the jodhpur boots, jeans, and sweat shirt he used for riding out of his closet; his mother's tailored shirt, English riding boots, and habit from another. He hurriedly smoked a cigarette to try to calm himself a little. Still nervous, he took out two riding crops, one his heavier jumping bat, and wrapped on a robe before going quietly downstairs with his bundle.

His plan was perfect if he wasn't too shaky to carry it off. It used to work quite well with prostitutes before he advanced to his current level of need. All it required was a little cooperation from Diane. He was pretty sure he could get it if he made whatever happened seem like something kicky, and maybe kinky, but not . . . sick. He opened her door quietly and laid the clothes across a chair with the crops on top. He pulled the chair close enough to the bed so he could reach them without getting up.

Diane pretended to be asleep. He sat on the bed beside her and touched her cheek. When she opened her eyes, he said softly, "I have our riding things with me, but there's not enough light yet. Can I join you?"

"Uh-hum," she answered, moving over sleepily, eyes half-closed, as he pulled back the covers and climbed in with her. She'd barely turned lazily from her side to her back when he mounted her abruptly, without warning. He shoved her long nightgown up above her hips and quickly

231

inserted his thick penis into her comparatively unlubricated vagina.

"Ouch, take it easy!" she cried out as he plunged in and out of her bruisingly.

"Excuse me, I'm sorry I'm hurting you," he panted. "But if you hurt me a little by scratching me and biting my mouth and ears, I'd love it."

"All right, darling," Diane agreed. She was determined to be a good sport, no matter what, this time. She began tentatively scratching his back and nibbling at his ear, trying to ignore his jarring thrusts.

"Harder, please, Diane, please try to hurt me," he implored. But while she managed to increase the pressure of her teeth and nails, it wasn't enough. He felt himself growing limper.

Diane noticed it too, but found it less irritating. She forgot her biting assignment temporarily to tell him he wasn't hurting her much anymore. The next thing she knew, he'd thrown the covers off his back and snatched the nearest riding crop from the chair. She was surprised when she saw it.

"Please, Diane, don't say anything nice. Here, use this on me like you hate me, and tell me you're the boss." As he spoke, he was slipping outside her. He buried his face in her shoulder and tried to hold himself inside.

Diane had such sympathy for him that she wanted to do anything she could to help him. She took the crop and gave him a lick on his behind.

"Harder, please, that's not hard enough. Use all your strength and *hurt* me." He could hear the growing desperation in his voice. But he couldn't control it. Diane gave him a good second whack that made tension start returning to his deflated organ. "That's better, Miss Diane. Don't be afraid to punish me hard. I know I'm naughty." His voice had become unintentionally high-pitched as he'd become aroused again.

"My God, Bob, stop talking like that. You scare me!"

Her words and the sound of the whip dropping on the rug completely demolished Butchie, his desire, and his brief dream of success. Bob got off her and out of bed. He struggled to remain controlled. "I'm sorry I frightened you. To my knowledge, it's the first time I've had that effect on anyone. Don't worry about any more ordeals with me."

He turned his back to put on his shorts. Diane began weeping. It was like a recurring nightmare. Chuck and Fire Island all over again. But she felt more desperate this time. She hated to see it end like that after all their plans.

She jumped from the bed and rushed to him. "I didn't mean it like it sounded when I said you scared me," she sobbed, pressing herself to his back to avoid looking at him. "I just got a little nervous. That's all. But I'm all right now." Remembering Morty, she added, "A lot of respectable men like unusual things in private. Maybe if you got a little counseling, you wouldn't be that much different from anyone else."

If Diane had been able to see Bob's eyes and drastically changed expression in time, she wouldn't have tried to offer him her advice about getting help. She never would've embraced him to sustain the illusion that she loved him, any more than he loved her. She would've kept quiet and stayed away from him instinctively. The man she clung to had very little resemblance to the old Bob as she'd perceived him.

He whirled and flung one arm out stiffly with a guttural cry. It hit her so hard across her face she was knocked to the floor several feet from where she'd stood. His eyes were glazed and his mouth twitched as he advanced on her.

"Who are you to tell me I need help? Why is it always orchestrated to make it look like I'm the sick one . . . no matter how people treat me. Pretending to care about me when they don't . . . using me until they get tired. They're healthy. I'm not. I'm supposed to be nice, gullible little Bob. Well, I'm tired of it. You're not so well your own self!"

Diane held her painful cheek and inched backward. Horrified and disbelieving. She had no idea what he'd do next. But he was standing directly over her, and she was afraid to get up. "I never said you were sick. I know

233

you're all right. And I already admitted something's wrong with me when people always end up turning against me. Look at you. I know it's my fault."

"You're damned right it is. You're worse than any of the others. You're the kind who likes to make a fool of anyone who treats them too nice. You'd rather get your ass beat. That doesn't scare you like what I ask you to do."

"I don't—"

"Shut up! I know what you're used to. I never should've pretended I believed you in the first place. You thought you were pretty smart with your lies, didn't you?"

Diane had no idea what he was talking about. "I never lied to you, Bob, honest. Please let me get up."

"Why don't you get on your knees and try 'pretty please'? That would've been all right for *me*. You think you're too good for that?"

Diane looked at him nervously, and obediently got into a kneeling position.

"Can I get up now?" she pleaded.

"What's your hurry? I canceled my only appointment to be with you. I kind of like this. Maybe if I'd been doing it all along, no one would say I needed help. I didn't know it felt so good." He reached inside his shorts and began stroking himself.

"This isn't you. Please . . . don't act like this," she stammered, trying to rise while he was preoccupied.

"I didn't give you permission. Whoa!" He gripped her shoulders and shoved her back to her knees. "You'd better do what I say. Don't forget, there's no one around to call the police for you this time."

"Why should I need the police? I know you wouldn't hurt me." It was hard to get much conviction in her voice.

"Who knows? If I did, would you make up a story to protect me like you did your other boyfriend when I called the police? What was he doing to make you scream like that? It didn't occur to me then that you might be getting your kicks when I interrupted."

Chapter 13

Diane had never stopped to wonder who'd called before. Maybe because of the nuisance phone calls. She knew it was important to explain carefully. If only her throat wasn't so tight. Her mouth so dry. She swallowed and licked her lips. "It wasn't a boyfriend. I swear I didn't know who it was, because I was blindfolded before the man forced me upstairs. I didn't lie before, I just didn't want to upset you by telling you everything. Honestly. You might have saved my life by calling at just the right time."

"I wanted to ask if I could bring your suit up. I was still dumb enough to think I could please you then. It's too bad you'd still rather lie than tell me what it is you go for. That means I'll have to experiment." He grabbed her hair and pulled her forward as she gasped in disbelief.

"Down on all fours!" He kept a firm hold on her hair while stooping for the whip lying near her.

Diane grabbed it first and clutched it tightly. "Please let me up, Bob. Remember how I couldn't hurt you before? That's because you've always been so nice to me. That's when you're the happiest. This is all my fault, but you don't really want to be naughty anymore. Now, let go of my hair like a good boy."

Bob released her hair without answering. Diane raised her head gratefully. But when she saw him stalking jerkily around to the other side of the bed, she could tell she hadn't reached him with her amateur, first-year psychology. It was the first time he hadn't been between her and the open door. She raced through it and reached the living-

235

room door. Because it was latched, she couldn't get out. A painful lash across her back marked Bob's arrival. He grabbed her hair again and dragged her back into the room so viciously, part of it was painfully torn from the roots.

He slammed the bedroom door and stood facing Diane as she cowered and whimpered.

"Where were you going without good old Bob? We were supposed to be going riding together. I think you're deliberately provoking me. Just asking for it. Look at you, panting like an animal for me to take care of you." His breath had gone foul, and an unpleasant odor was about the room.

Diane had never before experienced a cold sweat. The handle of the crop was slick in her hand. She was thinking of the notorious tenderness of men's genitals. The possibility of hurting him enough to reach his car. The irony of converting the dignified sedan into a getaway car from its ostensibly proper owner didn't escape her. But with all the force she could find, she struck him across his sex organ.

Bob yelled in pain and clutched himself. But instead of collapsing like most men, or being completely immobilized, he leaned against the door, moaning. He released himself and looked at Diane with the hungry slave look that would have been unmistakable to a prostitute. He moved toward her unsteadily, longing for another blow that would release him. Diane unfortunately thought he was moving in to retaliate.

Aiming carefully, she landed a resounding blow across his ear, another sensitive spot she was familiar with through her aunt. But it had no erotic associations for him. He was stunned. She'd perversely denied him the overdue climax well within her power. He felt a ringing in his ears, throbbing pain in his head, and a staggering hostility that had usually been suppressed. Diane had badly underestimated his threshhold for pain.

He lifted his jumping bat and struck her deliberately across her breasts. She screamed raggedly and managed to turn in time to block the next hit with her shoulders. She received one on her buttocks as she ran for the protection

236

of the bedcovers. Storm windows made the windows unassailable.

"In God's name, Bob, please don't hit me anymore." Her appeal was made after she'd jumped in the bed, pulled the quilt up to her neck, and was scrunched against the headboard.

For a moment there was a look of uncertainty on Bob's face. He squinted his eyes as if to shut out the conflict. When he opened them fully, he fixed Diane with a penetrating look and moved forward excitedly. With a sudden, stabbing movement, he grabbed the covers from her and flung them almost completely to the floor. Diane wrapped both arms around herself automatically. But he took hold of her demure eyelet gown and ripped it off her easily.

It was impossible to protect herself from the carefully aimed blows. Her pleas for mercy seemed only to incite more violence. There was so much pain from her breasts to her thighs, she couldn't think clearly. There had to be something she could do. An idea came to her, but it was repugnant. Being in New York hadn't changed her that much. She remembered how she felt when she first arrived. That was really something. Seemed longer than five months ago. Maybe if she thought hard enough about the trip, or whatever, she could imagine somebody else was getting beaten up. She'd try to act completely unconscious. That way, the beating might stop before she was more seriously hurt. . . .

Grunting and sucking in his breath, Bob was so carried away he'd overlooked Diane's scissors, still lying on the table beside them. Diane could easily have picked them up. Thrust them into his abdomen before he could've stopped her. But she was chilled by the thought of cold-blooded murder. It would've been hard enough to kill the man who forced himself into her studio at knife point. But she could have. As horrible as her ordeal with Bob was, he wasn't a strange nobody from off the streets. Badly disturbed, but not the type of person who went around killing people, any more than she was. . . . She remembered her revulsion for the *Last Tango* murderess. As she forced her face into a mask and tried to breathe as shallowly as possible, she had an intuitive certainty she'd survive her first nightmarish summer in New York. And learn from it. . . .

Bob lifted Diane's limp body from the bed and managed to move her to the blanket he'd draped across the sofa near the front door. He was trembling and perspiring profusely. Drained and terrified. He put his head to her chest, but wasn't sure if she was breathing or not. He pinched her cheeks and decided to give her some strong brandy to see if it would revive her. He put one of the snifters they'd used for engagement toasts to her lips. But the sight of the red liquid mingling with a creamy substance on her mouth and chin nauseated him. He wiped some of it off before pouring the brandy directly into her mouth from the bottle. Most of it still spilled over and trickled down her face.

She should've acted differently. But he never meant to hurt her as bad as he had. She had to be alive. If she could get the proper medical attention, he was sure she'd be all right. He pressed his fists to his temples and began marching back and forth, trying to clear his head and decide what to do. Where to take her. As long as she was alive, he couldn't see how he'd be in any trouble.

She'd be so grateful that he'd taken care of her, she'd never press charges against him. He'd visit her as soon as she regained consciousness. Pay her bills and promise to make it up to her. Even if she wanted to be vindictive, he could easily prove he'd called the police when she claimed she was attacked before. They'd believe it was more likely the same unknown assailant *if* the hospital was near her. There'd be plenty of likely suspects. Drifters and everything.

But he was confident it wouldn't go that far, because she'd remember how much she was to blame for what happened. The crucial thing was to make sure she got the right medical attention without implicating himself. He hated to see her hospitalized with no clothes on. But after he got her into her bikini panties, he decided it would be too difficult and time-consuming to dress her.

He hurriedly finished dressing himself, brought the jeep Wagoneer right in front of the door, and lugged her out in the blanket. He wouldn't have been comfortable in the Mercedes, so sweaty and dressed the way he was. Or doing what he had to do. His Rolex showed twenty to seven as he wrapped the blanket around her on the rear seat. He tucked it under her chin so it wouldn't interfere with her breathing. He shoved on Diane's hat at the last moment so he wouldn't have to worry about his hair.

Bob wished it were still dark so there'd be less chance of her being noticed. But if he left right away, there shouldn't be much traffic headed for the city at that hour, in the middle of the holiday. The only problem was the toll booths. He decided to put her on the floor to make sure she wasn't seen by a collector. Her reputation was being protected too. It wouldn't do her any good for people to know she'd been spending the weekend with a man.

When he got to the Kingston Thruway entrance, he was seized with panic. He would've backed up and turned off, but another car was in the lane behind him. His heart pounded as he took the ticket and drove through. At the Harriman exit, forty-five miles later, the seventy cents in exact change was noticeably wet when he handed it to the toll taker with his ticket. Shattered glass and automobile fragments nearby were reminders of the badly timed accident the night before.

By the time Bob reached the Henry Hudson Parkway, the muscles of his face were moving steadily without his control. His eyes strained from darting suspiciously from the rearview mirror to the road beside him. The ashtray overflowed with his butts. His thoughts were too jumbled for him to settle on a hospital. He drove downtown slowly and decided to turn off at the Seventy-ninth Street exit.

It wasn't quite nine as he slowed down at the entrance to the boat basin and rounded the turn through the park to Riverside Drive. When he emerged from an enclosed part of the turnoff, trees practically hid the jeep from the two or three people strolling near Seventy-eighth Street. A temporary construction site occupied the uptown side of the park, and he was a good distance from buildings facing the Drive. Trees shielded him from many of the lower floors.

With a minimum of conscious deliberation, he stopped beside the park path. A single car passed him, hurrying to make the light. When it crossed the Drive, he got out quickly and opened the back of the jeep, alert for other cars. He saw little change in Diane. He wanted to touch her face to see if it was warm. But he was afraid of what he might discover. He lifted her out, carried her across the narrow walk, and deposited her in the blanket beside the nearest tree. He hesitated, then yanked it from under her and ran back to the jeep. He made a quick U turn over to the uptown entrance to the highway. Sped onto it so fast that no one could possibly read his license plate, no matter what they'd seen or how hard they tried.

From his eighteenth-floor terrace at Sixty Riverside Drive, Arnold Denker had seen and did try. The sixty-two-year-old engineer had come out to see if there was enough of a breeze to make sitting outside comfortable before the sun turned the terrace into an oven. When he arrived in time to see Bob snatch up the blanket and spill something out on the grass, he was furious. Outsiders like him were ruining the park. He was too high up to identify what was dumped, but he would have taken his license if he could have read it. To show the bastard he couldn't get away with dumping his trash wherever he damn pleased.

After Bob shot off, he waited awhile to see if anyone else saw what happened and did anything about it. When several cars passed without noticing and no one walked down that way, he decided to call the police. Not 911, though, and risk looking like the kind of person who used it improperly, when there wasn't an emergency. He returned to wait impatiently on the terrace after reporting what happened and giving his name and address peevishly when asked.

Almost ten minutes passed before an interlocked young couple crossed Riverside Drive and entered the park. He shook his head disgustedly as they appeared to be turning downtown, too hugged up to notice whatever it was a few yards away. But then he saw them stop. He observed intently as they rushed to it. Suddenly the quiet morning was shattered by the girl's hysterical screams. As the young man ran for a phone, Denker hurried back inside to wake up Mrs. Denker. Her bursitis had kept them in town, but he knew she'd want to see everything firsthand in spite of her discomfort. He pulled back the drapes and raised the venetian blinds so she could remain in the cool bedroom without missing too much. Hurrying for the elevator, he was glad he'd given his name to the police so the youth wouldn't get credit for the report. He also rehearsed his description of the stocky, swarthy, long-haired man, unaware of the distortions caused by sunlight, his location, and Bob's outfit and Diane's hat.

Within the few minutes it took the police to arrive, more than a dozen people had left their cars or apartments or normal routines to push their way as close as possible to Diane. But no one touched the savagely beaten, half-nude girl. There were lines of congealed blood across her nipples and swollen breasts. A patchwork of deep red welts and cuts from her stomach to her open thighs. Her "man in the boat" was the center of a thick crimson patch. The dried pasty-looking substance about her puffy mouth was quickly identified as "come" or more polite terms meaning the same thing. Bob's semen. The brandy was mistaken for blood.

"It'll be a long time before she bites another prick, I'll bet," one motorist declared loudly. A man with a dog named Mia looked at him with disgust.

The first two officers who arrived had to get another radio car immediately to help control the crowd until the ambulance arrived. The girl who was first on the scene wept inconsolably, but wouldn't be led aside by her boyfriend. An old lady from a nearby nursing home talked to herself and made crosses. A dirty transient black looked around self-consciously and shambled back toward Broadway. But mostly there was shoving and cursing and booing as the policemen covered Diane with a blanket and tried to make everyone move on.

241

The ambulance came almost ten minutes after the police. "A DOA," the officers told the attendants when they got through.

"Yeah, not dead long, though, must've been a strong girl to hang on so long," one remarked after a brief examination.

By the time the detectives put out an APB based on Mr. Denker's statement, Bob was across the George Washington Bridge and well into 9-W. He had barely half an hour's drive ahead of him when they finally finished taking their pictures of Diane at every conceivable angle, made diagrams, and released her to the covered litter to be transported to the city morgue. He'd ripped the plain dark blanket into small pieces with the help of his screwdriver and disposed of it in miscellaneous out-of-the-way spots.

Disposing of the blanket stopped the tears that began to fill his eyes as soon as he started up the West Side highway. Although he'd done his best to wipe them away with the back of his hands, the road and traffic around him had soon become a blur. Everything returned to focus when the last shred of the blanket was gone. He stopped telling himself she was all right and decided instead that if she was dead it was due to untreated injuries from her other attack. That wasn't his fault.

He'd hurt the prostitute who'd called him a "sick freak" pretty badly, and she'd pulled through. For a minute he allowed himself to remember the mind-blowing peak of power and relief he'd reached on both occasions. He forced the memories aside with difficulty to concentrate on the careful cleanup job that remained ahead of him. He set his mouth into a tight, firm line. He was up to what he had to do.

Chapter 14

On Monday, September 3, the *Daily News* carried a prominent third-page story about the beautiful young brunette who'd been sodomized and sadistically beaten before being found dead in Riverside Park. The *Post* wasn't published on the holiday, and the *Times* had a small story above the advertisments on the eighth page. Death was attributed to a ruptured spleen, although the autopsy continued at the New York County Medical Examiner's office. Detectives of the Twentieth Precinct were seeking clues to the girl's identity. The motive for the slaying was unknown.

"Why couldn't he of dumped her above Eighty-sixth Street?" Detective Lucas groaned for the third time that day, not to mention the day before. "What makes the Twentieth so popular with the psychos? The way we keep losing men every year, we can hardly take care of cases that are supposed to be ours. This one's going to be a real ball-buster. Especially till someone misses her."

"Yeah, I would've made book on a yellow sheet for pros or some kind of bust she'd been printed on. Her long-haired pal's getting a lot of breaks."

"I don't know. What bugs me is whether he's just been lucky or smart. Why the hell do people pay the rents they do for those apartments when they've got to clear out like it's a plague every time a holiday comes along? He couldn't have picked many places in Manhattan where we'd be so fucked up for witnesses in broad daylight!"

On Tuesday, someone missed Diane. Her supervisor, Mrs. Morganlander, when she didn't show up for work.

The operator informed her there was a dead line, when she wasn't able to get anything but a silence after dialing several times with increasing impatience. When neither Miss Peretti, from advertising, or Miss Chernock admitted having any more information about Diane's vague travel plans than she did, she was very annoyed. Her attitude prompted Mona to suggest that she and Jacky go to Diane's at lunchtime. She remembered the recent murder practically on Diane's doorstep, and that made their supervisor agree. Mona was delighted at the unexpected excuse to see the scene of the crime and get an extra hour or so for lunch on company time. Jacky couldn't see why her boss had let her get dragged into the silly business.

When no one answered Diane's bell, the girls rang Mrs. Kraemer's garden apartment. Mrs. Kraemer didn't bother to conceal her annoyance at being disturbed, or her hostility toward Diane. She agreed to open the foyer door, and finally Diane's private one, only because it gave her an excuse to look around without worrying about the Sterns. She'd convinced Mr. Hannah to give her duplicate keys for security reasons. The young women were unprepared for the costly-looking ensembles in Diane's closet. They never dreamed she'd made them herself, because after her first days in the office she'd deliberately stuck to her simpler things.

But while they couldn't imagine her going home for any period of time leaving such things behind, it was the phone that made them act decisively. Finding it torn from the wall, they insisted on immediately notifying the police that Diane was missing. Mrs. Kraemer objected furiously, telling them the police already knew about the phone. She said she'd call herself when they made it clear they'd use the nearest public phone otherwise.

"Two girls are making trouble at my home . . ." she began. By the time she repeated the earlier story and the current developments to officers of increasing rank, they were all but certain Diane was the corpse from Riverside Park. Within a few minutes police cars interrupted the serenity of her quiet block. Soon afterward Jacky and Mona were being rushed to 502 First Avenue. At 1:25 P.M.

on September 4, 1973, Diane's body was pulled out of a large stainless-steel refrigerator on a metal tray. She was positively identified and tagged.

Mona vomited and required a sedative after seeing Diane. She had to be talked out of going home before answering questions at the precinct. Jacky was badly shaken. But she was anxious to give the police all her "knowledge" about the victim. When they were later photographed and exposed briefly to excited members of the media, both girls were impressed with their sudden prominence. But Mona bristled at the excessive attention Jacky received. By the time they returned to the office with two plainclothesmen, they felt more like celebrities than mourners for a friend.

Richard Fenster turned chalky when told detectives wanted to see him. He wanted to take sick time as soon as he heard Diane was the park victim. But he was afraid it might look suspicious. The officers didn't take him in for questioning because both his parents confirmed he'd been at home from about midnight Saturday evening until late the next afternoon, and didn't drive. But he acted so nervous, they questioned him about Diane's earlier complaint.

Once he saw he wasn't a prime murder suspect, Richard regained enough composure to give them his fantasized account of "making it" with her. "Man, I was flattered as hell when she first accepted a date with me. But who wants a broad who's so hot she'll open her legs to anything with pants on? As far as her almost getting raped, that's got to be a crock!" As soon as the officers left, he moved competitively into the spotlight occupied by Mona and Jacky.

Mrs. Kraemer reached her son, Bernard, on the phone the moment the principal detectives left for the morgue. "Policemen are all over the house," she whispered hysterically. "Did you do anything to that girl?"

"Who, Diane? Of course not. I already proved I was at the beach when she said she was attacked. I'm beginning to wish I'd never called her or rung her bell for you, the way you keep bugging me."

245

"She's been murdered. They found out she's the girl in the park. For God's sake, did you do it?"

"Oh, shit, this isn't real. I don't believe it."

After his mother assured him it was true and he assured her he had a solid alibi for the murder period too, he caught a cab and arrived unexpectedly at her doorway. Tangle-haired and dirty.

"I didn't tell you to come here," she told him as he pushed past her. "It's just my son," she called to the curious policeman in front of the house.

"You're the one someone should kill," he hissed when they were alone inside. "First my baby sister, now a poor chick I've barely laid eyes on. I should start doing something to earn my reputation besides getting stoned and making an ass of myself with a couple of your protégées." He glared at his mother menacingly.

"Now, don't get yourself all worked up about nothing. You should know that even if you'd been responsible, I would've done everything in my power to protect you and keep from having our names dragged through the papers. She's not worth it. I called her aunt, but I hope it doesn't get out that I helped her come here."

"Wonder who did it?" he mused, less disturbed than before. "Remember the guy I bumped into that night coming from upstairs? He looked mad enough to do anything. Maybe I should tell the cops about him."

"I don't think so. The less involved we are in this sordidness, the better. It would be too much of a coincidence if he was the one she went off with. And if he was, assuming he could be located and arrested, how much time do you think he'd get for killing a girl like her, even if a jury found him guilty? I'd be a lot more worried about him after he was released than I am now. I can't really feel threatened having him go free. He doesn't sound like the kind who'd be any trouble to normal respectable people."

Bernard was a little concerned about not telling the police all he knew when they questioned him shortly after this conversation. But he needn't have been. Richard Fenster had remained aggrieved enough to beat Diane home and watch for her from the park before following her

246

inside in new high-heeled shoes. He'd dug up an old fountain pen to scare her. He felt justified in taking what he believed he had coming to him before she left town. He would've screwed her good a couple of times before putting on his afro wig and sunglasses and leaving her tied up. But he wouldn't have harmed her. Certainly, he was no murderer.

Walking over to take the number-five bus home, Richard remembered how close he came to taking Diane. Passing the spot where she'd been found, he wondered what kind of a sick bastard would hurt a girl like that. But for the rest of the long trip home, he couldn't stop thinking about all the things the murderer must have done with her before he killed her.

When Carol Stern told Detectives Lynch and McLaurin she and her husband had actually met the guy with the Mercedes, known only to her co-workers as Bob Smith, they thought they were finally on to something important.

"How's about a description?"

"He was about twenty-nine or thirty, around six feet or a little taller, and slender. Maybe 160 to 170 pounds. Kind of sandy-haired and clean-shaven. He didn't have sideburns or a mustache or anything. His hair was quite short. He was very straight-looking, the way he dressed and all."

"What about his eyes?"

"I guess they were brown, maybe kind of light."

"How'd he act?"

"Well-educated and friendly. Really beautiful manners."

"You know what color the Mercedes was?"

"Yes, maroon, I think. Or dark gray."

"Year, model?"

"You know they all look so much alike, but it looked beautiful, no more than a year or two old. A fairly large sedan."

"Anything else you can tell us about him?"

"I can't think of anything . . . except his family has a business with a European branch. I think it was something to do with imports."

"Know if he was married?"

"I'm sure he wasn't." Then she thought awhile "Actually, I didn't talk with Diane that often, but I do recall she said she couldn't reach him until he called her at work when I invited them someplace once. But I never had the idea he had a wife. I'm pretty sure she wouldn't have gone out with a married man."

"I don't know. I spoke with a guy named Abrams who thought she wouldn't mind his being married if he'd wanted to set her up in a new apartment."

"That's ridiculous!" Carol snapped.

"Did you meet the colored guy she was seeing?"

"Yes, I did. You seem to have picked up a lot of information about her. What does he have to do with anything? Aren't you looking for a white man?"

"That's right. But the more we know about what kind of girl she was and the friends she had, the easier our job'll be. Mind telling us anything you know about him?"

Carol described Chuck accurately, and reluctantly told what happened at Fire Island, avoiding any conclusions at first. "I think they were just friends," she added when she was through. "He's supposed to live around here."

"Uh-huh," McLauren said, "we'll check with her other friends about him. Any other boyfriends you know of?"

"No," she replied tartly, "and I resent your implications. I know women always have to defend their morals if they're raped. That's disgusting enough. But if you're sexually assaulted and brutally murdered by a strange man who obviously forced you to accompany him somewhere, it's a goddamned shame the police spend more time looking for things to distort your character than in trying to catch your killer!"

"Sorry you think that, ma'am. We're not trying to make a case against her. But we've found she left with a piece of luggage and a small case, according to the lady in the garden apartment."

"They didn't get along. Are you sure they were really gone? I've seen the train case. I'd recognize it."

"You're welcome to go up, but it's not there. Her

toothbrush and some of her clothes were gone, too. Her girlfriends from work verified that.''

Carol was silent. She didn't know about the rape attempt or Diane's moving plans. She remembered her negative vibrations from the Dunes business. ''Maybe her judgment of people could've been better,'' she said sadly, almost to herself. ''After all, she was just a kid. I don't think she knew a soul when she came. Young women like that are fair game. But even if she was an out-and-out prostitute, which she wasn't, she'd still be entitled to the same kind of investigation your ninety-year-old grandmother would get.'' She was trembling, but braced for an open confrontation.

''Come on, Mac. She's upset. Would you have Mr. Stern call us? Maybe he can remember something you overlooked. A license number for Smith would be a big help. Even though neither he nor this Chuck sounds like the actual suspect, we'd like to speak with them if they could be located. We'd also like you and the husband to come over and look at mug shots, although I don't think we'll have anything on the white guy.''

''Naturally,'' she said caustically as she let them out.

''A real-live feminist.'' Lynch laughed when it was safe.

''Yeah. It's beginning to look like she had *some* taste in friends.'' He shook his head resignedly.

Chuck Johnson wasn't a *Daily News* reader and also knew nothing of the park corpse because he'd been away. He learned it was Diane on the six-o'clock TV news. He contacted an attorney friend, who accompanied him to the precinct the next morning. He told the detectives when and how they'd met, who she knew through him, and when he last saw her. He said he'd returned from a Westhampton weekend late Monday evening. Lynch pressed him for the reason he hadn't seen Diane since Fire Island. His ''no particular reason'' didn't satisfy them.

''Did you quarrel about another man, for instance?''

''No, we weren't that tight, it wasn't anything dramatic. I had other friends, and I suppose she did too, but not many.''

Chuck's friend objected when they proceeded to interrogate Chuck about Diane's attack. However, Chuck said he'd worked overtime the day they said it happened. When they next asked about the obscene calls, Chuck again answered over the lawyer's objections.

"Man, I didn't even know she had a phone. Besides, that sounds more like whitey to me. Cats like me save the heavy breathing for when it counts."

Lynch's face and neck burned a deep red, but he controlled himself because the lawyer was there. He told Chuck he could go, but to remain available for possible future questioning. He was surprised when Chuck hesitated and asked if it was possible to see Diane's body. He gave him the city examiner's address and called to request a detailed report of his reaction when he saw her. Chuck hadn't proved he wasn't involved. His pal, Tony, fit the murderer's description very well. But if he had a solid alibi, that would be that. He wasn't surprised the so-called Smith fellow hadn't shown up.

"You could hardly blame him, a guy like that with everything going for him. Probably a family too. The poor guy's probably going through hell, worrying about getting dragged into a mess like this."

Paul Slattery had no worries like that because Jacky never mentioned his name to the police. Relief soon superseded his shock.

Francis R. Smith Jr.'s face was impassive as he read the inconspicuous *Times* follow-up story on Diane in his old barber's chair. There was a ridiculous sketch worked up by an unidentified eyewitness and the police artist. It made him more confident no one could ever connect him with Diane or what happened to her. If they did, he'd removed every trace of evidence that she'd been in the country with him. He wouldn't have an alibi, but they'd never dare arrest him on circumstantial evidence. He hated her for the trouble she'd caused him. But tremendous doses of his medicine had helped. He was a picture of calmness as he turned to the stock-market section. His hair was being cut shorter than when Diane first met him. His clothes were again typical Wall Street. But after work he was buying

Screw magazine to look for a replacement for Miss Vera. He'd also become interested in people seeking punishment. Unfortunately, he was more stimulated by the idea of random encounters.

Detective Lynch had just referred Diane's puffy-faced, bewildered father to the morgue when they called him back about Chuck. Mr. Keely had come alone to arrange an inexpensive New York burial. His sister-in-law, Elizabeth, had gone into seclusion as soon as Emily Kraemer notified her of Diane's death the day before. She couldn't face anyone. The story was on the front page of the Newton *Daily News* that morning. If a lot of people missed it in New York, no one did in Diane's hometown.

"Johnson almost cracked up," the coroner's assistant reported. "I haven't seen many grown men behave like that. He nearly became violent when we tried to get him to leave. He was still crying and shaking when he finally went. If it was an act, he belongs in Hollywood."

"Our Mr. Cool lost his cool downtown. Looks like he was fucking her too. It's a good thing her old man didn't get there while a stud like him was blubbering all over his daughter."

"Yeah, you have to feel for the family. They end up suffering, and the department gets a black eye, all because these young broads have to come to New York to 'do their thing.' It's a damn shame."

Lester Haynes hid his shock and sorrow behind "we-were-only-friends" type remarks after seeing the local three-column headline and sordid wire-service story. But at Miller and Sons, Mrs. Corbett claimed Diane almost as a daughter. She was unable to forgive herself for her last-minute liberality. "Poor Annie, if she'd just listened to what I used to tell her up to then and looked for herself a nice husband, she'd of been alive today," she wept.

MORE BERKLEY BOOKS
YOU'LL WANT TO READ NOW